Short Trips: Seven Deadly Sins

A Short-Story Anthology
Edited by David Bailey

Published by Big Finish Productions Ltd
PO Box 1127
Maidenhead SL6 3LW

www.bigfinish.com

Range Editor: Ian Farrington
Managing Editor: Jason Haigh-Ellery

Doctor Who and TARDIS are trademarks of the British Broadcasting Corporation and are used under licence. Doctor Who logo © BBC 1996. Licensed by BBC Worldwide Limited.

ISBN 1-84435-146-7

Cover art by RED INK 2005

First published March 2005

The Duke's Folly © Gareth Wigmore
That Which Went Away © Mark Wright
Angel © Tara Samms
Suitors, Inc. © Paul Magrs
The 57th © John Binns
Telling Tales © David Bailey
Too Rich for My Blood © Rebecca Levene
Foreword and Afterword © David Bailey
Introduction, linking material and Conclusion © Jacqueline Rayner

Chris Cwej created by Andy Lane and appears with kind permission

With thanks to Robert Dick, Gary Russell, Steve Tribe and Vicki Vrint

Typeset in Quadraat

The moral rights of the authors have been asserted.

All characters in this publication are fictitious and any resemblance to any persons, living or dead, is purely coincidental.

All rights reserved. No part of this publication may be reproduced or transmitted in any forms by any means, electronic or mechanical including photocopying, recording or any information retrieval system, without prior permission, in writing, from the publisher.

This book is sold subject to the condition that it shall not, by way of trade or otherwise, be lent, resold, hired out, or otherwise circulated without the publisher's prior consent in any form of binding or cover other than that in which it is published and without a similar condition including this condition being imposed on the subsequent purchaser.

Printed and bound in Great Britain by Biddles Ltd
www.biddles.co.uk

Contents

Foreword	1
Introduction	3
Sloth	7
The Duke's Folly	
Gareth Wigmore	11
Wrath	27
That Which Went Away	
Mark Wright	31
Envy	71
Angel	
Tara Samms	75
Lust	93
Suitors, Inc.	
Paul Magrs	97
Pride	111
The 57th	
John Binns	115
Avarice	137
Telling Tales	
David Bailey	141
Gluttony	161
Too Rich for My Blood	
Rebecca Levene	167
Conclusion	189
Afterword	195

Foreword and Afterword by
  David Bailey
Introduction, all linking material and Conclusion by
  Jacqueline Rayner

CAMDEN LIBRARIES	
4108944	BFS
Aug 2005	£14.99
B	

Foreword

David Bailey

I never bothered to close the curtains at night any more, didn't worry about keeping the light in, keeping it cosy. Instead of the warm, smooth light from the lamp swelling and pooling in the corners of the bedroom, I just let it all leak out and soak uselessly into the gloom.

I wasn't going to miss it, after all. It wouldn't do me any good anyway.

So, there I lay – after I'd struggled into bed – and let my mind wander. When these sleepless nights first started, I used to think of Ellen, remember the times we had spent together. For many, many nights, that had been a comfort, even fun. I remember I laughed once or twice, catching myself by surprise with a suddenly surfacing memory: the squirrels in the park, crawling all over my chair, or the cat that spent a whole afternoon following us, but not letting Ellen get anywhere near it. That frustrated her so much. 'But I am the archetypal cat person!' she'd huffed. And then we laughed, comparing her to the women in that dreadful old B-movie.

'A kiss could change her into a monstrous fang-and-claw killer!'

Not that I ever got the chance to find out.

Thinking of Ellen wore out its welcome after a while, sure enough. The hollow, jolly memories would be trampled over by other invaders: bitterness like I'd never known, sharp and sour. For every smile I would recollect, a hundred cloudy, drizzly days would follow, pushing at the edges of my mind's eye. A hundred days on that hill, looking down at the obscured view, hearing her betrayal again and again and again.

So, after a while, I stopped thinking of Ellen. (At least, I tried, but *not* thinking about things often takes more effort than bringing them to mind.)

Instead, I focused on the Doctor. Rattled those last words he'd said around in my brain, over and over.

'Laurence, I'm so sorry you got caught up in this. I'm sorry for what's happened to your life, and I promise you I will make it all better. Undo it. Put it right again. But...'

There's always a 'but'. The Doctor had cast his eyes down, poured his shame on to the carpet, instead of having to face me, face what he'd let happen.

'But I can't do it yet. One day, but not yet.'

There's still no sign of one day. But there have been many nights like this.

Filled with nothing but emptiness and the stories of my past, played out in the theatre of my memories. Played by fickle actors, who change their costumes at a moment's notice – at *their* whim, not that of the director. My mind a whirl with them, shouting and echoing and begging for my attention.

So, I decided, it was time to bring them order, get them in line. Time to sort out the stories once and for all. I was going to get it straight in my mind, exactly how I got here, ended up alone in this flat, with the light escaping through the windows.

But my story isn't mine alone. I have to start somewhere else.

Introduction

In isolation they would have looked dignified, but the showman's behaviour towards them was so ridiculous that it bathed all around it in absurdity. He capered around them, a fool in green velvet, welcoming the four men and four women who stared at him derisively.

'Roll up, roll up!' he called, gesturing wildly at the stone doorway as if it led to a circus tent, as if he were talking to mothers and fathers and scabbed-kneed children, all smiling and chattering and candyfloss eating, rather than to kings and queens. 'Roll up for the experience of a lifetime!' He leaned towards a tall, beautiful woman with snow-white skin, and hissed, 'Purgatoria!' The woman leaned in to meet him, her eyes wide, but at the last minute the wavy-haired showman sprang away. He jogged through the doorway, waving a hand to beckon them on.

The tall woman went first, with barely a pause. Her scarlet gown swept along the richly carpeted floor, creating a path for those who came after her. She didn't look to her left or right, hardly noticed the doorways to each side of the corridor that led to rooms that could have been made for her, opulent displays in red and black and gold; her eyes never left the showman's back. But finally he stopped at the door to a room and requested that she enter. There was a sign stuck on to the door with a drawing pin, a piece of paper on which was handwritten: 'The Purgatoria Experience'.

The woman seemed reluctant to venture too far from the showman, but beneath the smiles and the jollity, he was insistent, so she went through the door. What she saw there shocked her, and she stopped, turning back. But the showman was already speaking to the next guest.

Slowly, they all filed into the room: a tall man with tanned skin and film-star good looks; a hunched-up little man in purple robes who could not stop scowling at the showman; a large woman in some sort of military uniform: dark blue and formal and covered with medals; a man of oriental appearance, dressed in sumptuous silk robes; a dumpy, sharp-suited woman. The last ones at the doorway were a tall, fat man with heavy-lidded eyes and a short, skinny woman who hopped restlessly from foot to foot. The showman put out a hand as they began to cross the threshold. 'No retinue, I'm afraid. The rules were explained.'

The man just stopped and gave what might have passed for a shrug. The woman, however, grabbed at the showman's velvet sleeve – then snatched away her hand, as if scared how much the gesture of desperation had revealed. 'I have to be here too,' she said, unable to hide the edge of pleading in her voice. 'The effort it took to get him here! He wouldn't do it without me. And he has to do it. He has to.' Her voice sank into a whisper. 'It's my last hope.'

The showman frowned for a moment, then suddenly gave her a beaming smile. 'Then I'll have to stretch the rules just this once.' A hint of compassion crept into his smile as he said, 'And how about I move you to the front of the queue.'

So the fat man and the thin woman moved into the room, and the showman shut the door.

Immediately, the military woman turned on him. 'What sort of place do you call this? I didn't spend –' she glanced round at her fellows and decided on discretion '– a considerable sum of money to be treated like a pauper.'

The showman glanced around himself and shook his head, as if he didn't understand. 'I thought you'd all like it,' he said, gesturing at the cold, tile-covered floor, the one-piece, solid plastic chairs, the featureless expanse of dull grey wall. 'As I understand it, each one of you has everything money can buy. You want for nothing. So you've come to me because...' He paused. 'Well, let's just say that this seemed like a good start. Something out of the ordinary. Something you wouldn't countenance in your day-to-day life.' He hissed conspiratorially to the skinny woman, who hadn't yet taken her orange plastic seat. 'I based it on a twentieth-century Earth school room. About as miserable as you can get, really. Lunch is mince and over-cooked cabbage.'

The military woman wasn't appeased. 'I call it a disgrace! And what's more –' she pointed at the skinny woman, now perched on the edge of a chair '– we were expressly told that we must come alone. No retinue, no weapons, no communicators. And yet now it seems as though the rules don't apply to everyone.'

'That's because the rules are at my discretion, madam,' said the showman, bowing towards her.

'So you admit you are giving them preferential treatment?' The woman looked like she was about to explode.

'Uh-huh.' The showman was unconcerned. 'Of course, if that makes you really angry... well, I'm not keeping you here.' He nodded his head at the door.

The woman opened her mouth – but shut it again. Looking unhappy, she subsided stiffly into her chair.

But another person had something to say, this time the silk-robed man. He unconsciously stroked his long moustache as he spoke. 'I can't say I am entirely happy about this "group session",' he said. 'Discretion guaranteed, I was assured. Unless I'm very much mistaken, you have some of the richest people in the galaxy in this room.'

'Probably the universe,' commented the showman happily.

The moustached man waved away the interruption. 'Important people. Very important people. Who don't –'

'Who don't want it widely known what they do for kicks,' the showman interrupted again. 'Oh, I'm quite sure everyone will be discreet. Like it says in the brochure – I can't quite believe there is a brochure, but this is a commercial enterprise – no harm will come to you, and discretion is guaranteed. Happy now?'

He didn't give anyone time to answer. Looking suddenly serious, he drew himself erect and began to address them.

'You all know why you are here. This may not be what you expected, but I can assure you it will be everything you hoped for – and more. And yes,' he said, holding up a hand to forestall the military woman's question, 'if you are not satisfied, it comes with a money-back guarantee. Although I can't help feeling that's self-defeating; if there's anything that's likely to inspire misery in at least one of you, it's losing a king's ransom for no good purpose.' The dumpy woman shivered.

The showman grinned. 'Now, as we're all sitting round in a nice circle, I thought we could start with some group therapy...' Several chairs were pushed back in involuntary alarm. 'No? Well, then, here's what's going to happen.

'I'm sorry you all had to come on the same day – usually our services are much more... individual. But Purgatoria is no ordinary experience; extraordinary even within the realms of the extraordinary with which we are dealing. And I can promise truthfully that it is a unique experience, a genuine one-off, a never-to-be-repeated offer. Out of our many thousands of prospective clients, you are the ones who have been specially selected for this phenomenon. Ladies and gentlemen... you are blessed.'

The short, purple-clad man made a 'hrmph' sound of disbelief.

'In a few moments, I will ask each of you to go to your appointed room. Technicians will be round to ensure you have the appropriate implants. And shortly, I will join the first client.' He nodded towards the fat man, who made no response. 'I regret that some of you will have to wait longer than others for your... session, but it will be worth the wait.'

He smiled, a big beaming smile that took in the whole room. 'Trust me... You'll never have anything to worry about again.'

Sloth

As he promised, the showman went first to the room where the fat man and the small, skinny woman were waiting for him. He noted the shiny silver discs on either side of the man's head, and nodded in satisfaction.

'Your Majesties,' he said, sketching a bow that was not deferential, yet was too polished to give offence. The woman inclined her head; a jerking nod full of restless energy. The man grunted.

'It's very unusual for this service to be requested by someone who is not the client,' said the showman to the woman. 'In fact, I don't think it's ever been done before. And if it had been, we probably wouldn't have agreed to provide it. My... colleagues may not have a conventional morality, but there are some depths to which even they won't sink. And carrying this out without the express consent of the client is one of them.'

'But you have agreed, haven't you?' said the woman nervously, desperately. 'You will do this for us?'

The showman nodded.

'The circumstances seem to be exceptional.' He paused for a moment, and when she said nothing, continued: 'Perhaps you could tell me something of yourselves. Your lives, your history.'

The woman took a deep breath.

'My husband was born to be king, and I have known him almost since that birth. We are cousins, brought up together, and we were betrothed before we could walk.' She gave an unhappy laugh. 'Perhaps not the best example to give. I could walk long before he could. He was not a stupid child, but even then... Ah, well. That is long ago now.

'Everything was done for us. We were fed, bathed, clothed, not just as small children but for year after year after year. It is something that, if you are born to it, you just accept – you know nothing else. Yet even then, I was determined not to let anyone else live my life for me. I explored. I investigated. I discovered things. I interested myself in what was going on around me. While Loesin...' She sighed, looking at her husband. 'Loesin found no reason within himself to do even that. He relied on others entirely. I suspect that if no one arrived to give him breakfast, he would starve to death before he could be bothered to fend for himself.' She glanced at the silver band on her finger. 'It was down to the efforts of others that he even turned up for our wedding, and still it was probably only because it would have been more effort to resist. Between our wedding and his coronation, he didn't travel further than from his bed to his chair.'

A tear trickled down her cheek, and she wiped it away fiercely. 'He has advisors, and I do all I can, but some things just have to be agreed by the king himself. And he will not do it. Our people are a placid race, yet they are being driven to despair. Crops are failing and industry is collapsing, and he will not so much as raise himself to put his signature to a law that might save us all. I thought...'

She sighed again. 'This is my last hope. He is, perhaps, happy. Certainly he wants for nothing. He has had every opportunity man could have; if one could have made him happier then he could have grasped it. So I thought... if he could experience misery. Know what it's like to be the farmer whose crops have failed and who will have nothing to sell and nothing to eat, whose children face starvation. Know what it is to be surrounded by disease and pain, as a city falls around him. Know how it feels to be the man of industry who sees all his work go for nothing, watches it fail despite every effort, who is close to putting a pistol to his head to take away the pain.'

She held the showman's gaze, took a deep breath. 'Our people are dying, and our world is collapsing around us. We have no heirs. You must save us.'

The showman dropped his eyes, then looked up at her again. 'I will do my best,' he said. 'It may not be quite as you expected it... no, don't worry!' She was looking anxious. 'I promise you that your husband will not be harmed.'

He jumped up and rubbed his hands. 'To business! Your Majesty, I need you to tie me up.' He held out a coil of rope, but she just gaped at him. He laughed. 'I assure you, it's all part of the plan.'

Slowly, reluctantly, she listened to his persuasion, and then she took the rope. The showman took off his green velvet jacket and hung it over the back of the chair – 'might get a bit hot' – and then sat down on another one. Unlike the plastic chairs of the meeting place, these were wooden and very solid, a heavy base making them impossible to overbalance, with carved decoration in the backs through which a rope could be twined.

For someone who'd never had even to tie her own shoelaces, she made a good job of the knots, and in only a few minutes the showman was fastened tight: wrists, waist, ankles.

'Good,' he said. 'Now, I must ask you to leave us.'

She looked surprised. 'But what can you do, like that?'

He grinned. 'Like this, I'm ready to begin. Would you just push that button on the way out? The one on the right.'

He nodded towards it, and she made her way over there. The tiniest pressure from her finger... and suddenly a siren wailed, and a screen lit up, and there on the screen were numbers: 100, a countdown. 'What is it?' she gasped.

'Oh, just a bomb,' said the showman, casually.

She took a step backwards – then forwards, rushing to untie him.

'No!' he barked, and she halted, hands still outstretched to the ropes. 'You will leave us now. It is necessary!'

And such was the power, the command in his voice that she believed him and obeyed. The bound showman and the indolent king were left to their fate.

'Well,' said the showman, wiggling his eyebrows, 'this is another fine mess you've got us into.'

The king didn't speak.

'Okay, okay, I take your point,' the showman continued, 'I do, perhaps, share some of the responsibility for this situation. But let's not argue about apportioning blame. The question, which I'm sure you're pondering, is how to get out of this!' He leaned his head to one side. 'This is the way I see it. There are four possible courses for you to take. Number one. You get out of that chair, and you disarm the bomb. It's very easy, I could give you instructions from here.

'Number two. You untie me, and I will disarm the bomb. If you're a bit nervous about wires and things, that's the one to take.

'Number three. You leave the room. I'll still die, but you could be fine. Collect your wife, and get as far away from here as possible. Not that you have to go very far, actually, the explosion will be very localised. Just enough to kill anyone in this room, and, oh, maybe a person or two standing outside. Where your wife is at the moment.

'And number four, of course –' he sighed '– is that you do nothing at all, in which case you will die, I will die, and your wife will die, and, from what I've learned, your planet will descend into chaos.'

The showman looked at the king. The king's eyes showed that he had heard and understood, but he made no move.

'Ah, you think that I'm bluffing, do you?' said the showman. 'Let me tell you, I never bluff. Can't do it, just can't do it. You can see in my eyes if I'm lying, everyone says so.' He batted his eyelashes at the other man. 'See, telling the absolute truth. Not a shadow of a doubt. Besides, what's the point? Get caught out once and no one'll ever believe you again, and what good's that in my line of work?'

But still the king showed no signs of moving.

'I've been scared to act, sometimes,' the man went on, conversationally. 'Should I do this, should I do that? What's for the best? Do I have the right? That sort of thing. But what it usually came down to was that doing something – anything – was better than nothing.'

The screen read: 50.

'Still plenty of time,' said the showman. 'Do you want to die? Is that it? Do you want to die, and don't care if you take me, your wife and your planet with you? Am I doing you a favour by offering an effortless method of suicide? Well, we aim to please.' He shot a frown at the king. 'Or is it just that *not* dying requires so much more effort than dying...?'

The screen read: 40.

The showman began to struggle against his bonds. 'You know, I thought this'd be enough to snap you out of it,' he said. 'Oh, I know it's not what your wife signed up for, but I reckoned she wouldn't say no to a nice straightforward cure, thank you very much. I'd even have refunded your money. Not going to work, though, is it? It's up to me to save us, and admit defeat.'

One hand was free. The screen read: 30.

'Lessons from Harry Houdini,' the man called out between deep breaths. 'He'd have met his match in your wife, though. There's someone who knows how to tie a knot.'

His other hand was free. The screen read: 20.

He pulled at the rope around his waist, wincing with pain as he tried to twist the knot round to where he could get at it. But it was easier than his hands, and the cords dropped to the floor. Only his ankles to go. And the screen read: 10.

Nine. Tugging at the knot.

Eight. Working it loose.

Seven. One ankle free.

Six. Turning to the other one.

Five. Almost free.

Four. Lunging towards the controls.

Three.

His other ankle hadn't been fully untied. As he pushed himself forward, across the room, the foot was caught up in the rope, and the showman slammed to the floor, ending up on his hands and knees. He looked up with panicking eyes at the still ticking display, turned to the fat man and flung out an arm, pleading: 'You must do it! There's still time!'

Two. Struggling to his feet. 'Please! Help me!'

One. 'I need your help! There's not enough time!'

Zero.

'Okay,' said the showman, 'sometimes I bluff.'

He was panting with exertion and emotion, but grinning now too. 'Thank you,' he said. 'That's exactly what I was after. A greater display of sloth I have never seen. Which leads me to this...' He reached out for another switch, beyond the redundant countdown display. 'What you came for – well, what your wife wanted for you – to live the life of someone else. I tell you now, what you're going to get is not exactly what she signed on for. But I think she'll be all the happier for it...'

The showman grasped the switch, and pushed. 'You're going down in the world now: a duke, not a king,' he told the other. 'But that won't be the biggest change for you today, believe me...'

The Duke's Folly

Gareth Wigmore

The chapel bell rang for a twelfth time at one end of the strip, and Slim gulped back a mouthful of bile and clammy saliva. He was about to die. A breath of hot wind took a hold of the desert dust on which the wooden buildings of Thorpesville sat, and threw a little in Slim's eyes. Aw, shoot, that was all he god-damn needed at a time like this – a man with a reputation facing him at twenty paces, with his hands ready over his guns. How in the name of all that was good had he got himself into this mess? What would his momma say when she knew it had all ended for her boy this way? He rubbed hard at his wet eyes with filthy, shaking hands.

'It don't have to be like this, kid,' came that funny-sounding voice from twenty paces away. 'You just take back what you said about my Sue, this whole thing'll be like it never even happened. You and me, we'll go back to the Tambourine, get comfy, drink some bourbon, play some bridge...'

What in hell was bridge? one part of Slim's brain asked while another tried to keep control of his bladder, and failed. 'Aw, son, that just ain't dignified,' he heard the mayor say. 'Listen to the man; he gonna let you live, you just ask him nice!'

'I don't care!' Slim squawked, his voice cracking with tension. 'His girl was all over me, flirtin' an' cuddlin' an' such. Man oughta keep control of a girl like that; I just said so.' He could feel his heartbeat pulsing in his temples, in his fingers.

'My God, Slim,' the mayor said from where he stood halfway down the strip, in between the two men, 'you think he's got that name for nothing – "Dead Man's" Chestington?' He shook his head. 'Let's get this over with; I got work to do today. You know what: I drop this here hankie, when it hits the dirt, you go for it. And may God have mercy on the both of you.' It occurred to Slim that the mayor sounded bored. What a stupid way to go.

Slim squinted in the noonday sun. He saw the gunslinger's girl – that prissy, no-good tease – rush over to her man and kiss him on the cheek, only for him to push her away, back into the crowd that had lined Thorpesville's main strip to see the show. It wasn't every day they saw something like this; maybe it was every other day.

'Okay, boys,' the mayor called, his little white cloth stretched out in his hands above his head. 'Get ready; here it comes.'

A message raced through Slim's skull: *Oh, God, oh, God, oh, God, I'm gonna die!* Twenty paces away, his opponent looked set, calm, ready; his face was grim, his jaw tight behind the stubble and grime, and his eyes didn't blink under the big brim of his hat. This was how death looked.

The handkerchief was falling from the mayor's hands, the wind playing on it for an instant to keep it hovering around his waist. Slim didn't even look; there was warm metal in his grip – the butt of his daddy's old Remington – and suddenly he felt the recoil, almost before he heard the thunder from its long barrel.

The handkerchief touched down on to the dust floor.

'Oh, boy,' said the mayor, and solemnly took off his bowler.

The gun dropped from Slim's hand. He gulped, and forced himself to look dead ahead. His opponent was still standing there, twenty paces away, a wolfish grin splitting his face, his hands still hovering over his guns. *How come he's got so many of his own god-damn teeth?* Slim couldn't help thinking.

Nothing happened for a moment. The crowd seemed to have drawn in their breath and didn't seem to be letting it out again. No one moved. Then, the stranger's funny voice came from behind that smile: 'Is it my turn now, Mr Mayor?'

Before there was a reply, Slim felt his right ear split into a thousand splinters, and was on his backside in the dirt, howling like a dog. It had been so quick he hadn't really seen it – the man's hand taking one gun from its holster, aim being taken, the flash of fire as the bullet clipped his head. Where his ear had been were just red flaps of skin.

'Let me see,' came a girl's voice, the voice of that girl who'd been the cause of all this, that pretty black-eyed Susie who'd seemed so obliging to him before... before... Colours flashed across his vision, and he passed out.

'Oh, Ian!' Susan said, kneeling down beside the boy. 'What have you done to him? There's blood everywhere!'

'Dead Man's' Chesterton knocked back the brim of his hat and shuffled resignedly up to the two of them, holstering his six-gun, muttering under his breath, 'Perfect shot... National Service handgun prize... cheating idiot had to flinch so I clipped him...' He cast a shadow over Slim's pasty face as he leant over, checking what was left of the boy's ear. 'He'll be all right, Susan. I had to shoot; you know I had to shoot.'

'But did you have to hit?' Susan asked, wiping her bloodied hands on her dust-brown canvas blouse.

'Reckon he did, miss,' said the mayor, a tubby little man, extending a hand to Ian. 'Boy may not hear too well from now on, but at least he'll be livin' to beg folks' pardon, and ten other men outta ten wouldn't have left him the luxury of breathing. I ain't seen sharp-shooting like that since... Well, I ain't never seen sharp-shooting like that.'

Ian shook the mayor's hand, and inwardly cursed the Doctor, imagining him sitting in comfort on those red leather benches on the other side of the world.

'Mr Mayor,' he said, in a none-too-good Wild West accent taken from a thousand B-movies, 'would you be so kind as to help me get this boy to Doc Bell's to be cleaned up? I'm kind of eager to get a bite to eat and a drink inside of me.'

'Chestington,' the mayor said, looking up into Ian's tired face, 'it'd be my very great pleasure.'

Across the Atlantic, the Doctor was sitting in an armchair, a delicate china cup laden with tea balanced in his hand. He was dressed in his frock coat and check trousers, his long white hair spread out on to his shoulders and a crooked smile on his old face. A trip out to the English countryside was a splendid thing, no doubt, he was thinking, and a pleasant change from the hustle and bustle of London. It would be a few decades before the motor car began to invade the city, but it was still a noisy, restless place, and a well-prepared cup of tea in the quiet was very welcome.

Not that it would be quiet or restless outside, he reminded himself. Oh, how he wished Barbara hadn't gone out with the hunt. 'I do wish you wouldn't ride, my dear,' he'd snapped at her earlier, in the carriage.

'But they expect it, Doctor,' she'd replied, almost laughing; it had been a conversation they'd had more than once before.

'Would it be so hard to concoct an excuse, hmm?' he'd pleaded. 'After all, you don't see me gallivanting around on horseback, chasing a poor, defenceless creature, do you? No, I just say I'm too old, and everyone leaves me alone.'

'You *are* too old,' the young woman had teased, putting an arm across the seat to his waist.

'Stuff and nonsense,' he'd said, waving her comments away. 'There's life in these old bones yet. I could ride twice as far and twice as fast as young Chilgrove – that good-for-nothing – and still get down to the House for the evening.'

'To take a snooze?'

'Oh, I suppose you think you're very funny.' He'd tried to keep up the pretence of seriousness for a few seconds, before he found himself smiling along with her. And now he recollected the conversation, he found himself smiling again. Well, he may have dozed off in the Lords a couple of times, he supposed; some of those debates could be a bit much to sit through late into the night, and he was an old man – older than any of his fellow peers supposed.

But Barbara was right, of course. It would have looked strange had the daughter of Earl Foreman not taken an active role in country pursuits, even the more barbarous ones. And it brought them here for the weekend, into contact with Chilgrove and all that was important about being in this time and place – all that was important about having sent Ian and Susan off to goodness knew what in America. Some of the journeys they made in the TARDIS were scenic, just stopping by to view the surroundings; some ended in them saving worlds and whole species; some were about friendship and duty. This was one of the latter, and he hoped that his companions understood it. Perhaps they thought he was just a vain old man, enjoying pretending to be important. But, no, surely they respected him enough to know that there was method in his madness – to know that if he did something, he had good reason.

His concentration was brought to an end suddenly, as the door to the drawing room was flung open and the young Duke of Chilgrove himself burst through. He threw down his riding crop on to a chair, followed closely by his hard, black hat, and said, 'Damn it all!'

The Doctor rose from his chair with a little more awkwardness than was strictly necessary; he wanted to remind Chilgrove that he was there, that he was his elder, and that the boy's father had made him his guardian for the year, until he was of age. He coughed pointedly as he placed his cup down next to a copy of *The Times* on an ornate table by the chair's side.

'Oh!' the young man exclaimed. 'Earl Foreman! How are you, sir? I'd quite forgotten that you were in here; I apologise profusely – just had the deuce of some luck out there – you wouldn't credit it, you really wouldn't.' Chilgrove brushed the hat and crop off the chair straight on to the floor and sat awkwardly in it. A male servant scurried into the room after the duke, who stuck out his legs for his riding boots to be taken off. 'I suppose Samson is getting a bit long in the tooth, but he's been one of my favourites in the stables for years. Maybe I drove him a little hard. But he's taken that ditch a thousand times with me, and I haven't put on any weight recently. Have I?'

The Doctor threw his head to one side in consideration, before sitting down again. 'I wouldn't say so, Your Grace, but then I can't say I've studied your figure particularly closely.'

Chilgrove stopped and looked over at him as his second boot came off. 'Oh. Well, thank you, Foreman, nice of you to say so...' He dismissed the servant with a wave, then called after him. 'A glass of punch, Burton?' Then he looked back at the Doctor. 'And don't call me "Your Grace" if you can help it, Foreman; it's bad enough from the servants. Can't you call me what you used to, before Father died?'

'I used to call you "little David",' the Doctor replied with a confused wave of each hand.

Chilgrove grimaced. 'I see. No, that won't do at all, will it? I'll have to get used to "Your Grace" sooner or later I dare say, but it seems so very formal.' He slumped back in the armchair, every muscle seeming to relax.

The Doctor looked at this boy, this boy he was investing so much time and effort in. He was so like his father in looks it was hard to fathom – the same sandy hair, worn long, the same very blue eyes and sharp, near-handsome features. He'd known Chilgrove – the old duke, the boy's father – at much the same age, and the resemblance to that man, who'd saved his life again and again, really was striking. But not in temperament. In that, the young duke was every inch his mother's boy. My, she'd been an attractive woman, yes, but to say that she was flighty was an understatement. She had enthusiasms and crazes from time to time but she was, for the most part, a very lazy woman, content to stand on her husband's arm and be an adornment to him, his rank and his political gifts.

'You will have to get used to it, David,' the Doctor said, seriously. 'You know better than I do what it means to be a duke – to be as noble in rank as one can be short of royalty. You have a duty. The country expects a lot of you. Your father did, too.'

Chilgrove looked at him rather sadly. 'You don't think I'm good enough to live up to him, do you?'

It was true, and both of them knew it, but the Doctor shook his head. 'David, you're a young man. You have time and energy you can devote to living up to the man your father was. If I can help you, I shall. If you want me to help you, you have only to ask.'

'I know,' Chilgrove said unhappily, his features settling into a childish expression of frustration, including something of a frown. 'I know the trust the old man put in you. He was a good old stick, and I miss him. I miss Mother, too.'

The Doctor said nothing. He felt like reminding the boy that that 'good old stick' had been one of the most important politicians in England in the latter half of the nineteenth century, with a brilliant mind for financial affairs and an unparalleled sense of the duty that came with his rank. But he'd seen that look on young David's face before and knew what it meant – a childish sulk in which there was very little point talking to him about anything important.

'Miss Joy St Peter was just behind me when Samson failed at the ditch,' the boy said mournfully. 'She saw me look an ass; goodness knows what she must think of me now.'

Ah, yes: Joy St Peter, Joy St Peter, there she was. 'And the horse?' the Doctor asked, after a moment.

'He'll have to be put down. Poor old Samson.'

'And how's my daughter, hmm?'

'Lady Barbara? Oh, she was racing away with Major Giles and his brother, the reverend. That reverend's a dasher all right.' Chilgrove slumped back into his misery after this momentary enthusiasm. 'But what must Miss St Peter think of me now?'

The Doctor arched his eyebrows in resignation, and went back to his tea.

Ian gratefully shut the door on the rest of Edwardston, and sat down on the bed next to Susan, exhausted. It was an upstairs room at the local saloon, the Edwardston Bravo, about on a par with their usual accommodation these days – spit and sawdust, paper-thin walls and cheap furniture.

Susan groaned and threw herself backwards on to the fragile-looking bed. 'I thought that was never going to end.'

Ian lifted a gun from its holster, checked the safety, and slid it under the bed's one pillow. 'It was some evening.' His mouth was warm with bourbon, but he wasn't drunk – he didn't know when he'd need to be on alert. This was no place for a girl like Susan; it was no place for a man like him, if he were honest, although so far he'd pulled the wool over everyone's eyes. 'Dead Man's' Chesterton – of all the names he'd managed to pick up... Barbara would find it funny when he told her. He wanted to see her; how he wanted to see her.

'Not just the evening, Ian, the whole day.' Susan shot upright. 'When that man was talking to me and you had to warn him off, all I could think of was a few days ago and that poor boy's ear!'

'He'd have been all right if he hadn't moved, I told you,' Ian wearily said. 'Now maybe he'll be clever enough to stay out of trouble. We've all seen the movies – don't mess with the tough guy from out of town.'

Susan giggled and put her hand on his. 'Or his girl.'

'Or his girl,' Ian replied, smiling, and moved his hand away to put his gun-belt on the bedside table. No wonder Slim had tried to mess with Susan, Ian thought. She was slim and elegant, her eyes live with intelligence, her features delicate under that elfin hairstyle. Even in her grimy clothes, she was very beautiful. And she was the Doctor's granddaughter, and his job was to bring her home to that meddling old man he loved and respected – almost as much as he was driven mad by the caprice with which he directed his companions hither and thither.

'I want you to go to America, my boy,' he'd said to him. 'Yes, to America! And why not take Susan with you, for the trip? Find this St Peter woman's family and gather all the information you can about them. Her father has some extraordinary name or other, so it shouldn't be too hard. I smell a rat, Chesterton; David could give all that his father worked for up for her, and the whole Chilgrove name and everything it means would be gone like that.' And he'd snapped his fingers, then clapped his hands on Ian's shoulders and said earnestly, 'You know how much this means to me.'

So here was 'Dead Man's' Chesterton, gunslinger of some renown, apparently, and his girl Sue, stuck in the wrong end of Arizona on the trail of the St Peters – a trail that had gone cold some time ago. He and Susan had started in Boston as genteel travellers and worked their way ever further west, walking smack into trouble the way they always seemed to. There'd been an unfortunate incident in Omaha that had left a body in its wake; the law had tracked them as far as Sante Fe, by which time the nickname had stuck. The duel in Thorpesville probably hadn't helped cover their tracks. And the only thing that Ian could think of was to keep heading west, for California and passage somewhere – anywhere – and back to Barbara and civilisation.

'We ought to get moving tomorrow, early. I'll go and get cleaned up,' he said, rubbing his hands over his face before picking up his gun belt again.

'You're going to sleep in the bath again, aren't you?' Susan asked.

Ian adopted his Wild West accent again. 'I sure am, honey.'

Her head upside down off the far edge of the bed, Susan stuck out her tongue, and Ian closed the bathroom door behind him, his eyes already beginning to close.

Lady Barbara Foreman opened the curtains of her room and let the sun stream in. Then she frowned; Jess, her maid, would berate her for not letting her do that job. It was force of habit, that was all. Even three or four months in Victorian London, assuming the mantle of the only daughter of a peer of the realm, hadn't impacted too much on her routine, the way she did everyday things. It was hard to get used to servants, though it was harder still to get used to corsets; she'd never worn them outside amateur dramatics at university.

'You should have let me do that, my lady!' Jess cried, rushing in, and Barbara smiled. But her mind was heavy with the burden of what she had to tell the Doctor that morning – what her visitor of the previous evening had told her.

'Help me brush my hair, Jess,' she said, and sat down straight in front of the big oval mirror, her maid taking up position behind her, beginning their daily ritual with a large tortoise-shell comb. Barbara's dark brown hair was long and straight at the moment, no lacquer or spray, her face without make-up. There was a worried look in her eyes and the set of her mouth that she didn't really understand, until she realised that she hadn't consciously thought about Ian yet that morning. It had been weeks since she and the Doctor had heard from him by letter or telegram, and she knew that the old man was beginning to worry. They'd heard about some trouble in Omaha – there'd even been something about it in one or two of the papers – but little afterwards. Ian had been her first thought in the morning for a long time now; not to have thought of him for the good half-hour while she'd dressed and washed since waking upset her immeasurably. She shut her eyes and let Jess firmly brush the full length of her hair, concentrating on the sensation above all else.

Barbara opened her eyes again, and knew that that look of concern was going to stay on her face for the rest of that day. It was simply the way she looked now – the slightly raised eyebrows, a pinch above the nose, a quiver on her lips. She looked older than she was, she knew; she wasn't beautiful, like Susan, and her prettiness had a growing plainness about it. Susan was young and her looks were at the height of that gamine charm that men found hard to resist. Why couldn't the Doctor have sent her off with Ian to America? Why couldn't Susan have stayed in London to keep the old man company? She closed her eyes again, and enjoyed the broad strokes of the brush.

A few minutes later, she was downstairs in the breakfast room. 'Good morning, my dear!' the Doctor exclaimed, standing up at the table to greet her. 'I'm sorry I was late home last night; there was an interesting debate on the situation in Africa that kept us going till long past midnight.'

'Really?'

'Oh, yes, quite fascinating. I didn't contribute, of course, though I could have said plenty – but best if I lie a little low, hmm?'

'Any post?' Barbara said, changing the subject as she looked at the table, with its envelopes and papers scattered in front of the Doctor's plate of eggs, mushrooms and kidneys.

She watched the old man's shoulders fall. 'Well, nothing from Chesterton and Susan, if that's what you mean.' He sat down again, and motioned for her to do the same, ringing a bell with one hand to summon a servant.

'Can't we do something? Try to find them?'

'I'm worried about them too, my dear, but the best thing to do is sit tight and hope for the best.' He smiled. 'There's always hope, hmm? And they've been in plenty of tight fixes before. Chesterton's a resourceful young man; I wouldn't have entrusted Susan into his care if he weren't.' His eyes narrowed. 'Young Chilgrove could learn a lot from an Englishman like that, a good role model. Of course, he had his father to learn from and ignored that good example, so perhaps it's a moot point.'

Barbara had stopped listening. She asked the servant for some tea and a muffin and jam, and let the Doctor prattle on for a couple of minutes while he attacked his breakfast before she ruined his day. 'I think I should tell you, Doctor,' she said when he'd come to a pause, 'that I had a visitor last night, and you're not going to like what he had to say.'

A fork of kidneys and mushrooms stopped halfway to the old man's mouth. 'Oh?'

'The Duke of Chilgrove was here.'

'Young David?' The Doctor put his knife and fork down. 'And what did he want with you, eh? Why didn't he come to see me?'

'He was afraid to tell you, so he told me instead.'

'Afraid? Afraid?'

Barbara had known this wasn't going to be easy. 'He's been sent down from Cambridge.' The old man's face fell even further. 'He was at Doncaster. Rotten Row, that horse he part-owns was racing there. It didn't do too well, and he lost a substantial sum of money.'

'His father's money,' the Doctor snarled, his head pointing slightly downwards so his face was hidden from her a little.

'He went out with his friends and drowned his sorrows a bit too much, and missed the last train. The dean of his college had specifically ordered that he not go. When he found out, he said that the duke had used up all his chances, that he had no choice, could make no special exceptions.'

The Doctor pushed his plate away, and dabbed at his mouth with a white napkin in agitation. 'This is very bad,' he said. 'Very bad indeed. And I wish you hadn't kept it from me.'

'Oh, don't be silly, Doctor.' That made Barbara genuinely angry. 'The longer you play the role of some Victorian patriarch, the harder it seems for you to step away from it. I haven't kept anything from you. The duke left here at ten o'clock last night; I'm telling you this morning.'

'You're right, my dear, you're right – I'm sorry. I'm just upset. You know that.' The Doctor rose to his feet and turned to the big bay window, less to inspect the world outside than to look away from Barbara, she imagined. 'He's so gifted – he has his father's mind for figures, if only he'd think to use it. But betting! And horse racing! It's a waste, that's all. I'd hoped that getting his degree would settle him – wake him up to himself and what he's capable of. And now that's gone, gone...' He hung his head and leaned a little theatrically on his walking cane.

Barbara closed her eyes and wished herself somewhere else. She heard herself grunt in frustration and brought both fists crashing down on the table. When she opened her eyes, a china cup was on the floor in pieces, its saucer still rattling up and down in front of her, and the Doctor was facing her, open-mouthed. 'Why is this all so damned important to you, Doctor?' she shouted. A servant scurried in, surveyed her master and mistress, and scurried out again. 'I know the old duke was your friend. I know you feel responsible for his son. I know you want him to take his responsibilities seriously and follow his father into politics. I know you don't want him to marry that American – you even sent Ian and Susan off God-knows-where to try to stop that. But I just don't understand why it's so important to you.' She suddenly realised that this had been building up inside her for weeks now, and she had to let it out. 'We've spent months here, months pretending to be people we're not. You're indulging yourself in a fantasy life of luxury: servants, a seat in Parliament, a title – that you've concocted out of thin air – while Ian and your own granddaughter are in trouble thousands of miles away. There's no threat here, no menace to Victorian London, just a nice enough young man not living up to his potential. There's nothing unusual in that; I could have shown you half a dozen like him in Susan's class at Coal Hill. We should find our friends and get in the TARDIS and go.'

The Doctor bristled upright. 'For a historian, you're not very interested in your own history, are you? I'm sorry if living through one of the most important periods of your country's history, mixing with the politicians you studied at university and the society set you read about at school... I'm sorry if that fails to interest you.'

Barbara growled to herself at the back of her throat. 'You're not listening. Of course I've loved being here and seeing a new period of history, you know that I have, and of course I appreciate the doors your position here –' she threw up her arms and looked around her, indicating the opulence that the

Doctor's pocket peerage had brought '– have opened to me.' She stood up and went closer to him. 'But you once told me that you could never rewrite history – not one line. Do you remember?'

'Yes, I remember. Of course I remember.'

'I know my Victorian history, Doctor – I know the part that the old Duke of Chilgrove played, the good deeds he did. But I don't know a thing about his son!' She looked dead into his eyes, to make sure that he got the point. 'History forgot him. Whatever his potential, he didn't do the great deeds his father did. Do you understand? You can't change what has already happened!'

The Doctor glared at her with an emotion she couldn't quite fathom. Hatred? Outrage at being spoken to in such a fashion? Then he went to the table and tingled the bell. In a second, a servant appeared; she'd obviously been listening outside. 'I need a glass of water, Emma,' he said, breathlessly, 'a large glass, and fetch one for Lady Barbara too.' The servant left; the Doctor didn't turn back to his companion. The water came and he gulped it down, while Barbara sipped at hers. Then he turned to face her.

'In your history class at Coal Hill School, did you have a chance to teach Susan about the Indian Mutiny, hmm?' Barbara shook her head. 'Well, if you had,' the Doctor continued, 'you would have found that she knew rather more about it than the rest of her class. Yes, the Ship took us there, right to the middle of the carnage, a year or two before we met you and Chesterton. We saw some dreadful atrocities – and the only thing that kept us from death more than once was a young man called David Warblington – the Duke of Chilgrove. He watched his family butchered there, including his own father.'

Until then, the Doctor's manner had been stern and authoritarian, but Barbara watched his face crumple as the memories came back to him. 'Oh, Barbara,' he said, 'it was terrible, as terrible as anything we've witnessed together. A frenzy of killing, devoid of any sense. Chilgrove was our saviour – such courage, such strength and resource. Any life that I have from now on, I owe to him – and any life that Susan has, she owes him too. That man gave my granddaughter the chance of a life. I can't do anything as dramatic for his son, but I won't stand by while he sacrifices his talent and his ability altogether – not when David Warblington has put me in trust as his guardian.' He moved over to a group of chairs and settees in the other half of the room and sat down, seemingly exhausted.

'So that's why you sent Susan away,' Barbara commented after a moment. 'The old duke would have wondered why she was still a teenager.'

'Whereas an old man can just pretend to be a little older, a little more hunched, a little more unsteady on his feet.' The Doctor smiled gently at her. 'Maybe it's not pretend, hmm?'

She walked to him and handed him her glass of water, which she'd barely touched. 'Drink this, Doctor,' she said, putting a hand down on to his hair for a moment in affection. 'You want to help your friend's son, I know. But you can't make him into someone history says he never will be.'

He looked up at her, his face kindly and wise and sad, an expression on it that Barbara would always remember. 'But sometimes, Barbara, sometimes you can make history fight its hardest to have things its own way. And every now and again, you must.'

'I understand.'

'I know you do, my dear, I know you do,' he said, clasping her hand. 'That's another reason I wanted you here, with me, while I do what I can for little David.'

'"Little David" isn't so little any more,' Barbara said. 'And nor are his gambling debts. As his guardian, he's looking to you for a cheque...'

The Doctor rose to his feet angrily. 'Oh! That boy! His father must be turning in his grave, and he'll have me turning in mine too!' And off he stormed, shouting to himself and to anyone who could hear.

Barbara clapped a hand over her eyes. She was going nowhere fast.

Ian moved back through the San Francisco evening gloom with a spring in his step, if not a smile on his face. Everything was working out. He wore an overcoat under his low-brimmed hat; the coat was ludicrously heavy, even after dark, for such a warm night, but he could pull its collar up over the lower half of his face. The beard he'd grown in the last push west made him look pretty different from his face on the 'Wanted' posters, but there was no sense in being foolish now, when they were so close to passage home. He was taking backstreets as much as he could, ones without gas lamps and rowdy bars full of people who could bother him and say, 'Feller, ain't I seen you somewhere before?'

Down at the docks, he'd found a boat bound for Holland with a skipper who'd agreed to let him and Susan aboard for a pretty ludicrous sum, with a few provisos. He wasn't looking forward to telling her that she was going to have to spend the entire journey stuck in the cabin – that the skipper didn't want the crew to know there was a woman aboard – but he'd do it. And she'd damn well stay in that cabin for as long as it took them to get back to England, the Doctor, the TARDIS and Barbara.

The whole trip had been a disaster. He thought of that dreadful moment when he realised what Susan had done in Omaha, watching the body hit the ground, tossing the still-warm gun into the river. He remembered looking from the top of a ridge into a valley and thinking, though he knew it was madness, that he could only be looking at a dozen centaurs – half-men, half-horses – racing around down there, before realising with a lurch of his stomach that he was watching Red Indian braves at play on horseback, their movements impossibly polished and easy. His mind moved on to the duel in Thorpesville, the desperate search for water in Idaho, the time his horse had been shot out from under him and he'd gone sprawling into the dust of the desert floor. They were memories he'd always have, and always be quite happy to lose.

He rounded a corner, thinking about the present instead of the past. His job now was to get Susan out of that hotel and down to the docks as quickly as possible. The boat would sail in a few hours; he had to get her on it with the minimum fuss or noise. If he took this route with her, he hoped not to meet too many people. There were a few shops – it was a busier street than some of the others he'd been on – but there were no crowds.

Ian was feeling pretty single-minded, as though nothing could divert him from the job in hand. Then he passed a shop window and, before he knew it, he was staring at himself in the reflection performing a double take worthy of high farce. The sign said 'St Peter's Tailors' in large lettering, and underneath in smaller script 'Quality suits and coats made to measure – genuine woollens – low prices – prop. Robertson St Peter'.

There was a light on in there, in a back room with a half-open door. Ian could have knocked on the window and got someone's attention there and then. Instead, he blinked a couple of times, gulped, and reread the sign, transfixed. Robertson St Peter – that was the name all right, the name of the man the Doctor had sent him to find. Ian looked down and caught sight of his reflection again, that wild beard around the open mouth and under the staring eyes, and thought of the law closing in on him and Susan. As he turned on his heels and walked away, he began to plan a different route from the hotel to the docks.

The carriage pulled up at around the time that the lower chimney stack collapsed into the growing wall of flame below it. The house had been on fire for some time. The windows in the upper storeys were belching out flames twenty or thirty feet high, accompanied by columns of thick black smoke that towered into the air. The roof was almost lost altogether in the smoke, but the Doctor could see that parts of it were still there, although in other places the fire had burst through tile and brick and spewed into the air. The lower part of the manor seemed less affected so far, but he'd seen fires like this before – not for a long time, thank goodness – and knew that there was nothing of Warblington Place, the Duke of Chilgrove's Richmond home, that could be saved. The fire was even worse than he'd been told.

He felt Barbara's hand on his knee across the carriage, and looked aghast into her concerned face. 'I'm sure David's not in there,' she said, nodding at him.

'We must go and make sure!' he said, leaping out of the doorway, his night-cape flapping wildly behind him, in a manner that was perhaps ill-fitting the dignity with which an Earl Foreman should conduct himself. The heat was staggering, almost pushing him back into Barbara, who was shielding her eyes in the carriage doorway, her lips silently forming words of shock.

'The horses don't like it, my lord!' shouted the coachman, over the din of crackling flames, and the Doctor realised that the animals were snorting and stamping angrily at the ground, desperate to get away.

'Yes, Fletcher, take them out of here!' he called back to him, and then helped Barbara down to the turf. 'Come on, my dear!'

'Maybe we should stay in the carriage, Doctor. That heat –' she started to say, but the old man shook his head, grabbed her hand and started moving towards the fire as quickly as he could go.

There were plenty of onlookers gawping, of course, although plenty of other people in not much more than their nightgowns seemed to be assisting the firemen, reeling hoses down to the river, marshalling others to help, dousing trees and outbuildings in water so that they didn't catch fire as well. 'Get out of the sodding way!' someone screamed at them as he rushed past with a water bucket in each hand. But all that the Doctor could really hear was that immense crackling of the fire, brick and wood and glass being subjected to something against which it stood no chance whatsoever of survival.

Warblington Place was not a big house – perhaps twelve or fourteen bedrooms, as he remembered – but it was an old one, built with no real thought of defence against fire. When the roof collapsed altogether, it was with a crash like a hundred cannon being set off together and a sheet of flame jumping high into the sky. The Doctor heard himself cry out in shock, and felt Barbara's grip on him tighten. Then it started raining sparks and little flakes of fire all around them, coming down noiselessly in their hundreds. One caught in the centre of someone's hair as he stood watching, and the Doctor was quick to whip his cloak off and throw it over the unfortunate man's head as he hopped around, beating at the flames.

A fireman with a blackened face, his brass helmet clutched in his gloved hands, pushed them back. 'Get away, sir, madam!' he shouted, though the Doctor could barely hear his voice through his ringing ears. 'This is no place for old men and women!'

'The Duke! The Duke!' the Doctor hollered back. 'Where is the Duke of Chilgrove? I'm the boy's guardian!'

The fireman shook his head and motioned them back again, then turned to deal with other spectators. But the Doctor felt a hand on his shoulder; he looked round, and there was the boy.

'I'm here, Foreman, I'm here,' he called out, nodding, a weak smile on his face. 'Lady Barbara,' he added, and waved to her. He was in pyjamas, his face grimy, his hair askew.

The Doctor restrained himself from hugging young Chilgrove in relief. 'Thank goodness you're safe, David! What on earth happened here?'

Chilgrove groaned and put a hand to his face. 'A late night, one too many glasses of port, I think, and definitely one cigar too many...'

The Doctor stumbled, and put out a hand to Barbara for support. 'What's that you say, my boy? What do you mean?'

'Come away, both of you,' Barbara's voice sounded through the terrible noise in his ears. 'It doesn't matter what happened. David's safe. Is everyone accounted for?'

'Oh, yes, all the servants are out, the firemen said.'

'That's all that's important for now,' Barbara said, her hands beginning to push him away from the fire and directing David that way too.

'Yes, yes,' he heard himself say without conviction, blinking as he adjusted to the light away from the burning remains of the house, 'that's all that matters. So long as everyone's safe.' He knew what the boy had done. Warblington Place and all the family history in it were gone, just because David had been too lazy to make sure his cigar was extinguished.

The wedding of the Duke of Chilgrove and Miss Joy St Peter took place a few days after Ian and Susan had arrived back in England, only a fortnight after David Warblington had come of age; the Doctor had refused to let him marry his American bride before. The service and wedding breakfast were small in scale; again, the Doctor had prevailed on the young man to let the country slowly get used to the idea of one of its noblest families marrying into the colonies, rather than announcing it with the kind of society wedding that he had originally envisaged.

Few Americans were there, other than the new duchess herself. Her parents were not invited. She'd lost touch with them after her father had gone into prison, although she'd heard that he made an honest living these days as a tailor somewhere out west. She behaved with utmost decorum on the wedding day, and even charmed the Doctor a little – if only a little. Ian and Barbara were both there, though Susan had to stay away, to her annoyance. The Doctor was adamant that there might be someone there who'd recognise her from India or their stay in England after the Mutiny, and refused to allow her out of the house.

'But, Grandfather –' she'd said.

'You're not going out there and causing trouble for us, young lady, however much you "But, Grandfather" me,' he'd said, and she'd stamped her foot and slammed the door on her way out of the room. Given that she'd spent an entire journey back from the west coast of America under hatches, Ian felt a little sorry for her and brought her something to read he'd found in a railway station waiting room. It was a penny dreadful full of Wild West stories, including one entitled *Wanted: The True-Life Crimes of 'Dead Man's' Chestington and Black-Eyed Susan*, as told by someone rejoicing in the name of Slim McWatt.

'Your governor's played the old devil with me these past few months, while you've been sunning yourself abroad,' the bridegroom told Ian over a glass of champagne at the wedding breakfast.

'Didn't I hear that you gave him a reason or two?' Ian replied a little warily.

The duke shrugged. 'Suppose I did really. I was sent down, I got into debt.

And then I burned Warblington Place down, which wasn't too clever I admit.' He gestured around them to the opulent hall in which they were standing – the hall of another of the several Chilgrove family properties. 'The advantages of being a duke, eh? Burn one house down and you just move on to the next. I'm joking, really. I shan't do it again – I don't think my wife would let me.'

Ian decided to change the subject. 'She's from a rough old country, the new duchess.'

'Oh, don't call her that,' the duke said, quickly. 'She's just going to be Mrs David Warblington – they don't care for dukes and duchesses too much over there, apparently. She's taking me home in triumph for good, once we've had this grand new house built in somewhere unspellable or other. Somewhere with lots of dust, apparently.'

'That doesn't really narrow it down, Your Grace.'

'Oklahoma, I think. Did you see that on your travels?'

Ian shook his head.

'Well, make a point of looking in on us there on your next trip. Bring the old man, why not?'

Ian breathed out heavily. 'I don't think I'll be going back for a while,' he said, a wry smile on his face. 'I didn't like some of the company out there – and I'm not sure they much liked me either.'

The Duke gestured over to a servant to top up their flutes. 'Well, I hope your governor will make the trip one day. I know he thinks I'm an utter imbecile, but I am fond of him really. He's taken a damn sight more interest in me than my old man ever did, I'm bound to say, God rest his soul.'

Ian looked blank. From everything the Doctor had said, the old duke had been a paragon in every way. The duke saw the look on his face and laughed. 'He may have been the finest financial brain the Empire's ever had and all the rest of it, but he wasn't much of a father to me. You'd never have caught him chasing me into houses of ill repute, trying to rescue me from my own sins. He'd never have forked out all that silly gambling money either, of which there was rather a lot to be found, I grant you. Father to the country's balance books, but he didn't have much time for me. After Mother died, it was nannies and boarding schools all the way; he never did have a clue what to say to me. I think perhaps I reminded him of her a bit too much. Not that I'd complain about it – after all, I didn't turn out too bad, what? But I can see your governor, being a "can do" type of chap as a parent, so to speak, always getting his hands dirty looking after you one way or another. And let's face it, he's never wrong about anything. *Mea culpa*, I've always said when I've seen that disappointed look in his eye, because there's no point my arguing with someone who simply knows better than me. Think that's why the wife took to me too, ha!'

It was only when they were all back in the TARDIS, Victorian London left behind them, that Ian related this conversation back to the Doctor.

'Oh, Chesterton,' the old man said, his voice full of regret, 'don't make me think even worse of the boy by telling me that he spoke ill of his father. The old duke was ten times the man little David's become.'

'I don't think he'd argue with that, Doctor,' Ian countered. 'He knows his father's qualities as a public servant and he respects them, but you've got to admit that Chilgrove is more qualified than anyone to comment on what kind of father he had.'

'That boy is feckless,' the Doctor shouted over the console to him, looking down at one of its panels and angrily flicking a few switches. 'He's bone idle. He has a first-class mind which he can't make the effort to use. He has no sense of the duty to his country that comes with his rank – marrying an American and emigrating to Oklahoma! What's worse, that kind of laziness is dangerous. Some of those firemen were badly burned trying to put out that fire that he started with a drunken cigar, you realise.'

'What I think Ian's trying to say, Doctor,' Barbara said in a calm voice, trying to bring down the high pitch of the conversation, 'is that maybe David wouldn't be quite the way he is if his father had spent more time bringing him up to be a duke, and less time throwing himself into politics and government. Maybe he should have looked after his own family first.'

'I shan't hear a word of it, Barbara.'

'Maybe the old duke was the really lazy one. For him, being President of the Board of Trade or Chancellor of the Exchequer was second nature, as easy to him as breathing. Maybe that's how it was for him when he had to save your and Susan's lives in the Indian Mutiny too. But if he couldn't work at something important that was difficult for him – bringing up David properly – perhaps he doesn't deserve quite as much of your respect as you give him.'

The Doctor pushed back his shoulders and stood at his most upright. 'I'll show you,' he said imperiously, his eyes flashing. 'You only met him on his deathbed. Let's go and see what kind of father he was, and then we'll see who's right and who's wrong, hmm?' He scurried to the other side of the console, studied some dials on it, and pressed a few more switches. 'Let me see, let me see... London, 1865,' he said. 'That'll settle it.'

But when the TARDIS landed, the doors opened on a glass canyon a mile deep and a mile wide, its surface covered in grasshoppers the size of tables and with legs that could extend for five or six metres. The sky was yellow and had four moons in it, and there were green clouds.

Ian put an arm round the Doctor's shoulders as they stood in the TARDIS's doorway, and said, 'It's a shame you never bothered to learn how to steer the Ship properly...'

The Doctor just glared.

Wrath

The showman looked rather pleased with himself as he hurried down the corridor. 'Yes, yes, yes!' he was saying to himself. 'It's working! It's actually working! One down, six to go...'

He stopped outside the next room, drew himself up, and took a deep breath before popping his head round the door. Inside, tinny speakers were filling the room with music that was too loud to be called quiet, and too quiet to be listened to properly. 'Won't keep you a moment, Miss Candy,' he said to the imposing-looking woman in the military uniform. Her medals indicated she was no stranger to conflict.

'That's *General* Candy,' she snapped. 'And I'm not accustomed to being kept waiting.'

The showman nodded in polite agreement. 'I'm sure you're not. Which means I'm already fulfilling my part of the bargain; a whole new – unpleasant – experience for you.' He left, shutting the door behind him.

Half an hour later, he returned. 'I'm sorry, Mrs Candy, I'm afraid I've just been informed that we never received your fee, so we won't be able to go ahead today.'

The woman spoke through her teeth. 'You did receive my fee. I had a receipt.'

'Can I see this alleged receipt?'

She drew herself up. 'Are you suggesting I'm a liar?'

'No, no. Can I see this receipt?'

She shook her head. 'No, you cannot. It was requested as I landed. I handed it over to one of your staff.' She grimaced. 'And could you turn off this music?!'

The showman looked surprised. 'Twentieth-century advertising jingles played on pan pipes? You don't like it?'

'It's driving me up the wall!'

He smiled insincerely. 'I'll see what I can do. And I'd better go and investigate this receipt business. Please feel free to amuse yourself while I'm gone.' He indicated a stack of old newspapers and magazines. As he left, she went to investigate. The first bore the headline: 'Candy Responsible For Gemilt 3 Massacre.' The next carried an expose: 'Candy: "I saw her with camel," says aide.'

When the showman came back, the newspapers were confetti on the floor.

'I'm sorry, none of my staff have any recollection of that,' he said, still giving her the same inane smile. 'Now, I do have other clients waiting, so if you'll excuse me...'

The woman stared at him. 'I have paid a considerable sum for this service. A phenomenal sum. And you expect me to just skip off home thanks to the incompetence of your staff?'

The showman ran his eyes down her. 'Well, hardly *skip*... Come, come, Mrs Lollipop –'

'General. *Candy*.'

'– if you don't pay the fee –'

'I paid *the fee*.'

'– then you lose the receipt –'

'*I did not lose the receipt*.'

'– you can hardly expect us to provide the service. Now, if you'll stop wasting my time...'

'*Do you know who I am?*' Her face was brick red.

The showman nodded. 'Lady Toffee, or some such. Massacred all those children. Saw it in the papers.'

'That was all lies!'

He chuckled. 'They'd hardly print it in the papers if it were all lies!'

She raised a hand, looked like she might strike him. 'It was. All. Lies.'

The showman took the hand and patted it, like she was a child. 'Now, now, there wouldn't be any reason for you to get so defensive about it if it wasn't true...' He sighed. 'You've just gone and proved it, as far as I'm concerned.'

She snatched back her hand and swung for him, but he ducked swiftly out of the way.

'I will kill anyone who says I did such a thing!' she screamed.

'If you wait here, someone will escort you back to your ship, poor little cross general,' the showman said, standing straight and laughing in her face.

Her fist flew again; this time he leaned back, impossibly, and her arm soared over him.

He tutted. 'You really should try yoga, you know. Goodness knows what your blood pressure must be like... Go on, say after me, "Ommmm..."'

Her breath was coming in ragged gasps as she glared at him.

'Maybe not. Now, I really do have some more important people to see.'

'I have the forces of an entire solar system at my command,' she said.

The showman laughed. 'A woman, in charge of an army? Oh, I'm sure you've got some nice, safe figurehead role with a smart uniform and good childcare benefits, but they'd never actually put you in charge of an army...' He pointed at a golden medal on her chest. 'What did you get that one for? Flower-arranging? Careful!' He ducked again. 'If you don't watch out you'll break a fingernail...

'Look, I'll tell you what I'll do. You sit at that computer over there and fill in the registration form. I'll see if I can't sort out something about the fee.'

'What about the music?' she called after him. But he had gone.

General Candy kicked out hard at the chair in front of her. After a few minutes, when it seemed the showman was not going to return immediately, she stomped over to the computer and, grudgingly, sat down.

The screen said: Name?

She typed: General Candy. Too long since she'd had a first name. No one left to call her by it, be that informal, be a friend.

It asked her for personal details: age, appearance, career. Things that anyone could find out, but she was still reluctant to commit to type. But if she hadn't been convinced of the absolute discretion of the organisation here, she would never have come. Mind you, her confidence had been taking a bit of a battering thanks to that infuriating imbecile with his patronising smile and his inefficiency and his ridiculous pseudo-historical costume.

Still. She needed this. Andrea had suffered so much misery before her death. The only way Candy could get close to her was by suffering even more...

So she typed in her details, the barest bones of who she was.

But it wanted the meat. The screen asked her to tell her story. And, surprised at her sudden need, she began to do so. She began to tell the screen things she had never spoken of before. Slowly her life rolled up the page in front of her. An unhappy childhood, a small child raging against a world that seemed full of injustice. Her hopes, dreams, fears. Andrea. The atrocities committed against her people, that made her so full of rage... Joining the army together; the desperate desire to make a difference. Her rise to power; the righteous anger against their foes... Andrea's pleas for peace, a heartfelt plan that an enraged soldier could not contemplate. Her death, so easily prevented if only Candy had followed a different course – and after Andrea's death, the blind hatred that had consumed Candy utterly, made her determined to wipe the enemy off the face of the solar system, made her a vessel for wrath and nothing else. The campaigns that followed, military brilliance ruled by anger, no clemency for man, woman or child...

She told the screen everything.

It should have been cathartic. But the life on the screen was full of injustice, full of everything that was wrong with her existence, and it just made her furious.

Everything made her furious.

And the music wasn't helping.

The door opened, and she turned her head to see the showman enter. Then she turned back to the screen.

It was blank.

Where were the words, the thousands and thousands of words that cost her so much?

She hit out, her fist striking the wall. A hairline crack appeared.

'Something the matter?' said the ridiculous mountebank.

'Everything I wrote... gone.'

The showman leaned over the screen, looking. Finally he sighed. 'You obviously did something wrong. It's gone. You'll have to do it again.'

Do it again? Pour out her heart again? Recapture the words that had expressed her to herself, that had told her innermost secrets? The anger, already strong, began to build to even greater heights inside her.

The music went: 'Ooo-ooo-ooo. Ooo-ooo-ooo.'

The showman was bending over the computer. 'Oh, I see what's happened. Whoops. Somehow it seems to have sent it instead of saved it.'

Sent it?

'Sent it to all our clients... every one of your ships... oh, and the newspapers, I see...'

And as General Candy began to roar with all the rage in the world, the showman flipped a switch.

That Which Went Away

Mark Wright

Zoe was cold.

She had never felt anything like it in her life. A bitter, anaesthetising cold that cut through every layer of clothing she had pulled on before leaving the TARDIS. Even the enormous, shaggy fur coat, that the Doctor had helped her into before they stepped from the police box into this barren wilderness, wasn't doing the job he claimed it would. And as for the smell... Well, she'd rather not ask about that.

Zoe huddled deeper into the folds of the coat and looked over at the Doctor. He was walking happily along beside her, decked out in an identical coat that swallowed him up even further than her own. As he bobbed along, he occasionally blew absently into his recorder, a tune for a new composition that would, as usual, never get finished.

'You certainly know how to pick the perfect spot for an afternoon stroll, Doctor,' Zoe mumbled. The Doctor paused in his quest for musical mastery and glanced across, beaming widely.

'Glorious, isn't it?' He returned to blowing into the recorder, stepping his pace up a notch.

Zoe frowned as she struggled to keep up. The Doctor had missed the sarcasm brimming to the surface of her last comment. 'Glorious' this certainly wasn't. Wherever this was.

Freezing mist hung in the air all around them, clouding any sense of perspective and deadening sound to an eerie hollowness. Her booted feet squelched soggily through clumps of yellow, heathery grass, and occasionally she would have to stop to avoid deep, icy puddles of murky water. And, somewhere on the periphery of her stunted senses, waves breaking on a shore tugged at her hearing, close yet always out of reach.

Zoe sighed and stopped. She hadn't stamped her foot or stuck her bottom lip out petulantly for years, but she was close to it now. 'Glorious isn't the word I'd use,' she shouted after the Doctor, who had absent-mindedly pulled even further ahead. A long, drawn-out note indicated he had halted his progress. He turned, an instantly warming look of concern playing across his face as he jogged back to Zoe's side.

'And what word you would use, my dear?'

'Bleak,' she replied without hesitation.

'Oh.' The Doctor's face fell, his sweets taken by the school bully. 'But...'

'Bleak. Cold. Freezing...' The Doctor opened his mouth to speak, but realised it was no use. 'Subzero.'

Tucking his beloved recorder somewhere inside his coat, the Doctor put his arms gently around his companion. 'Well, why don't we compromise on baroque, and leave it at that?' His look of concern folded into a mischievous grin, to which Zoe couldn't help but respond.

'There,' said the Doctor. 'That's better.'

'Oi! You two!' A robust Scots burr cut through the dead silence. 'Come on!'

The Doctor clapped his hands delightedly. 'At least Jamie seems to be enjoying himself,' he commented, watching Jamie come towards them out of the mist. He moved with a powerful, animal grace, and if he was feeling the cold, he certainly wasn't showing it, despite only wearing a flimsy fleece jacket and bearing his legs to the elements from beneath his kilt.

He bounded up to the Doctor and Zoe like a faithful labrador, his skin pink and healthy with exertion, dark brown hair matted down over his forehead with sweat and moisture. 'Are you two comin' or not?'

'I think that's quite enough exercise for today, Jamie,' the Doctor told him, throwing a sideways glance at Zoe. 'We should, er, probably head back to the TARDIS. Baths and hot chocolate all round, I think.'

'Och! I'm just getting goin',' protested Jamie, but the Doctor was having none of it and started to usher his friends in the direction they had come from.

'Where are we anyway, Doctor?' asked Zoe, it suddenly occurring to her that nobody had bothered to ask that question.

'Do you know, I haven't the foggiest,' the Doctor replied in breezy honesty. 'The coordinates the TARDIS gave me put us smack bang in the middle of the Serpentine, jubilee week, 1977. Which, um, can't be right. I expect the old girl will make her mind up eventually.' Jamie and Zoe exchanged withering looks as the Doctor babbled away. 'I think it's Earth, but aside from that –' he spread his arms wide '– it could be absolutely anywhere!'

'At least you're consistent, Doctor,' said Zoe, poker-faced.

'Aye,' Jamie played along. 'It wouldn't do t'know where we were, would it?'

The Doctor frowned. 'Now listen, you two,' he grumbled, wagging a finger reproachfully. 'The TARDIS...' And then he noticed the grins on his companions' faces, which shattered into uncontrolled bellows of laughter. The Doctor smiled, and then joined in, and soon their guffaws were echoing back at them from the surrounding mist.

The Doctor suppressed his laughter enough to smile ruefully at Jamie and Zoe. 'Sometimes I don't know how I put up with you two, I really don't!'

'The feeling's mutual, Doctor,' Jamie said, smirking.

'Come on, then, back to the TARDIS.' The Doctor turned and linked arms with his friends. 'First one there gets a lollipop!'

They stepped forward as one, but stopped immediately.

'Oh, dear.' The Doctor sighed.

The mist had parted briefly, revealing an imposing line of twenty or so men blocking their path.

Very tall, frightening men.

Carrying swords and spears.

'Mebbe we should go round the other way, Doctor,' said Jamie, slowly and deliberately.

'I think that may be wise, Jamie.'

'They might be friendly,' Zoe whispered, always ready with the benefit of the doubt.

The man at the centre of the line, long blond hair blowing in the wind, scratched his beard before drawing a shining sword from the leather scabbard hanging at his belt. He was clearly the leader, and the men standing on either side hefted an assortment of spears and axes and less impressive swords.

'Ah. I think not, Zoe. Jamie.'

'Doctor.'

'Zoe.'

'Doctor.'

'When I say run...'

'I think we get the idea, Doctor,' hissed Zoe impatiently, adrenalin making her voice quiver with more than a little fear.

'Yes, quite. Run!'

The Doctor grabbed Zoe's hand and dragged her away, his feet sliding on the slippery grass but eventually managing to find purchase. Jamie broke in the opposite direction, springing like some wild cat to provide a second moving target and divide the attention of the attackers.

The leader of the men shouted once and they sprung into action with guttural cries, their leather-booted feet thudding and splashing through the sodden undergrowth.

Zoe cried out as a spear sliced through the air and buried itself into the ground next to her. She felt the Doctor, who was breathing hard with exertion, take her hand once more and pull her forward. 'Keep going, Zoe!' he shouted.

'Where's Jamie?' she gasped back.

'Jamie can look after himself. Come on!'

Jamie could see the Doctor and Zoe running as fast as they could across the way, a pack of the men in pursuit. He couldn't worry about that now and banished them from his mind, his battle sense, learnt in the wilds of the Scottish Highlands, kicking in unconsciously.

As he ran, he ducked down, deftly pulling a long knife from his boot in one fluid motion. Behind, he sensed movement and turned, kneeling quickly and assessing the danger.

A band of the men – definitely soldiers of some kind – bore down on him. He immediately jumped into action, his muscled legs propelling him forward. The lead soldier had a spear raised high as he stormed towards Jamie, and the young Scot went straight for him, shoulder charging beneath the line of the spear into the man's solid thighs, using his opponent's momentum to propel him up and over his back, depositing him with a sickening crunch on the ground.

Not even pausing to think, Jamie turned and lunged forward with his knife, catching the outstretched sword arm of another aggressor. The man yelped in pain but still managed to lash out, backhanding Jamie in the face. Jamie grunted at the blast of pain, tasting blood, but didn't go down, still clutching his opponent's sword arm.

'Think ye can take on a McCrimmon, do ye?' he screamed, bringing his knee up. It crunched satisfyingly into his attacker's forearm. The warrior howled in pain, falling to the floor and releasing his weapon.

In a flash, Jamie sheathed his dagger and picked up the fallen sword. It was crude. He swung it experimentally. 'Aye, that'll do it, I reckon.'

He turned once more to the pack of attackers, bringing his newly acquired sword up to eye level.

'Come on then, ye Sassenachs,' he breathed to himself, then stepped forward.

The Doctor and Zoe had managed keep just ahead of their pursuers, their size and relative nimbleness compared to the lumbering gait of the men giving them a slight edge. But it wasn't long before the stamina of the chasing force had them snapping at their heels. Spears thudded into the ground around them, and it was surely only a matter of time before one hit home.

Zoe was sweating under the weight of the heavy coat, and she knew she couldn't keep going for much longer. Capture and whatever fate awaited them was inevitable. The Doctor was running along at her side, shouting encouraging words, but even he was starting to flag.

One of Zoe's booted feet struck an unexpected stone hiding beneath a clump of grass, and that was enough to send her flying. She heard the Doctor yelp in panic before she crashed to the ground. Most of the impact was absorbed by her coat, but she now had a mouthful of soil and freezing water.

The Doctor hopped around in worry, before leaning down to see if she was hurt, just as the soldiers swarmed up to them. The air filled with the odour of fetid sweat and rank breath. The Doctor stood calmly, looking into the eyes of the front soldier, before kneeling down to help Zoe to her feet. Slowly, the men surrounded them, cutting off any chance of escape.

'What now?' asked Zoe, rubbing her aching, mud-covered jaw.

The Doctor raised his arms in the air. 'Surrender and smile nicely.'

Zoe followed the Doctor's lead, but screamed as one of the men roared and leapt forward. He scooped Zoe up in his arms and threw her like a sack of grain over his shoulder. The other men laughed and whooped, cheering their comrade on as he paraded backwards and forwards with his prize, who rained ineffectual blows down on the brute's broad shoulders.

'Put her down this instant!' the Doctor pleaded, jumping forward to help, but he was held back by one of the men, both arms pinned behind his back. 'Oh, no! Zoe!' he cried helplessly.

Zoe's captor stopped and looked back at his comrades, his show of bravado striking a popular note. He grinned stupidly at them, an arm raised in the air in triumph, his other holding Zoe firmly in place.

His grin suddenly became a wide-eyed cry of shock when a spear zipped through the air, ripping into the centre of his chest with a dull thud. His arms immediately went limp, and Zoe slithered to the ground, curling herself into a sobbing ball. The soldier just stared at the long, wooden-shafted weapon protruding from his chest for a few seconds before collapsing to the ground in a dead heap.

The Doctor's eyes widened before he turned to where the spear had originated. Not far away, standing atop a grassy ridge, was another line of very tall, very frightening men, holding spears and swords.

Swords clattered against each other as Jamie parried yet another blow, quickly returning the attack with a hacking cut to his opponent's upper leg. Cut. Evade. Thrust. Dodge. Parry. Smash.

Sweat was stinging his eyes, blood tasting bitter and warm in his mouth, muscles aching and tight, but Jamie kept going. He was made to be a warrior.

He smashed a blade to one side and brought the flat of his hand up into the face of yet another marauder. Bone cracked and blood spurted.

Breathing hard and fast, Jamie whirled around to face his next conquest, but there was none. As the red heat of battle faded from before his eyes, his first thought was for Zoe and the Doctor. Which way had they gone? His head snapped from side to side, looking desperately for his companions, but they were nowhere to be seen. What he did see froze the racing blood in his veins.

The man who obviously led the band of attackers stood watching Jamie curiously, head cocked to one side like a cat. He didn't seem concerned with the bodies of his fallen comrades, some of whom were starting to come to, groaning and crawling away from the wildcat that had cut them down. He just looked. Jamie knew he was being sized up.

The leader was taller than his men by a good foot, powerfully built. He wore a tunic of deep red, and, although dirty, it was woven with an intricate pattern that must have denoted some kind of leadership. His beard was long, but neat, and his blond hair hung down to his shoulders.

He raised his sword and looked directly into Jamie's eyes. 'Boy!' he bellowed, and sprang forward.

Jamie swallowed hard, caught off guard, and leapt to meet him, swords colliding with a dull, sickening clang. Jamie's arms rang with the impact and he was thrown off balance by the blow, stumbling on to the ground. He rolled immediately to evade the whistling sword that was thrust where he'd been a second earlier.

Jamie laboured to his feet. This lad was much stronger than the others. It occurred to the Scot that he might finally have met his match.

The Doctor didn't take his eyes off the new arrivals as he stepped slowly sideways and backwards, putting himself between danger and Zoe, who was starting to get unsteadily to her feet.

It seemed safe to assume that the new arrivals weren't friends of their attackers, but neither did it follow that they would be inviting the Doctor and his friends round for tea. It just added a new and possibly dangerous element to an already perilous situation.

The two gangs of men faced off across the grassland, and an imposing figure stepped to the head of the line of new arrivals, looking down from the rise.

He was imposingly handsome, his beard and hair a fiery, russet brown, contrasting with the blond of his comrades. He stared down for a second at the scene below, his keen, piercing gaze taking in the Doctor and Zoe, before sweeping to the ragged line of men standing by their dead comrade.

Spears were hefted, swords drawn and muscles tensed.

The leader looked quickly to either side and raised his sword before swiping it down.

No words had been necessary. His men roared into action, exploding from the rise, streaming towards the Doctor and Zoe.

'Doctor!' Zoe screamed.

'Oh, my giddy aunt! Not again!' The Doctor hugged Zoe to him protectively, expecting the cold bite of a sword blade to strike at any second.

The men ignored them, swarming around instead and going straight for the other band of warriors, their battle cry a terrifying roar. They easily outnumbered their opposition, who, leaderless, turned and ran.

The Doctor let go of Zoe, noticing that her eyes were screwed tightly shut.

'You can open your eyes, Zoe,' he said, smiling.

'Are they gone?' she asked through gritted teeth.

'Yes, for the time being.'

'They will not be back.' A rich, gentle voice spoke to them, the kind of voice that rarely spoke louder than it ever needed to. The leader of the men had walked over to the Doctor and Zoe without a sound. He sheathed his sword in the rough leather scabbard hanging from his belt.

The Doctor cautiously regarded their apparent saviour. 'You have my thanks. It seems we owe you our lives.'

The man dismissed the Doctor's gratitude with a grunt and relaxed wave of his hands. 'Think of it not. Vignor's tribe are no more than barbarians. I am Bior, drighten of my tribe. You are welcome here.'

The Doctor smiled in return. 'That's most kind of you. This is Zoe, and I'm the Doctor.'

Bior grinned widely, showing a full line of healthy teeth. 'Friends, you are welcome. But this is dangerous country to travel alone and unarmed.'

Zoe spoke for the first time, overcoming her awe at Bior's imposing presence. 'We were trying to get back to the TARD–'

The Doctor interrupted her. 'We're just travellers, making our way home.'

Bior nodded, understanding. 'As are we all.'

'Speaking of which, we really must be on our way. As soon as we've found...' The Doctor stopped short, remembering something. Zoe touched his arm in concern.

'Doctor?'

The Doctor's eyes widened in horror. 'Jamie!'

Jamie dodged another whistling blow as his opponent's sword swiped down to his side. Once again, he slammed his own weapon into the blade, trying to beat it down, but his rival was just too damn strong. Again he was thrown back, but managed to keep his balance and glance away the next thrust.

The challenger pulled back for an instant, regaining his own balance. Jamie could feel the sour breath of his attacker merging with his own, and Jamie's heart slammed blood through his veins, almost deafening him.

Their eyes met.

This would end soon, one way or another, but Jamie would not give up.

Jamie wiped away the sweat-soaked hair from his brow, before feinting to the left, then moving quickly to the right. But his opponent had not been fooled and had brought his sword swinging round in a wide, graceful arc. With a grunt of effort, he slammed the blade into Jamie's side.

'Jamie!'

Zoe saw the sword bite into Jamie as she ran across the plain, the Doctor and Bior right behind her.

Jamie dropped like a stone and lay still, while his attacker, alerted by Zoe's cry, looked round, ready for a new attack. When Bior saw the man, he immediately went for his sword, roaring a guttural battle cry and swinging the blade in a circle over his head. He leapt ahead of Zoe, storming down the gentle slope, an animal power propelling him forward – surprisingly quickly, considering his broad, tall frame.

Jamie's opponent simply grinned, raised his bloody sword in a defiant salute, before turning and sprinting away, spurred on by the threat of Bior's roaring pursuit.

'Oh, my word, Jamie!' the Doctor cried, hopping down the slope behind Zoe to where Jamie's prone form lay.

* * *

Jamie heard Zoe scream. His instinct, as always, was to protect her, but something was wrong. He heard her, but couldn't see. She was calling his name. He tried to call back, to let her know it was all right, that he was there, but speaking was painful, his voice coming as a feeble croak.

'Zoe...'

'It's all right, Jamie, we're here,' said Zoe, trying to sound calm, but wanting to break down into sobs at any moment. The Doctor knelt, a serious look creasing his face as he examined his young friend, opening the boy's ripped fleece jacket.

'Jamie, it's the Doctor.' The Doctor spoke loudly, surgeon to patient. Jamie moaned once as the Doctor examined the wound with practised hands. His face clouded as he brought his hand to show Zoe. It was slick and wet with blood.

Zoe balked, her stomach churning. 'Oh, no.'

Jamie was beginning to shiver violently and the Doctor immediately removed his coat. 'He's going into shock. Zoe, help me!'

Zoe knelt by the Doctor and helped to move Jamie as gently as possible. They placed the coat around him. He seemed light, suddenly insubstantial.

'Your friend is hurt.' Bior had abandoned his pursuit and stood looking down at them. They hadn't heard him approach. His men, having routed the other band, were starting to gather around, waiting for instructions.

The tribal drighten continued. 'It is not safe to remain here. You must come with my thanes and me to our village. We can tend to your friend there.'

Zoe was doubtful. 'Doctor, we must get Jamie back to the TARDIS. We'll have a better chance of treating him there.'

The Doctor chewed on a finger thoughtfully, his other hand resting on Jamie. 'We don't even know where the TARDIS is, Zoe. And, even if we do get back to the ship, actually finding the hospital room is a whole other kettle of fish.' Jamie moaned, and Zoe opened her mouth to protest, but the Doctor cut her off. 'Jamie doesn't have that much time.'

The Doctor stood and turned to Bior. 'Thank you. That would be very kind.'

Bior had sprung into action immediately, barking instructions to his men. There was nothing with which to fashion a stretcher, but after the Doctor had padded Jamie's wound as best he could – blood still trickled steadily around the makeshift dressing – six of the thanes gently hoisted the unconscious Jamie into the air.

And it was like this that they held Jamie aloft, their strong arms cradling the Scot as well as any stretcher, keeping him secure and supported.

Bior strode ahead at the front of the party, sword drawn, eyes searching. The Doctor and Zoe followed behind Jamie and his carriers, the rear brought up by the remainder of Bior's thanes, eyes bright and alert, spears held ready to fight off any attack.

As they jogged at a brisk pace across the countryside, the sky darkening towards dusk, a cold sleet began. The Doctor, now in just his jacket, didn't seem to feel the cold. There was nothing that could be done for Jamie until they had arrived at their destination, and the Doctor talked to Zoe quite animatedly as they moved along.

'Meeting these fellows has allowed me to make an educated guess as to where we are. I'd say Scandinavia, somewhere on the peninsula.' He sucked in breath through his teeth. 'Possibly about the eighth or ninth century.'

'Scandinavia?' Zoe gasped, a little breathless, trying to remember Earth's history. 'Vikings?'

'Technically, not quite. If I'm right, we're in the correct geographical location, but, temporally, we're just on the cusp of the vikings' voyages across the oceans into the rest of Europe and Russia. It's probably more correct to call these chaps barbarians.'

'I don't really care what we call them as long as there's help for Jamie at the other end and something approaching a warm fire.'

From his human stretcher, Jamie cried out before lapsing back into fevered oblivion.

The Doctor looked up grimly, and then put an arm out to Zoe in reassurance. 'I'm sure it won't be long now.'

Twenty minutes of hard jogging brought them to the village that Bior's tribe called home. Along with the driving sleet, the dense mist had fallen again, but as they began to descend a shallow, sweeping slope, Zoe could see the orange smudges of campfires lighting their way like a welcoming beacon.

As they descended lower, the indistinct black shapes amongst the brightening splodges of fire revealed themselves to be a collection of sturdily built wooden huts of varying sizes, dominated in the centre by a long, high dwelling that dwarfed the rest. In the fading light, she could just about make out grey smoke curling from a square opening in the roof.

Beyond the nestling of huts, Zoe could also see that her instincts about the ocean had been correct. The settlement rested on the edge of a narrow inlet of water, snaking away into the distance, and she had a brief sense of salt air on her face as a waft of breeze picked up.

As they made their way into the village, their arrival drew attention from the villagers, as women emerged into the cold from the smaller huts, ready to greet the return of their men.

A hubbub of cautious chattering began around the village at the sight of Jamie being held aloft by the six warriors, and Zoe could feel the eyes of curiosity on her too. Children peered out wide-eyed from between their mothers' legs.

They stopped in the centre of the village for a second. Bior spoke to one of the warriors. 'Take him straight to Hefn's hut.' The man nodded quickly and the six thanes carried Jamie to a hut on the far side of the village, one that was slightly larger than the standard dwellings.

Bior noticed the worried looks of the Doctor and Zoe as they watched Jamie manhandled through the low doorway into the hut. 'Fear not, my friends. My man, Hefn, is adept in the art of plants and herbs. He has closed many wounds of mine.' As if to demonstrate his robust health, he banged both fists into his chest, smiling a wide, reassuring grin.

'Husband!' A female voice called from across the encampment. Warming firelight spilled from the doorway of the large, dominating building as a fur drape was moved aside. A figure moved rapidly from shadowy silhouette into the dim twilight, revealing a striking woman walking towards them. She wore simply a long, blue dress, over which she had wrapped a fearsome-looking animal fur against the cold. Her blonde hair flowed freely, blowing lightly in the breeze. As she drew nearer, Bior took her in his arms, lifting her easily in the air. He kissed her with a sudden passion before lowering her with a gentleness that belied the big man's strength.

'My frawe, Aella,' he declared, with obvious love in his eyes.

Zoe mouthed 'frawe' at the Doctor with a questioning look. He responded, mouthing the word 'wife' in explanation.

'Father!' A whirlwind of movement flashed from the long house and barrelled up to the group. Bior laughed as a ball of energy slammed into him, and he picked up this whirling mass of arms and legs that turned out to be a boy aged, Zoe guessed, about five years old. He giggled as his father rubbed the roughness of his beard against the boy's cheek, and both then roared in mock drama, seemingly a tradition between father and son. The lad noticed the Doctor and Zoe and now eyed them with suspicion.

'What happened?' Aella asked her husband, also looking curiously upon the two newcomers.

Bior grunted. 'The Doctor and Zoe were set upon by Vignor and his dogs.' Both the Doctor and Zoe smiled and nodded awkwardly in greeting. 'Their thane, Jamie, took on Vignor himself and was hurt.'

'My thanks to your Bior,' said the Doctor graciously, 'but I think we should be with my, erm... thane, um, Jamie, that is. I may be able to offer assistance.'

'Yes, of course.' Bior placed his son gently back on the ground. 'Einar, go with your mother and help prepare the food.'

Jamie was alone.

He was surrounded by thick, cloying smoke. It was sweet and pungent, almost tangible, and however much he wafted at it, it would not dissipate.

He ran one way, then the other, trying to break through, but he was hemmed in, the thick smoke acting like a physical barrier.

He stopped, trying to get some bearing. Silence pressed in. He cocked his head on one side, listening.

Movement!
A flash of something moving quickly through the smoke. Powerful.
He ran after it, but it was gone.
He stood, breathing hard, the burning in his side getting worse.
Then, from somewhere out in the void, a low growl forced its way through the vapour.
There was something out there!
He ran towards the sound, but again, the same. Nothing.
Something was playing a game with him.
Whatever it was, it clearly wasn't safe. He had to find the Doctor and Zoe.

'Doctor!' Jamie moaned, sweat pouring from his forehead. 'Zoe!'
He thrashed around for a second, held down by the strength of one of the thanes.
 'It's all right, Jamie! We're here!'
The Doctor placed a hand on the thane's solid shoulder, indicating with a gentle smile that he should step aside. Zoe watched the Doctor take his place, kneeling down close to Jamie, so he could be heard.
The hut was deceptively spacious, but eerily lit by a single, large fire in the centre of the room, the roaring flames casting dancing shadows around the rough wooden walls. The smoke escaped through a square hole in the ceiling.
Jamie was stripped to the waist, sweating in the fierce heat cast by the fire. Zoe winced as she saw the sword wound, a deep gash running across his stomach, blood still running from it freely.
As the Doctor attempted to calm Jamie, a thin man was busy mixing something in a wooden bowl. He scattered a handful of what looked like berries into the mixture, and continued his work. His cheekbones were high and shallow and, even in the red-hot light, he appeared pale. He didn't have the same robust strength as Bior and his men, but the eyes burned with a clear intelligence.
Zoe was disturbed by Bior entering the hut behind her, the big man stooping to fit through the door.
'Hefn?'
The man looked up from his work, exchanged a look with his drighten, and then returned to his task. He spoke to the Doctor as he continued.
'Your friend's wound is severe.'
'Hmm,' the Doctor responded. 'Can you help?'
The man, Hefn, did not reply. He scooped a thick, black mixture of herbs and berries out of the bowl and dabbed it gently around the wound. Jamie's back arched for a second and he gritted his teeth, pain creasing his face, but as more of the mixture was added, he settled back, his breathing calmer.
'This should stem the flow of blood,' Hefn told them matter-of-factly. He carefully placed a last blob of the concoction on to Jamie's body, then turned

away and began sprinkling more herbs into a different bowl from a varied pile of dried preparations. The Doctor looked on in interest, passing comment on something that was being added to the mix. Hefn regarded the Doctor for a second, his eyes seemingly incandescent in the light of the fire. Then he smiled briefly and nodded in agreement. He added a small amount of something suggested by the Doctor.

Despite her concern for Jamie, Zoe's gaze, now accustomed to the intensity of the light within the medicine man's hut, began to wander around the walls, which were adorned with various ornaments.

There was nothing particularly spooky or macabre about anything in the hut. A branch was attached to a wall here, piles of drying grasses and plants lay in a corner there. She had expected something more... mystical, she supposed. No, this all seemed quite practical.

But as she gazed at the far wall, she saw something that almost made her jump. Stretched wide and pinned high up was the pelt of an animal. It was brown, and the edges of the skin had been roughly hacked away from the carcass of whichever beast it had belonged to.

Zoe shivered, despite the choking heat, and turned away from the stomach-clenching sight. Hefn was clearing away the first application of herbs from Jamie's stomach. The blood flow had stopped, as promised, but the wound still looked evil. Jamie looked much calmer and was starting to come round. Over the wound, Hefn now placed a much healthier-looking green mixture that he and the Doctor had collaborated over.

'This will begin the healing process,' he said simply.

'Doctor?' Jamie croaked weakly, his eyes flickering open. The Doctor smiled and gripped his hand. Zoe quickly rushed over to their side.

'Hello, Jamie,' said the Doctor.

Jamie winced. 'What happened?'

'You got into a fight, as always,' Zoe joked, trying to lighten the mood.

'It's all right, though,' said the Doctor. 'We're safe now, and you should see the other chap.'

Jamie smiled, but started to cough, the hacking running through his body. Hefn finished applying the new mix of herbs, and Jamie lost consciousness again. His chest rose and fell steadily, sleep taking him.

'Now he needs rest.'

'And prayer?' Zoe asked. Hefn glanced at her as if she was mad.

'If you wish.'

Bior laughed from where he stood. 'Hefn puts no trust in the gods. Come, my friends. We eat as a tribe, and you come as my guests. Maybe we can persuade the gatekeepers of the beyond to not let your warrior in just yet!'

Satisfied that Jamie was out of danger, the Doctor and Zoe were happy to be led across the small village to the long house that dominated the encampment. Night had fallen now, and darkness surrounded them. Zoe felt a sense of isolation, but that vanished as an animal skin was moved aside and she entered the structure.

The Doctor had explained that this was the central meeting point of the village, and would probably have served as the quarters of the drighten's family, with the thanes and other members of the community living in the smaller huts dotted around it.

The large room was more brightly lit than Hefn's hut, with torches around the walls, and this warming light gave Zoe some comfort after the bleakness of the Scandinavian plain. A large fire blazed in the centre of the room, the smoke blanketing up into the high roof, where it escaped through the hole in the ceiling. Zoe could see joints of meat and bundles of fish hanging there, and she guessed that smoked fish and meat provided the tribe with its staple diet.

Zoe followed the Doctor to where they had been invited to sit with Bior, Aella and Einar. The child sat protected between his father's crossed legs and shared food from the pile that sat in front of them.

Around the room, the rest of the villagers had assembled, and sat around in various family units. The thanes (or 'warriors', as the Doctor had explained) sat in more prominent positions, with the rest of the villagers sitting where they could. There were about fifty people in all, Zoe guessed, and there was a happy, if businesslike, air to the meal.

As Zoe picked at an unappetising but surprisingly delicious hunk of smoked fish, the Doctor spoke with Bior.

'We are just entering the winter months,' the drighten said through mouthfuls of meat, 'and we are gathering what final resources we can.'

The Doctor nodded, picking at his own food, but declining the mead that Aella had offered him. Zoe had no such qualms, and accepted the potent brew. She exchanged a conspiratorial look with Bior's wife.

'And our friends out there on the plain?' the Doctor asked, and Bior spat.

'Vignor. His village is not far from here and we compete for the same resources. I have lost several of my thanes in skirmishes between our people.' A look of angry pain flashed into his eyes, quickly replaced by a steely resolve. 'But he has lost many more.'

The Doctor finished off the last of his meal. 'You have my eternal thanks for your help and hospitality.'

Bior grunted. 'You must stay until your Jamie is rested. Hefn is skilled in his art, and he will heal quickly.'

'Thank you.' The Doctor glanced at Zoe as she drained her cup of mead. She looked back with a lopsided grin and sleepy eyes. The Doctor cast his eyes heavenwards with a smile.

Movement at the door attracted their attention, however, and they saw that Hefn had ducked under the covering animal fur. He stood at the door, not coming any further. A look passed between the medicine man and his chief.

'My friends,' said Bior. 'Aella will see you are provided with a warm place to sleep. I must go.' He kissed Einar on the forehead and the child crawled from his father into the arms of his mother, who was frowning worriedly at her husband. Bior hardly acknowledged her as he rose to his feet.

Around the hall, the thanes also stood, as one, and they followed the drighten to the door, filing through it into the night, one by one. The Doctor watched curiously as the last man disappeared, then noticed that Hefn was still there, staring at him.

The Doctor looked away, and when he looked back, Hefn was gone.

Zoe awoke, her head thick with the effects of the mead. She tried to move, but she was weighed down by a thick covering of animal skins.

She had vague memories of being led across the village to a small hut, but sleep had taken her immediately as she was cocooned in the warm pile of furs.

Silence surrounded the hut as she lay there, listening, her eyes growing accustomed to the dark.

Just as she was about to close her eyes and let sleep take her once more, a long wail sounded somewhere out on the plain, the cry of some animal.

She sat up with some difficulty, listening again. There it was, a howling, almost a growl. She shivered.

'It's all right, Zoe. Go back to sleep.'

She hadn't seen the Doctor sat cross-legged in the darkness by the open doorway. She could just make him out, peering out through the opening, eyes narrowed in concentration. His recorder was clutched in his hands, and he was blowing into it absently, but barely strongly enough to form a note.

Happy that the Doctor was keeping watch, Zoe flopped back down beneath the pile of bedding and was soon drifting back to sleep.

Long after Zoe had returned to her slumber, the Doctor remained in his position at the door. The growling wail came again from far off on the plain, and the Doctor blew a long, quiet note into his recorder.

Watching.

Listening.

'Doctor!' Jamie's face brightened as the Doctor and Zoe entered Hefn's hut. He sat atop a pile of furs, barechested, the area surrounding his wound still covered in the herbal sludge. Colour had returned to his cheeks, and he ate from a wooden plate piled with smoked meat and fish.

The Doctor clapped his hands together. 'Well, you look much better!'

'Aye, I feel it,' replied Jamie through a mouthful of food. He shifted slightly, wincing. 'There's still pain though.'

'Maybe this will teach you not to go running into battle against an army of barbarian warriors,' Zoe said with mock admonishment.

It was the morning of their fifth day in the village, and Jamie's recovery had been remarkable. The first two days had seen the boy drifting in and out of feverish consciousness, tended to by Hefn with the Doctor's assistance. Between them, they had coaxed Jamie away from the brink of death and by now he was well on the way to recovery.

Jamie grinned at Zoe. 'Not likely!'

Zoe frowned. 'I didn't think it would.'

Hefn removed the green sludge from Jamie's side. The wound was still an angry red, but it had closed, and it looked clean.

'I believe,' said the medicine man, 'that you can be moved to your friends' quarters. There is nothing more to be done except rest.'

'Splendid,' said the Doctor. 'A few more days, and we should be on our way.'

Hefn nodded but said nothing.

As Hefn cleaned up the area surrounding Jamie's battle wound, the Doctor and Zoe promised that they would return shortly and then left them alone.

Together they walked across the village. For the last few days, they had been readily welcomed into the bosom of the tribe, helping wherever they could.

Zoe had, to her satisfaction, surprised the farming men of the village, helping out with manual tasks and the gathering of supplies, even going out in the small wooden boats on to the inlet to gather fish. Used to being slaved to a computer console and throwing numbers around in her head, she relished the physical nature of the work, gaining the grudging respect of the men in a short time.

The Doctor, typically, made himself popular with just about everybody. He would flit around the village, helping the women prepare food, making them laugh with stories, or entertaining the children with games or a tune on his recorder. Zoe had seen him on more than one occasion being chased across the village by a gang of children, giving one of them a piggyback with obvious delight on his face. Or he would talk with Bior about the trials of their existence on the plain and the approaching winter.

In the evenings, they would eat as a tribe in the long house, followed by songs and merriment. The men would wrestle each other in shows of strength, and Zoe found herself developing a taste for the musty, powerful mead that was passed around.

But at the same time every night, Bior would hug his son, pass him to Aella and leave the long house with his thanes as Hefn appeared in the doorway. On the second night, she had seen the Doctor looking on the ritual with those curious eyes of his. When he realised that Zoe was watching him, he smiled at her sheepishly.

On the fifth night, Zoe left the long house, pulling her fur coat around her to cross the village to the hut she shared with the Doctor. She was about to head across the darkness, but a movement behind caught her attention.

The Doctor leant against the wooden wall of the long house, hand in his pockets.

'Doctor?'

He jumped slightly, suddenly realising she was there. 'Oh, Zoe.'

'How long have you been out here? You didn't come in for dinner.'

'No. I wasn't hungry.'

'What the matter?'

'Who says anything's the matter?'

Zoe cocked her head on one side. 'Doctor,' she said warningly, and the Doctor smiled. He'd been seen through.

'Look.' He gestured across to the far side of the village.

Torches had been lit, and this allowed Zoe to see the village thanes standing in a huddle around Bior and Hefn. Seconds later, the group turned as one, and they began to run out of the village, Bior leading them. Zoe and the Doctor watched as the torches were quickly swallowed up by the night.

'Where are they going?' Zoe asked.

The Doctor shrugged. 'I have no idea, but this has happened every night since we've been here. They leave, and return just after dawn. Like clockwork.'

'Doctor, don't worry about it. It's got nothing to do with us how Bior and his people go about their business. They've been kind to us and without their help, Jamie would be...' Zoe didn't want to finish the sentence.

'Yes, I know. I just have...'

'A feeling? You always have a feeling, Doctor. Let them get on with their lives. With luck, we'll be gone in a few days. Stop looking for trouble.'

The Doctor frowned, but his expression quickly softened. 'Yes. Yes, you're absolutely right, Zoe.'

Zoe smiled, bid the Doctor good night and made her way quickly towards the hut and her pile of warm furs.

As she left, she saw the Doctor return his gaze in the direction that Bior and his men had taken.

And now, in the cold light of the following morning, it seemed they would be leaving very soon.

Making their way across the village, the Doctor and Zoe greeted people who had become friends, and Zoe had a pang of regret that they would be departing in a day or two. She stretched, barely worked muscles coming alive, and breathed in fresh air. There was something nurturing about this environment, and it was no wonder that Jamie had healed as quickly as he had.

'You like it here, don't you?' the Doctor asked.

'Yes. Friendly people, fresh air, hard work. It makes me realise just how privileged and easy a life is in the future.'

'Indeed,' the Doctor agreed.

Ahead they could see Bior chasing Einar round in a tight circle, making the boy laugh uncontrollably. He scooped his son up from the ground, swung him round and plonked him easily on his shoulders. He saw the Doctor and shouted a greeting as he strode towards them.

'Good morning!' the Doctor called, winking at Einar, who giggled at the funny man who had been so entertaining for the last few days.

'My friends, you are well?'

'Very much so, and so is Jamie. It seems we shall be leaving you soon.'

'That is good, but a shame also. You are welcome here always.'

'Thank you so much for your help,' Zoe added.

'But you will stay for at least a few more days.'

'I'm sure that would be best, just so Jamie is properly well again,' said the Doctor.

A curious look had crept into Bior's eyes. 'Oh, he will be fully healed, of that you have my word.'

As the day wore on towards the rapidly approaching night, the village went about its life as normal. Jamie was moved from the medicine man's hut, supported between two thanes, to the Doctor and Zoe's hut.

Zoe wandered behind them to make sure he settled, and she reflected on how at home he seemed amongst these warriors. They had taken Jamie as one of their own, impressed by his prowess on the battlefield, and Jamie happily laughed and joked with the two men who carried him now. They spoke the same language, the language of battle, of fighting men.

He slept for most of the afternoon and Zoe sat with him while the Doctor wandered the village, blowing into his recorder. Something was troubling him, but she had no idea what. He was probably just getting itchy feet and ready to leave, no doubt eager for more adventure.

As usual, the communal meal took place just after sunset, and it was the usual raucous occasion. A place had been opened out for Jamie amongst the thanes, and he ate heartily. There was much laughter and drinking of mead, and Jamie joined in enthusiastically. He would look over occasionally and grin at the Doctor and Zoe. Zoe knew this was good for him, but she could tell that the Doctor wasn't entirely comfortable. If she didn't know better, she'd say he was jealous.

Later that night, the Doctor, Jamie and Zoe slept, huddled beneath piles of animal skins. A soft rain pattered down on the roof of the small hut, and a mist had fallen, entwined with the night.

Torchlight flickered outside the door of the hut and a figure, steeped in shadow, stepped through, taking care to make no noise. The figure held the torch up, regarding the sleeping forms of first the Doctor, then Zoe, the torch highlighting their faces in a contrast of orange glow and dark shadow.

The figure moved across to Jamie, stepping gently, kneeling down next him. The torch lit the intruder's face. Hefn looked down at Jamie, face serious, and gently shook him until he woke, indicating he should be silent.

'Come, boy.' he whispered. 'Your healing is just beginning.'

Jamie climbed to his feet. With a last look at the Doctor and Zoe, he followed the medicine man from the hut.

For several minutes, the only sound in the hut was that of the Doctor and Zoe's steady breathing and the rain, getting heavier, pattering down on the roof.

The Doctor's eyes snapped open. He reached out for his jacket and coat and moved towards the door. He looked back to make sure Zoe was sleeping soundly, before tiptoeing out.

Jamie ran into the night, a refreshing shower of rain spraying across his face. He felt protected at the centre of a running pack of thanes, all bearing torches, Bior and Hefn leading the way.

He didn't know where they were going, and despite the pain that crept across his stomach from his healing wound, it felt good to be running, his muscles, cramped for the last week, stretching with use.

Cold air blasted his face as the pace picked up, and one of the thanes gave him an encouraging look, slapping his back in comradeship.

Jamie grinned and ran on with his brothers.

The Doctor followed.

Rain battered down from the heavens, plastering his unruly mop of hair into a sodden, tangled mass that persisted in slithering down over his eyes. He was forced to slick it back every few seconds to see where he was going, as his boots slipped and slid across the waterlogged terrain.

Combined with the dark of the night and the seemingly ever-present chilled veil of mist, the Doctor felt as if a barrier weighed down on him from every angle as he forged ahead. But somehow he managed to keep pace with Bior's relentless progress across the plain, moving further away from the safety of the settlement. Ahead he could just make out the dirty orange smudges of the warrior band's torches, bobbing along like fiery will-o'-the-wisps, their light not extinguished by the barrage of falling rain

The Doctor wrung his hands with worry as he jogged along. Jamie had recovered his strength remarkably quickly, and he had a level head on his shoulders, but his ready acceptance into the warriors' circle had filled him with something that he hadn't seen in the lad since their first meeting all that time ago. It was that shared fighting spirit, the energy running through a band of men or brothers united in war and conflict. In his own mind, as he had done so many times, the Doctor thought he could channel that spirit in the people he encountered, shaping and planing it into something more subtle. The education of the noble savage?

No. That was unfair. Jamie was loyal and unswerving, and that should, and could, never be changed, no matter what. And no doubt the company of likeminded men – fighters, soldiers, warriors – had infused something in the lad – a healing energy, a noble sense that had possibly helped the recuperation process along. But, with what else he'd seen in the village, whether fair or foul, was Jamie being drawn into something that he couldn't control?

The Doctor muttered – almost sobbed – under his breath with worry as he stumbled over a sodden clump of grass. But then, in a moment of clear resolve, he shook his head to banish that last thought to the back his mind. With eyes narrowed and jaw set in a determined line, he strode forward.

Ahead, the murky glow of the torches carried on into the night.

After another twenty minutes of tramping through wet, rough terrain, Bior's party came to a rest. The Doctor watched from a good distance as, one by one, the men disappeared into a gully cut into the terrain. When he was sure he couldn't be seen, the Doctor crept forward.

The gully led down into a deep bowl that seemed to have been cut out of the ground, although the Doctor could tell it was a naturally occurring feature of the terrain. Fires had been lit below, and an eerie, red-orange glow fired up the surrounding area.

The Doctor crept up to the edge of the bowl and, using a rock as cover, looked down upon the scene below.

Bior and his thanes gathered around a blazing fire, moving slowly around the crackling flames, intoning a low hum as they went. The Doctor's eyes widened as he saw Jamie walking with them.

Set to one side stood Hefn, his face smeared with something from a large bowl in front of him, a dark red substance. Around his body was pulled an animal skin, and the Doctor recognised it as the bearskin that hung in his hut.

One by one, each of the thanes stepped up to Hefn, and the medicine man daubed the red substance on to their faces. They stepped aside once this had been done, and dragged a similar bearskin from a pile next to Hefn, pulling it around them.

Jamie stepped forward, allowed Hefn to paint his face, and, directed by the medicine man, took a heavy bearskin for himself.

Soon every man wore a bearskin, Bior putting on the last one before taking his place at the front of his warriors, standing before their medicine man. It was a macabre scene and the Doctor was repulsed by the grotesqueness of the ritual.

At a signal from Hefn, the humming increased in volume, and the men began to stamp their feet on the ground, the thumping mixing in with the humming to be almost deafening.

Hefn raised the bowl over his head. The humming reached a crescendo, then ceased, leaving silence.

The bowl, held aloft, was turned upside down, the sticky substance pouring down over Hefn, over his face, into his mouth and dribbling down his chin to splatter on the ground in a growing pool.

The Doctor watched in horror. What had Jamie been pulled into?

The bowl clattered to the ground, released from Hefn's grip. Then, slowly, Hefn began to shake uncontrollably, the shivering taking over his whole body, making his thin frame convulse.

The tremors seemed to spread out from the medicine man, moving throughout the warriors as they all began to jerk and spasm. The Doctor saw a look of terror pass through Jamie's eyes as he too was taken by whatever force was causing this.

The Doctor tensed, ready to run down into the bowl and haul Jamie out of there, but what he saw next froze him to the ground in terror.

The skin of the warriors' hands and faces seemed to be bubbling and flowing, as if something were trying to break through. The same thing was happening to Jamie. He scrabbled at his face wildly, then pulled his hands away. The bones in his fingers began to crack and pop, changing shape before his eyes. All around, the same was happening to the other men.

The Doctor was horrified and fascinated at the same time, drawn between helping Jamie and his scientific curiosity. He saw one of Jamie's arms elongate with a painful cracking, the muscles expanding as it did. He fell to the ground, putting his deforming arms out to break his fall.

The bearskin began to tighten around his body, hair and muscle fibre merging, growing, the human flesh and dead animal skin fusing into one. Jamie, if indeed it still was Jamie down there, screamed as his back arched, the bearskin now expanding as a great, gnarled mass of muscle simply grew around his shoulder blades. His screams became more guttural, as did those of the rest of the pack, everybody undergoing the same transformation.

Jaws lengthened, hair sprouted around the bearskins, engulfing the once-human forms, encasing new muscle and bone structure. Screams became growls, hands became paws, hair became fur.

The warriors had transformed before the Doctor's eyes into a pack of bears. The animals examined their surroundings through new eyes, eyes shining in the light of the fire. As they moved forward on muscled limbs, their bodies rippled with a calm, suppressed power that seemed to stem from the mass of muscle centred around shoulders and neck.

One of the animals, the biggest of the pack, stood on its hind legs, snout snuffling in the air. It sent forth a low growl, which was taken up by the pack, and the leader – the Doctor guessed that this had to be Bior – fell nimbly back on to its front legs and bounded forward.

As one, the pack followed, twenty or more bears that seconds ago had been men, thundering out into the darkness.

The Doctor almost fell as he sat back heavily against the rock, breathing hard.

Helpless.

'Jamie,' he muttered under his breath.

The sun rose over the village, fighting its daily battle to bring some warmth to the cold of the Scandinavian plain.

The encampment was quiet, the smoulderings of dead fires acting as markers against the white of the sky.

The long house was empty, light beginning to seep in from the day through the door. Bior entered, followed in single file by his thanes, with Jamie bringing up the rear.

They fanned out into the room, talking animatedly, some of the men picking up scraps of food that had been left from the previous evening's meal.

'I must say, you all seem rather chipper this morning,' a dark voice said from the shadows. The Doctor stepped into view. He glared at them from under darkened brows, anger clear in his expression.

'Doctor...' Jamie stepped forward enthusiastically, but stopped as he noticed the unmistakable anger on his face. 'What's the matter?'

The Doctor was silent, but then it seemed he'd come to a decision. He addressed Bior. 'I saw everything last night.'

Bior shook his head slightly, bemused. 'Saw?'

'Everything. I followed you. Saw where you went. Saw what happened.'

'What of it?'

Agitated, the Doctor stepped forward to face Bior, looking up at the man's great height. 'You decide to tamper with nature and you ask me what of it?'

'Tamper with nature? I do not understand.' He looked to his thanes, confusion lining his features. 'What is it to you how I choose to protect my people?'

'Protect?' The Doctor exploded with anger. 'I witnessed what you did to yourselves. It is an abomination! An abhorrence!'

'It is protection,' a quiet voice cut in from the doorway. Hefn stood, his face still daubed with what the Doctor could now see was blood.

'Protection? Poppycock!'

Hefn moved into the centre of the room. 'It is the way it has always been for our people. The passing from one form into another. Very few have the gift and it is never spoken of, but this...'

'Magic?' the Doctor asked accusingly.

Hefn shrugged. 'If you wish. Whatever you call it, the passing of forms is, and always shall be, protective.'

'It's true, Doctor. I can remember everything!' Jamie said, excitement in his voice. 'I was frightened at first when it happened, but that didn't last. It was like looking down from a great height on myself, running across the night.' The Doctor listened, but still glared, nostrils flaring. 'And I could hear the voices of everybody else, talking to me. Doctor, it was amazing.'

Bior spoke. 'We live good lives, Doctor, but there is danger, and we have been in conflict with Vignor's tribe for several seasons. When we cross over, we simply protect the borders of the village, keeping our tribe safe. Would you have me do any less?'

'Well...' The Doctor had no answer for that. He raised an arm, pointing at Jamie. 'Why take Jamie?'

'His healing was not yet complete,' answered Hefn.

The Doctor's brow creased. 'I don't understand.'

Jamie untucked his shirt and lifted it over his head. 'It's completely healed, Doctor.' Where the angry red mark of the deep sword cut had been, Jamie's skin was unblemished. Not even a scar remained.

'We would have taken the boy earlier,' Hefn continued, 'but he was too weak. Now the process is complete.'

'Yes,' the Doctor muttered. 'But at what cost?'

'We protect our own in whatever ways we can, Doctor,' said Bior reasonably.

'I can understand that.' The Doctor was calmer now. 'But I cannot condone it. I have seen people meddle with the laws of nature, thinking they are in control. Sooner or later, it controls them.'

The Doctor breathed out heavily and began to move towards the door. 'My friends and I owe you a debt of gratitude, Bior, and to you, Hefn, but, with what's happened, it's time we were leaving. Jamie.'

'No.'

The Doctor stopped halfway to the door and turned. ' I beg your pardon?'

'I'm not ready to leave yet.'

'I'm afraid, Jamie, that's not your decision to make.'

'Well, whose is it? We always go where you go, leave when you decide. I'm decidin' this time, and I want t'stay for a while.'

'Why?'

'Och, I don't know! Just trust me, will you?'

'You want to leave Zoe and me?' The words sounded hollow.

'I didnae say that! Just let me get my bearings. Please.'

The Doctor and Jamie stared at each other, the tension uncomfortable. Eventually the Doctor broke the silence. 'I can't promise how long I'll be here.'

And then he left.

Zoe poked her head out of the hut, yawning away the last traces of sleep. She saw the Doctor heading towards her across the encampment and smiled in greeting. She was taken aback when he didn't return the gesture.

'Stupid, pigheaded idiot!' she heard him mutter as he approached.

'Doctor...?'

Movement at the entrance to the long house caught her attention as Bior and his men filed out. They were carrying spears and belting up their swords. Among them, carrying his own spear, she spied a familiar figure.

'Is that Jamie?'

The Doctor wasn't listening, chewing on his finger, deep in thought. 'What?' He followed Zoe's gaze. 'Oh. Yes. I expect so. Joining his new friends for a spot of hunting, no doubt.'

Zoe watched the group headed away and out of the village, then turned and looked sternly at the Doctor. 'Have you two had an argument?' The Doctor looked sheepishly back at her. 'Oh, Doctor.'

The Doctor smiled gently. 'Zoe,' he said seriously. 'When we leave here, it's entirely possible Jamie may not come with us.'

The Doctor wandered out of the village, towards the shore of the inlet where the water lapped gently. Soon the men remaining in the village would be readying the boats for another precious day of gathering resources on the water.

The Doctor shoved his hands firmly into his pockets and looked out across the water, sighing heavily.

When the attack came, it came quickly.

Zoe was helping to pull a boat up on the shore when she heard the screams from the village. She let go of the boat and began to run towards the collection of huts.

Spears thudded into the ground seemingly from all angles, many hitting their mark. A village woman cried out as a spear glanced off her, ripping into her throat. As she went down, her cry became a strangled gurgle, and she lay twitching on the ground.

Then came the men, running into the village, swords raised to hack at anything that came their way.

Zoe ran and crouched in the cover of their hut. She recognised the attacking men as those who she had encountered with the Doctor and Jamie days previously. At their head ran Vignor, his massive gait unmistakable as he sprinted into the centre of the village. He swept his sword into the belly of one of the men who was too slow to run away, ripping him open in one easy movement.

He signalled his men to move through the village, and women, children and men ran screaming in all directions before them.

Zoe looked around desperately for the Doctor, but couldn't see him anywhere. Without protection from Bior and his thanes, the village would be decimated.

A young girl ran screaming across the expanse of grass, away from the long house, seen by one of the marauders who began to move after her, his sword hefted and ready to strike. The girl lost her footing and fell to the ground heavily, the wind knocked from her. The attacker smiled cruelly, and Zoe desperately wanted to rush in and save her, but she wouldn't have stood a chance.

She was about to look away as the sword was raised high in the air, but at the last second a flash of black ran beneath the sword, and she realised it was the Doctor, who scooped the little girl up in his arms and carried on running, knees pumping, making towards Zoe's hiding place.

The warrior began to give chase, and would soon gain on the Doctor and the girl. Zoe looked down and saw a nasty, jagged rock. She lifted it, testing the weight. As the Doctor and his pursuer came closer, she stood and closed one eye and, with good aim, she flung the rock as hard as she could over the Doctor's head.

The warrior stumbled as the rock struck his unprotected head, a jagged edge smashing into his eye. Blood flowed freely from a gash in his head and he staggered to his knees, disorientated with pain.

The Doctor ran into hiding next to Zoe, placing the child on the ground. 'Oh, well done, Zoe!' he smiled triumphantly at her, then turned to the child to check that she was okay.

'Doctor, we've got to do something!' Zoe pleaded.

'This is the world of fighting men, Zoe. Sticks and stones. All we can do here is keep running and survive the best we can.'

As swiftly as they came, the attackers left.

It seemed their intention was to raid, not to destroy, and they had carried away baskets of meat, fish and berries. Many had fallen, many were wounded, but the settlement would survive.

The Doctor and Zoe walked from where they had sheltered. The Doctor looked around sadly at the devastation, shaking his head. The child they had saved saw her mother and, with a happy cry, she ran towards her. Mother and daughter embraced.

The Doctor saw Hefn kneeling over a body in the grass. With a look to Zoe, he walked over and knelt down next to him. Hefn looked at the Doctor, shaking his head to indicate that nothing could be done to help the fallen villager.

'Einar!' The scream pierced the now relative calm of the village as Aella appeared at the door of the long house. She looked from side to side, eyes wide with a mother's fear. 'Einar!' she called again and ran forward. 'Where is Einar? Have you seen him?'

She ran up to Zoe, her eyes pleading. 'Have you seen him?' The same mantra repeated over and over again. Zoe put a hand out to her and she held on to it for support, for the touch of another human being.

And then she saw it, an indistinct shape, obscured in some tall grass a little way off. Aella seemed suddenly calm as she walked towards the bundle. She looked down at it for a second, and then began to wail as she collapsed on to the ground, throwing her body over what was undeniably the body of her son.

The Doctor closed his eyes.

Bior and his thanes returned to the devastation of the village a few hours later.

The Doctor and Zoe assisted wherever they could in tending to the wounded, helping Hefn apply similar remedies as he had done to Jamie only days ago. A few were beyond their help – a woman passed away in the Doctor's arms, and all he could do was offer words of comfort in her dying moments.

Jamie helped the surviving thanes in the grim task of gathering their dead. Five of the warriors had fallen in the attack and several more had been wounded, and those that remained helped their comrades to the safety and care of the medicine man's hut. The dead were gathered and prepared, but already there had been cautious talk of the beyond.

Zoe applied a herbal preparation to a flesh wound on a young, fresh-faced farmer. He winced at the stinging pain, but smiled gratefully through it.

Light spilled in from the doorway as the skin was thrown aside to admit Jamie and one of the thanes, bearing a dead body between them. They placed the corpse carefully on the ground and stood as Hefn bustled across to see if anything could be done.

Their charge delivered, Jamie and the warrior made to leave. Zoe tried to catch Jamie's eye, to offer a sympathetic smile of encouragement, but he had not even acknowledged that she was there.

From the other side of the hut, the Doctor raised his eyebrows in support and smiled sadly.

A little later, the Doctor and Zoe emerged from the stifling atmosphere of the hut, blinking in the daylight that was frayed at the edges with greying storm clouds. The Doctor pulled his jacket on against the sudden bite of cold. He looked across to the centre of the encampment and frowned grimly at the tableau laid out before him.

Bior stood over the broken body of his son.

Einar lay where he had fallen, the ground around the corpse churned and slicked red with blood that had long since stopped pumping.

'He's still there?'

'Ah, yes. I'm afraid so, Zoe,' answered the Doctor quietly.

Zoe sighed heavily, unable to imagine the weight of pain that must be crushing down upon the proud man. 'How long can he keep this up?'

'As long as he has to, I imagine.'

The drighten had been like this for two hours, his sword hanging uselessly in his hand, hollow eyes staring down at his son. He had refused any attempts to offer comfort or efforts to move Einar's body into shelter.

A calm seemed to descend upon the village, along with a sharp breeze, that brought with it a mist of threatened rain. Zoe looked past the tragic scene in the centre of the camp, to where she could see Jamie and several of the warriors splashing themselves with water at the shore of the inlet, cleaning away the stench of blood and death.

A flurry of movement at the doorway to the long house attracted her attention away, and she clutched the Doctor's arm as Aella appeared. Her eyes were as hollow and tired as her husband's, punctuated by dark patches. She spoke to one of the women at her side and then turned her pale, beautiful face towards Bior and strode out into the centre of the village.

Jamie and the thanes halted their bathing, turning from the water to see what the commotion was.

Aella's pace did not slow as she grew close, and she too looked down at her fallen son, tears glistening on her cheeks. She stepped next to Bior, and touched his arm gently. A plea.

Zoe gasped as the tribal leader lashed out at his wife, striking her across the cheek with such force that she cried out in pain and fell to the floor. Zoe felt the Doctor tense as he placed his arms protectively round her shoulders, but neither spoke.

Aella pulled herself upright, massaging her bruised face. Bior had returned to his vigil over Einar's body. Slowly his entire body began to convulse: his face strained, and it seemed he was fighting some great force within.

Tears began to flow freely down the imposing man's face. He fell to his knees, his sword slipping from his loosened grip and dropping to the ground as he flung his arms out wide and threw his head back.

Zoe buried her head in the Doctor's chest as Bior screamed into the heavens. It was a primal roar of rage, and it cut through every fibre and sinew of her body. Zoe screwed her eyes tight, trying to block out the ungodly sound.

She could hear Bior scream for a second time. She knew that if any man with guilt in his heart heard that cry, he would know that vengeance was coming. Zoe looked up and watched through reddened eyes as Bior, his chilling bellow of rage receding into nothing, collapsed to the ground. His muscles seemed to lose all substance, and he began to sob like a child, choking into the ground.

It was a show of emotion from the chief that no one ever thought they would see, and the tribe could do nothing but stand and watch, dumbfounded. He clawed at the ground with his hands, churning up the bloody mud that marked Einar's position. Aella crawled on her knees and pulled at her husband's tunic, attempting to draw the big man into an embrace, but he suddenly found a final sliver of resolve from somewhere within and, with a sweep of his arm, cast her aside.

Zoe wanted to rush forward and help Aella, unable to bear seeing her flounder in the filth surrounding her son's corpse, but she knew the Doctor would hold her back. This was the beginning of grief. Or was it something else?

Bior stood, struggling and slipping to his feet like a newborn foal. His sobbing had been replaced with choking, rasping breaths. Now standing, he bent down and lifted Einar's shattered corpse into his arms, plucking him from the earth as easily as driftwood from the inlet.

'What's he doing?' Zoe asked in alarm.

'I doubt he even knows himself,' replied the Doctor.

The drighten strode across the length of the encampment, resolve and calmness returning with each step, although his eyes seemed to blaze with some manic intent. He stopped before a particular hut – Hefn's.

'Oh, dear,' remarked the Doctor quietly. 'I don't like the look of this.'

Bior stood for a few seconds before the doorway into the abode of his medicine man, before stepping through.

The Doctor squeezed Zoe's shoulder and smiled at her kindly. 'Zoe, stay here. See to Aella.'

Zoe nodded. 'All right, Doctor.'

The Doctor trotted across the camp, the only movement in a freeze frame of confusion. He stopped close to Jamie and fixed him with a firm gaze. The Scot returned it unflinchingly. 'Jamie. Watch after Zoe.'

'Doctor, I...'

'I'm not asking, Jamie.'

Jamie stepped back, stung by the seriousness in the Doctor's tone. The Doctor turned away from his friend and stole towards Hefn's hut.

'I will not!'

'I am your drighten! You will do as I command!'

'No! This is not yours *to* command!'

'I strongly suggest you listen to your medicine man.' The Doctor spoke quietly, moving from the fur-covered doorway into the fire-lit warmth of Hefn's hut. He found Bior, tall and imposing, his hair matted with sweat, confronting Bior at the centre of the room. Hefn stood, his cloak wrapped around his slight frame protectively. He had been glaring at his chief from beneath dark, heavily lidded eyes, but now both men turned to look at the Doctor.

Between drighten and medicine man lay Einar's body, small and broken. The Doctor glanced down, sadness flashing across his mind, before he returned his gaze to the two men before him.

'And what business is this of yours, Doctor?' Bior spoke surprisingly quietly, and this worried the Doctor even more.

'When you involve my friends in whatever...' the Doctor floundered, his choice of word sounding clumsy and ridiculous, '... magic it is you use here, then it becomes very much my business.'

'Your friend is unharmed and healed thanks to our... magic.' Bior spat the last word.

'That remains to be seen.'

Hefn spoke. 'I told you, Doctor, this magic, as you insist on calling it, is protective.'

'I don't doubt it, and Hefn, you have my grateful thanks. I'm convinced your intentions are true, but I suspect your chief is asking you to use your skill for a much darker purpose.'

'I will not do it!' Hefn exploded, whirling his cloak to one side in agitation, stalking towards Bior.

Bior stood his ground at the ridiculous sight of the thin, bony Hefn facing up to his own huge frame. A mocking smile whispered at the corner of his mouth before he pulled himself up to his full height.

'I will rip his heart from his chest and hold it beating in my hand. I will see his lifeblood flow away and I will watch as his sons are forced to eat their own father's heart.'

The Doctor watched in alarm as the fire in the hut seemed to grow in intensity and the shadows swept away from around Bior. His eyes narrowed as he saw that the drighten was framed against the outline of the bearskin that was stretched and pinned to the back wall of the hut.

'You must not strike out with vengeance in your heart,' Hefn whispered. 'The beast will better you, and you will be lost from the sight of this world.'

'Superstition! You have sent the young scurrying away in fear with less.'

'I find that where there's superstition,' the Doctor interjected, 'the cold bite of reality is never far behind.' The Doctor had now stepped up close to Hefn and the two men faced Bior defiantly.

'I will not do it! I *cannot* do it!' Hefn pleaded.

Bior smiled again. 'You will do as I command.'

The Doctor shivered, suddenly ill at ease in Bior's gaze.

Hefn stood proud and defiant. 'I will not be coerced.'

'You have no choice.'

The Doctor frowned. 'What do you mean?'

At that moment, a chink of white light sliced through the room, and two black figures stepped into the hut. The light fell away behind them and the Doctor saw it was Jamie and one of the thanes.

'Jamie, I told you to stay with Zoe.'

Jamie did not answer, standing impassively with his companion. Waiting.

'Jamie, what's the...' The Doctor looked quickly at Bior, as the drighten began to laugh. A deep, throaty, mocking laugh. His eyes flashed a bright red in the darkness for a brief moment and the Doctor stepped back in shock. When he spoke, his voice seemed deeper, thicker.

'Take them.'

The Doctor gasped as Jamie and the thane walked forward, drawing swords. Their eyes flashed the same red as their leader's had.

'Jamie! What on...' he murmured curiously.

Hefn answered. 'The beast has them already. It can sense that blood has been spilt and more is to come.'

The Doctor cried out as Jamie stepped closer and clamped an iron grip on his arm. He began to drag the Doctor to the door. 'Oh, Jamie,' the Doctor exclaimed, struggling against his friend's strength to no avail. Hefn struggled similarly with Jamie's comrade.

The Doctor wriggled round against Jamie's vicelike grip so he faced Bior as he was dragged to the door. 'Bior! Listen to me! This is not the way! Take control of your emotion. Think of your honour, your tribe!' Einar's body caught the Doctor's eyes and, with his free arm, he gestured to the ground. 'Think of your son's memory!'

Bior stared down at the corpse, and for a second he wavered, swaying, but then he shook his head, clearing some nagging doubt from his mind. He turned away from Einar's body and strode confidently towards the door after his prisoners.

'Doctor!'

The Doctor was dragged blinking into the sunlight to find Zoe and Aella being held by two thanes. The rest of the warriors stood, unmoving, around the centre of the village. The rest of the tribe cowered in groups around their dwellings, fear clearly marking their faces.

'Zoe,' the Doctor gasped as Jamie threw him forward with some force towards where Zoe stood with her captor. The Doctor winced in pain.

'What's happening?' Zoe asked, eyes wide with shock. 'One second Jamie was talking normally, the next he just walked across to Hefn's hut without saying a word.'

'He's not himself, Zoe,' the Doctor explained. 'I think there's a nasty case of bad medicine brewing.' The Doctor bit at a nail worriedly and turned to Aella, whose face was drawn and pale. 'Aella, your husband is heading down a very dangerous road that we may not be able to turn him from.'

'He is a proud, stubborn man, Doctor. When anger is on him, he will listen to no man.'

'That's what worries me. Hefn, what can we do?'

The medicine man had been deposited next to the Doctor. Jamie and the three thanes stood a few feet away, and escape was clearly not an option. Hefn spread his arms wide. 'I do not know, this is beyond my experience. Perhaps we have become too bound up with the nature of the beast, but if the ritual is not performed, it may be possible to banish it from Bior.'

'Hmm,' the Doctor said, frowning. 'Let's hope so.'

Bior strode forward and regarded his captives. 'Bring them,' he commanded.

The Doctor, Zoe, Hefn and Aella were dragged through icy mud. Dark clouds were forming overhead. A growl in the distance hinted at a gathering storm.

The party made its way in silence across the plain. The Doctor was deep in thought, glancing between Bior and Jamie as they moved, helping Zoe and Aella along if they stumbled in the mud. Hefn walked at their side, his cloak drawn about him as he mumbled under his breath.

At all sides strode the silent thanes, their faces blank, some carrying torches, all carrying swords, even Jamie. Zoe had tried talking to him, pleading with him to come back to them, but he just stared straight ahead.

And at the front of the group was Bior, eyes fixed on the horizon, leading them onwards. It hadn't taken the Doctor long to work out that they were being taken to the site where he had watched the ritual take place the previous night.

They soon arrived at the fissure in the rock that led down into the natural bowl in the plain. As darkness fell, the Doctor and his fellow prisoners were led in single file down the roughly hewn pathway, torchlight glinting off rock slick with moisture.

The four prisoners were pushed into the centre of the bowl. The Doctor looked around – things had been left as they were the night before. The fire burned, casting an eerie, devilish light as the day receded above them.

'What is this place, Doctor?' Zoe asked, face white with fear and exhaustion.

Aella answered for him. 'It is the place of protection.'

'If your husband has his way, your place of protection is about to become a place of death and destruction.'

'He will be destroyed.' Hefn broke his silence, watching the proceedings around him.

'Along with half his tribe, no doubt,' said the Doctor grimly. 'We have to talk sense into him, appeal to the humanity inside that clouded mind.'

'It is beyond my ability to reach him. I fear he listens only to the beast now.'

'You control the beast, Hefn.'

The medicine man laughed. 'Only a fool would think that.'

Around them, the thanes moved silently, setting up the ritual as before. They pulled bearskins from the pile, enveloping themselves in the heavy pelts, the remnants of the animal providing a macabre, pantomime image of what the Doctor knew would follow.

Bior stood where Hefn had before, already wearing his own bearskin, face smeared with blood taken from the same bowl. One by one, the thanes lined up before their leader, allowing their faces to be similarly marked, before stepping back into formation. The Doctor noticed Jamie had also taken a place in line before Bior, the lad's eyes flat, his face expressionless.

'Can Bior perform the ritual himself?' the Doctor whispered to Hefn.

'Only I possess the skill.'

'That's encouraging.'

Zoe's eyes followed Jamie as he walked slowly back to stand by their side with three of his fellows, his face now painted. 'Why is Jamie affected by this, Doctor?'

'He's been part of it, Zoe. He doesn't know what he's doing.'

'And why do they need us to be here?'

As if in answer, Bior raised a hand towards the four prisoners, their captors pushing them forward towards the drighten. Bior regarded them, focusing his gaze on Hefn.

'Medicine man,' he sneered. 'You will perform the ritual.'

'I will not.' Hefn folded his arms defiantly.

'Unless you have turned your back on the honour of this tribe, you will do as I command.'

'Bior.' The Doctor stepped forward. 'Without Hefn, this is all in vain. Are you going to kill him if he doesn't do as you say?' He held out a hand to Aella, who took it and stepped forward, looking up with pleading eyes at her husband. 'This is not the way,' the Doctor continued, smiling benignly. 'Come home, be with your wife. Mourn your son, don't destroy his memory with more death.'

For a fleeting moment, Bior seemed to waver. His gaze cleared and he looked at Aella with the eyes of a loving husband.

A rumble of thunder in the distance broke the moment, and Bior's eyes darkened once more. 'You are not a warrior, Doctor. I would not expect you to understand.'

With a signal from Bior, Hefn's guarding thane pushed him forward as the chief drew his sword.

'You're going to kill him?' The Doctor's voice grew agitated. 'Where will that get you, hmm?'

'You think me a fool, Doctor.' Bior gazed down at Hefn. 'Medicine man, will you perform the ritual?'

A last moment of defiance. 'I will not.'

Two swords were drawn, and before the Doctor could react, Zoe and Aella were dragged forward. Jamie held the Doctor firm.

'Zoe!' the Doctor shouted as the two women were thrust to the ground by the thanes, who then raised their swords high above their heads.

'Doctor!' screamed Zoe.

'If he refuses again,' said Bior, his voice thick and slurred. 'Kill them both.'

Hefn looked on at the two women, cowering on the ground, anguish showing clearly in his eyes.

'Will you perform the ritual?'

The seconds leaked past with painful slowness. Hefn looked to the Doctor, eyes pleading, but the Doctor could only look back, helpless. Aella climbed to her feet despite the sword wavering above, ready to strike down at any second. Hefn turned and she met his gaze with stony eyes, head shaking slowly from side to side.

The two faced each other for what seemed like hours, until Hefn finally sagged in defeat. His shoulders fell and the breath left his body. He closed his eyes and nodded.

'Forgive me,' he said to nobody in particular, before shuffling forward. In a trance, he picked a bearskin from the pile and pulled it round himself, then went to stand beside Bior.

The Doctor felt Jamie's grip on him release and the Scot walked forward to join the pack of thanes who now stood in formation before their drighten and medicine man. Zoe and Aella had similarly been abandoned.

As a low hum began to rise from the group of warriors, the Doctor ran to Zoe and Aella.

'There's nothing we can do now,' he raised his voice over the rising volume of the chant.

'What's happening?' Zoe shouted as the thanes began to stamp their feet in deafening unison.

'Too late for that,' said the Doctor apologetically. He looked up to see Hefn raising the wooden bowl high above his head. 'We need to get under cover.' The chanting and stamping ceased. 'Now.'

The Doctor put his arms around Zoe and Aella and he swept them to the side of the rocky hollow. Hefn turned the bowl upside down. The Doctor, Zoe and Aella ducked down into an overhang of rock. Blood splattered in thick rivulets over Hefn's face and chin.

'Don't look!' commanded the Doctor.

All around, the thanes began to convulse, their skin flowing and bubbling. Bones began to crack and pop, lengthening and changing, muscles being ripped away and reformed, bound with gristle and sinew. Zoe screamed as she saw Jamie, his entire body contorted out of shape, reforming before her eyes. The Doctor put a comforting hand on her shoulder.

The Doctor looked around, horror replaced with curiosity. A fizzing, popping sound echoed around the hollow and began to drown out the brutal sound of transformation. The Doctor glanced furtively from side to side, his eyes coming to rest on Bior, who appeared to be the source of the sound.

Where the drighten had stood seconds before was a half-man, half-beast as he too was caught in the grip of the change, but something different was happening to him. As he became more bear than man, his back arching over with powerful muscle, his entire body began to glow a deep, burning red. The air around him began to shimmer and haze, as if he were drawing energy from the very air, the fizzing shifting into an angry buzzing, growing in intensity with every passing second.

The hair on the back of the Doctor's neck stood on end, and he could almost feel the air crackling with energy, filling his nostrils with a bittersweet odour.

'Doctor!' Zoe had emerged from the overhang of rock and was pointing towards Jamie. Somehow the transformation had not taken him as far as his fellows, who now stood on all fours, growling and snarling in their new bodies. Jamie convulsed and shook, his face a bizarre amalgam of human and bear, his jaw elongated, thick hair sprouting across his arms, but the cry that came from his mouth was definitely human.

The buzz of energy practically throbbed in the air like a swarm of hornets, and the air around Bior was incandescent with power. He was now fully transformed, standing on all fours, clawing at the air.

The Doctor sensed that something was about to happen and, without thinking, began to sprint across the ritual site. 'Stay back, Zoe,' he shouted over the unbearable wall of noise. He saw Jamie before him, still fighting against his change.

The build-up of energy peaked as a scream of power.

The bear that had been Bior roared in triumph.

The Doctor sprinted for Jamie, launching himself into the air.

And then the world fell silent.

The Doctor and Jamie crashed to the ground as a ring of fire exploded outwards from Bior, rushing overhead, expanding rapidly. It sliced through the air above the Doctor and Jamie, leaving the smell of charred flesh behind it. The blast of energy passed through each of the bear-thanes, and their huge bulks glowed with power as they absorbed it into themselves.

As one, the bear pack roared, filling the hollow with their battle cry. The bear that had once been Bior padded slowly over to the Doctor and Jamie, eyes glowing a deep red. He sniffed the air in front of them and the Doctor placed himself between the creature and the convulsing and shaking Jamie, fearing the worst.

But the beast simply turned and ran from the hollow, powerful legs propelling him forward. The rest of the pack did the same, following their leader until the only sound in the bowl of rock was Jamie's ragged, violent breathing.

The Doctor immediately attended to Jamie, who seemed to be calming.

Zoe ran from out of the cover of the rock, followed by Aella. 'What's happening to him, Doctor?' she asked worriedly, kneeling down next to the Doctor and Jamie.

'Jamie,' the Doctor called, placing a calming hand on the lad's chest. 'Come back to us, Jamie.'

Slowly, the convulsions eased and Jamie's breathing became easier. The tufts of fur that covered his skin began to recede, and half-formed bones cracked and popped back into place, displaced skin flowing around them to form what was undeniably Jamie McCrimmon.

His eyes opened. 'Doctor?'

The Doctor smiled. 'Hello, Jamie. Welcome back.'

'Where have I been?' he asked, confused.

'What do you remember?' the Doctor enquired, helping Jamie into a sitting position.

'It wasn't like the first time,' he said. 'That was safe. I felt protected.'

'And now?'

Jamie shivered, memories coming back. 'It was all wrong. I just knew I had to pull away, fight back against whatever was trying to pull me in. It was horrible.'

'We're very glad you did.' The Doctor sat back on his haunches thinking fast. 'But it's not over yet. Bior has blood in mind.'

Jamie suddenly got to his feet, alert.

'Jamie, you need to rest,' Zoe protested.

'They're heading for the other village,' said Jamie, eyes bright and alert.

'How do you know?' The Doctor's face was lined with curiosity.

'I dunno. It's like I can still feel them. Smell them, I suppose.'

'We have to go after them,' said the Doctor.

'What can we do against a pack of slavering bears?' asked Zoe.

'We have to warn those villagers before it's too late!'

'The Doctor's right,' Jamie piped in.

'They'll get there way ahead of us,' Zoe countered, logically. 'It's pointless.'

'People are going to die, Zoe. We have to try. Come on!'

The Doctor and Jamie began to make their way to the fissure that led into the hollow, and after a second, Zoe and Aella began to follow, but they were stopped by a groan. The two women looked about them and Aella saw a body almost hidden by a rock.

It was Hefn.

Aella knelt by the unconscious form of the medicine man, the Doctor, Jamie and Zoe standing behind her. Like Jamie, Hefn was clearly human.

'He had more control over the beast than he thought,' the Doctor concluded.

Aella looked up. 'I will remain here. When he has regained consciousness, we will return to our village.'

The Doctor nodded reluctantly. 'I don't want to leave you,' he said.

'You must,' replied Aella clearly.

'We'll do what we can for Bior,' Zoe smiled sadly, placing a hand on her shoulder.

'I fear my husband is beyond anyone's help.'

Jamie grabbed a lit torch from where it had been placed in the ground and looked to the Doctor and Zoe. 'Ready?' he asked.

'Yes,' said the Doctor gravely. 'Let's go.'

★ ★ ★

The three time travellers made their way across the dark plain in silence, Jamie's torch encasing them in a fervid bubble of light.

It seemed to Zoe that Jamie had picked up the torch not for his benefit, but that of herself and the Doctor. He walked, almost stalked ahead, torch held high, head bowed low, staring into the night. Was the effect of whatever he had been through in the last hour lingering within him, infusing his senses with something extra? None of them had been to the rival village, but Jamie appeared to know without doubt which route to take, and one that was clear of rocks and rough terrain to make it easier for the Doctor and Zoe to traverse.

Zoe glanced across at the Doctor who walked by her side. His faced was still lined with worry, but something seemed to have lifted from him. She hadn't been party to what had gone on between her two friends, but what she had seen tonight made things clearer in her mind. Jamie had been pulled into the tribe in a unique way, but turning his back on it tonight, being able to pull away from the forces at work, had shown the Doctor where Jamie's heart truly lay.

Whatever happened tonight, Jamie was with them.

'Do you think we'll be able to do anything?' she asked the Doctor.

The Doctor shrugged. 'We can only try, Zoe.'

Ahead, Jamie had come to a halt. He was on one knee, examining the ground and... was he actually sniffing the air?

'There!' he pointed.

On the horizon they could see an angry glow. Something was on fire. A breeze picked up across plain, bringing with it the sound of people screaming in terror.

The Doctor's eyes closed in resignation. 'We're too late.'

Dawn was clawing back the night as the Doctor, Jamie and Zoe ran down towards Vignor's village. The screams grew louder as they approached, and they saw that the source of light came from several blazing huts, including the large central hall that could have been a mirror image of Bior's own.

Large brown blurs flitted rapidly across the encampment, chasing down running figures. The pack of bears was running berserk through the village.

It would be a massacre, and there was nothing they could do.

The three friends walked cautiously along the main approach into the village, then peered around the side of a hut.

Jamie spotted a bear lumbering after a woman, her eyes desperate with fear, screaming as she ran. The Scot immediately leapt forward, brandishing the torch before him.

'Jamie, no!' the Doctor shouted, but Jamie didn't hear, or chose not to.

Jamie ran between the woman and the rampaging bear, cutting off the animal's path. It reared up on its hind legs, roaring angrily, yellow teeth showing. Jamie thrust forward the torch, the flame flaring and dancing.

The Doctor and Zoe stepped out of the cover of the hut and gestured to the fleeing woman, who changed direction and ran towards them, the pair pulling her into the relative safety of their shelter.

Jamie continued to fend off the bear. Its claws swiped down towards him, but each time he managed to evade their bite, swinging the torch in a wide arc to force it back. The bear screamed in rage and reared up once more, before slamming down on to its front paws, glaring at its human opponent. Jamie too dropped to all fours in an approximation of the creature's stance.

Bestial eyes locked with Jamie's, and the two stared each other down. Seconds past. The bear growled. Jamie breathed in and out heavily, bearing his own teeth. The bear sniffed the air, a silvery line of saliva stretching out from a sharp fang. It hung in the air for a split second, glinting in the light of the burning buildings, before snapping. The bear stood for a second longer before its muscles relaxed and it turned, padding away into another part of the village.

Jamie closed his eyes and breathed out, almost collapsing in sudden exhaustion as the Doctor and Zoe ran up to him.

'That was amazing!' Zoe breathed. Jamie just nodded.

'Zoe, get him into shelter,' the Doctor commanded. 'He's weak again.'

Together they helped Jamie to his feet. 'Where are you going?' Zoe asked.

'To see if I can find Bior. He's the key to stopping this madness.' Zoe looked around doubtfully, the battle massacre still raging. 'Don't worry,' the Doctor smiled. 'I'll be fine. Look after Jamie.'

And with that he was gone.

The Doctor dodged through the village, running from hut to hut. The bears were everywhere, roaring and growling. Bodies lay here and there, blood seeping into the ground. Women, children, men, there was no distinction.

And then he found them, in the centre of the village.

Dawn slowly filled the village with grey light, but the blaze from the roof of the great hall provided a fiery backdrop to their battle.

The Doctor recognised the beast that was Bior, a huge, powerful paw raised in the air, swiping down towards a human opponent, who managed to dodge the blow, stumbling backwards. It was Vignor.

Bior's shaggy hide was matted and wet with blood, his muscled body covered with cuts where Vignor's sword had hit home. Vignor's hair was similarly matted, and he was covered in scratches and deep wounds. Blood spread in a dark, wet patch across his tunic and his face was white with pain. But still they fought.

Claw swiped. Sword cut.

The Doctor could only watch. If he tried to intervene, he would be cut to pieces.

And then it ended.

Vignor thrust forward with his sword, finding flesh, cutting deep. Bior roared, eyes burning, hatred firing his actions. His muscles rippled with effort and power, claws sang through the air, ripping and tearing through the man's flesh again and again. Eventually the mauling ended as Bior's claw ripped through Vignor's chest, blood erupting around it.

The Doctor turned away, impotent, unable to watch any more.

When he finally turned back, Vignor's body, or what remained of it, lay on the ground, the creature of his destruction standing triumphantly over the object of its vengeance.

The Doctor walked forward slowly, silence suddenly reigning. The rest of the pack seemed to sense that their reason for being here was at an end. They stood in a circle, motionless. Movement caught the Doctor's eye, and he saw Jamie and Zoe at the edge of the circle.

Bior growled, regarding the Doctor through eyes that shone with the power of the beast he had become. The Doctor stared back, unflinching.

And then the angry, red glow began to fade from his eyes, a hint of humanity returning. Bior's powerful form began to glow as it had done earlier that night, energy whirling in a kaleidoscope around him.

The Doctor took a step back as the creature's entire body began to agitate and shake, and it fell to the ground, roaring in agony. All around the village, the same thing was happening, as the change began to take Bior's warriors. Slowly humanity began to reclaim what was rightfully its own, leaving a pack of unconscious warriors in its wake.

Except for one.

When the glow of fizzing, sparkling power dissipated from around Bior, it had left him unchanged, still trapped within his bear form. The anger was no longer in the eyes; it had been replaced by sadness.

What terror must be running through the drighten's mind, the Doctor could only guess at. He reared up once more on his hind legs and released a long, mournful animal cry into the dawn sky.

And then he turned and ran from the village.

The funerals of all who had perished from both tribes took place a few days later.

Smoke from the funeral pyres snaked up into the sky, a marker for death and mourning, and, according to Hefn, rebirth.

The Doctor had worked alongside Hefn and Aella to broker an uneasy peace with the rival village. Aella and Vignor's widow approached the situation with a solid practicality that began to return some dignity to the tragedy that had unfolded over the last few days.

The thanes had been returned to the village safely, disoriented and remembering nothing, but seemingly unharmed. Of Bior, there was no sign, but the Doctor had a sense of something on the edge of the village, a presence watching from afar. On more than one occasion, he came across Jamie looking sadly out over the plain, but had said nothing to him.

The Doctor had tried to speak to Aella about what had happened, but she refused to acknowledge even the existence of her husband. The Doctor didn't know whether to admire her or pity her.

The day after the funerals, shortly before they were due to leave, the Doctor took a walk in the area surrounding the village. He came across Hefn, alone, standing next to a blazing fire. One by one, from the pile at his side, he fed the fire with bearskins. The stench from the fire was overpowering, and the Doctor covered his mouth with a handkerchief.

The two men stood in silence, watching as the flames and bitter, black smoke erased the memories of the last few days.

'Our people will have to find new methods of healing and protection,' Hefn said to the Doctor. The Doctor just nodded.

And then the travellers were on their way again.

In contrast to their arrival, the sun shone brightly across the bleak Scandinavian plain, its fingers stretching down to brush the barren landscape through fluffy, grey clouds. It was a last act of defiance in the face of the coming onslaught of winter.

As the Doctor stepped up to open the door of the TARDIS, Zoe looked out over the landscape, shielding her eyes with a hand, while Jamie looked on beside her, hands thrust deep into the pockets of his fleece.

'It's really beautiful here, isn't it?' Zoe remarked, as if seeing her surroundings for the very first time.

'Aye,' Jamie agreed quietly, breathing out heavily.

Zoe looked over and the two friends exchanged a look. Zoe smiled. No more needed to be said.

The TARDIS door creaked open and the Doctor replaced the key in his pocket. He walked back to where his companions stood, stamping his feet. Despite the sun, it was still bitterly cold. He placed his hands affectionately on Jamie and Zoe's shoulders.

'I think it's time we were on our way.'

Jamie nodded, all awkwardness between himself and the Doctor gone.

Zoe continued to gaze out towards the horizon. 'What happened here, Doctor?'

'I don't really know, Zoe,' the Doctor replied.

'It's just so... absurd!' she exclaimed. 'Men turning into bears. It's, well... magic.'

'To Bior's people, the things you can achieve in your time, Zoe, would be seen as magic. It's a simplistic outlook, but the chasm of understanding between science and nature is minute.' The Doctor gestured the infinitesimal with his thumb and finger. 'I don't claim to understand any of it. Jamie here has a far greater perspective in this than you and I. To Hefn, what we would call "magic" was a tool. Something to use, something he understood as you would an atomic fusion generator.'

'That really doesn't help,' sighed Zoe.

'Unfortunately, in this case, Bior chose to abuse that tool, to ignore the advice of somebody who knew far better than him.'

'Is that why he stayed as a bear, and the thanes were released?'

'Who can say? The thirst for vengeance was Bior's. He almost destroyed his warriors along with himself, but they were lucky.'

'What'll happen to the tribe, Doctor?' asked Jamie.

The Doctor blew out a long, thoughtful breath. 'Aella is a strong woman and has the respect of the tribe. They have as much chance as any of surviving the winter.' He held out his hands in a shrug of uncertainty.

Jamie began to wander towards the TARDIS, followed by the Doctor. Zoe stood for a few seconds longer. Just as she was about to follow her friends, she caught sight of something at the edge of her vision.

She pointed. 'Look!'

The Doctor and Jamie came back to her side. Some distance away, they saw the silhouette of an animal lumbering atop a rise in the plain. It stopped and sniffed at the air, before rising up on powerful legs. It dropped back to the ground and lumbered away, disappearing into the haze of the sun.

'Do you think that could have been Bior?'

'Impossible to tell,' said the Doctor.

'He was a good man,' Jamie thought aloud. 'With a warrior's heart.'

'Yes,' agreed the Doctor. 'But, as you have shown on so many occasions, Jamie, a warrior's heart must be tempered with compassion and humanity.'

'I hope he'll find that humanity on whatever road he travels now,' said Jamie, sadly.

The Doctor patted Jamie's shoulder. 'So do I, Jamie. So do I.'

One by one, the three companions turned and filed into the reassuringly solid, blue frame of the TARDIS. The door clicked shut and, seconds later, the time machine faded and vanished.

As the laboured breath of the TARDIS's engines whispered into nothing, somewhere, far away, a long, sad howl wailed out across the plain.

Envy

The showman shook his head in relief as he moved on to the next room. 'Lucky to get out of there with all my bits intact. Who'd have thought this would be such a risky business? Now, next, next, next... ah.'

A look of sorrow, perhaps regret, flitted across his face, but was banished by a smile. He tried on several smiles before settling on the most patronising, a smile that radiated ego and disdain for others. Then he reached out a hand and, with a sigh quite at odds with the expression on his face, grasped the door handle.

The showman bounded into the room, rubbing his hands. 'A-ha!' he said to the room's occupant, the short, pinch-faced man who was wearing heliotrope robes and a matching skullcap. 'I've been looking forward to this one. Such a bore to have to listen to other people's stories, don't you think? But I knew that I'd get to do all the talking this time, because you really don't have anything to say, do you?'

The short man turned eyes of loathing on him.

'Funny, really, how things turn out,' the showman said, flopping into a chair and crossing his legs. 'Remember us back at the Academy?'

The man nodded, reluctantly.

'And that's what's so funny, because I don't think there was an "us".' The showman's grin got broader, seemingly unaware of the other's flinching. 'I seem to recall we were only in a few classes together. You got much higher marks than me, but it didn't seem to make you happy. You'd watch me, though, me and my friends, you'd watch us constantly. You seemed to hate me. You seemed to hate the fact that I had friends.'

The dried-up old man roused himself to speech. 'Because you were nothing special! I was special. I had so much talent; my intellect was greater even than the teachers'! All your little escapades – I could have contributed so much.'

The showman shrugged. 'But you never had the bottle to get involved, did you? Still, never mind. You must have been relieved when you heard I'd fled Gallifrey in a stolen TARDIS. A life of crime! You couldn't possibly have wanted to be part of that.'

But there was such longing in the man's eyes...

The showman continued, smiling all the while as though what he said was of little consequence. 'Of course, that was what led me to have such thrilling adventures. I've met all the Gallifreyan heroes: Rassilon, Omega... you can't tell me there are many Gallifreyans of our generation who've done that. You, as a devotee of history, must be green with... Well, let's not go there. Green's the colour for Arcalians, not Patrexes! Mind you, I'm a Prydonian, as you know. The chapter that's produced more Time Lord presidents than any other. And I've been Lord President of Gallifrey myself, of course. I didn't exactly enjoy it, but still, strange to think that my name will be in the history books, long after all my contemporaries have crumbled to forgotten dust. Not one of them even meriting a footnote. Not a trace of them remaining.'

He mimed blowing a pile of dust off his hand. 'Not a trace. And of course, it's not just in the chronicles of Gallifrey that I'm to be found, important though those are. Just look in the annals of Skaro, of Telos, of... oh, what's it called, that one whose name I never can remember, you know, where I met a bloke made out of sweets? No?' He cleared his throat. 'I mean to say, how many times have I defeated the Daleks now? It's got almost embarrassing. Lucky I did, though – do you remember the time they invaded Gallifrey? You'd probably be stuck down a mine, or exterminated or something, if it wasn't for me.'

'I was off-planet at the time,' muttered the man, scowling.

The showman snorted a laugh. 'You're joking! The one big thing that happens in your lifetime, and you miss it! All the excitement, the danger, the heroics... Can't be a hero if you're not even there. Still, I expect you were away doing something just as thrilling and important.'

'I was monitoring lichen growth on Verana Delta.'

This time the showman clapped his hand over his mouth, but the guffaws still escaped. 'Oh, no. Oh, how sad. So while I was rescuing Romana – you must know Romana, everyone knows Romana, of course she's president now but still a lovely girl – you were off observing simple non-flowering organisms?'

The man gave a curt nod.

'Romana used to be a companion of mine, did you know?' the showman continued. 'Came on board when I was saving the universe one time. I'm not entirely sure how many times I've saved the universe now. You stop counting after the first two or three. Come to think of it, I'm not entirely sure how many companions I've had, either. Sarah Jane, I remember... young Jamie... Liz, very clever girl, you'd have liked her... Bernice, now she was something and a half... Jo, sweet thing, you'll be seeing a bit of her shortly. The prettiest and brightest and best, from all over space and time, they all wanted to travel with me. One lad even hopped across from another universe, believe it or not.'

'Other... universe?' One of the man's hands was starting to twitch, and he used the other to hold it down. But both hands began to twitch in unison.

'Oh, yes,' said the showman. 'I've been to a few. I know, most people don't even believe they exist. The universe is infinite, they say, it is everything. How can there be another everything, there'd be nowhere for it to fit! But yet, somehow – I know you're a bit of a whizz at physics, but I won't bore you with the details – there they are. You can probably count on the fingers of a Sontaran's hand how many people have been to more than one... Ooh! Sontarans! They invaded Gallifrey too. I foiled that one as well. Were you there for that?'

'I was ill.'

The showman slapped his forehead. 'No! To miss one invasion is unfortunate; to miss two... Still, no doubt you were in deadly peril. Spectrox toxaemia, perhaps. Dreadful injuries from a fall off a high gantry? Perhaps you'd been riddled with bullets from the shooting of a street gang. Or a burst of deadly radiation did you in, just after you'd saved a planet or two.'

'I had a slight chill.'

The showman looked as if he were about to laugh again, then stopped. He was suddenly serious, suddenly real.

'That's why you're here, isn't it? You've never had some great tragedy. Never been a dramatic figure with your world falling apart around you. You look at me and see me smiling throughout the death and disaster and doom, and you think that's how you want to be. You see the excitement and the danger, and equate that with terror and misery. And you're right. But you're looking at it all topsy-turvy.'

The showman smiled now, but a sad smile, a true smile. 'I wouldn't give it up for the universe, but that doesn't mean I'm someone to be envied. I have to go on, but sometimes that's the only reason I can go on – because it's impossible for me to do otherwise.

'I meet people, make friends, and they all die around me. I see pain and suffering wherever I go. And I have to think, the whole time, *without me this would be worse*.' He thumped the table. 'I do it to stop the misery, not to experience it!'

They were both silent for a few minutes. Then the showman said, 'Another thing about being me. Sometimes things are worse because of me. A couple of lives ago... well, perhaps that's another story. Let's just say that because of who I am, a lot of extra misery was spread. Hunger. War. Pestilence.' A pause. 'Death, of course. I lost someone... I lost someone I cared about. And you can envy me for the wonders I've seen, and the places I've been and the sheer, adrenalin-filled thrill of it all... but you can't envy me for that.'

But as the showman looked into the eyes of the other, still full of hatred and longing and discontent, he knew that the Time Lord did envy him for that.

He sighed. 'I shouldn't have said that, any of that. It's not what I'm here for. It's not what you're here for. I need to tell you more, more about my travels, about my fights with Cybermen and Ice Warriors and the terrible Zodin. I need to tell you about being chosen above all other Time Lords to serve the White Guardian, the most powerful entity in the universe. I need to tell you about travelling back to the dawn of time, and forward to the end of everything. I need to tell you about finding enlightenment. About picnicking on Mars and swimming on Florana and strolling through the Eye of Orion.'

The showman looked at the pitiful figure before him, and saw that the Time Lord had tears in his eyes. 'That should have been me,' the Time Lord whispered. 'I was the bright one, I was the better one. I could have done so much more. I would have succeeded where you succeeded, but succeeded where you'd failed, too. My birth is more noble than yours. I am cleverer than you. I could have done it all. But you have everything, and I have nothing.'

'That might be true,' said the showman. 'But you never took the first step on the path, whereas I have never given up walking onwards, forcing myself to take one step after another, however rocky the road.'

He stood up. 'But right now, I need you to know why it is bliss to be me, and hell to be you. And you do feel that way. And I am so, so sorry that you do, because it has destroyed your life. A life that could have been truly great. But at the moment – I'm afraid it's how I need you to feel. I'm going to turn on the machine now. There is so much misery this time...' He gave a small chuckle. 'I don't envy you!'

And then the showman walked sorrowfully over to the wall, and pushed down on a switch.

Angel

Tara Samms

I

I think it was a Friday when they told me I was going to die, but it's hard to recall. There are no divisions here. Each day is the same. The harsh, inflexible monotony of the regime is as much an enemy as disease or injury.

The lights stay on at night, shine in your eyes, you can't sleep. When you fall to fatigue at last they wake you and feed you pills that snag in the throat.

A long day of nothing begins.

The food, dry and tasteless, clings to your teeth and tongue. It does not nourish. I always get the worst and last of the stuff anyway, because of where my bed is. The hollow thump of feet on floorboards wears on your mind; it is a great clock ticking a resentful rhythm all around you. As the days and weeks blur, its purpose escapes you entirely. Sheets are swapped, curtains rattled round, fluids emptied, half-hearted baths attempted. A cold flannel on your armpits, between your legs, knuckles kneading into your breasts. But the smell remains, it's old in the air and the boil-washed sheets.

You stay here on your grey slab, an effigy that fools or satisfies no one. The wrong colour, too thin. Too hot or not responding. Parts of you inside are incompetent, or rotten. Hard to reach, hard to mend.

But the more time they take with you, the less you have.

This place steals your strength to feed itself.

Some will survive and pull clear, they will heal despite themselves.

I shall remain; I've always known that. While these old crones pull clear all around me. Their sainted aunts and lucky stars cluster around them, queuing up to be counted.

No one comes to me without purpose. To prick and prod and poke me, to take numbers and sounds and fluids from me. They give a tight smile, mumble a pleasantry, their smart shoes clip-clop away like they run on hooves. All the day this treatment goes on. I look at the crones beside me, across from me, and see the brave-faced, happy people in bright clothes and glossy hair who have come to see them, to distract and amuse and push the hurt into the background for a time.

I am sick-jealous of them the worst. Sick-jealous of these plump, ripe people. The young ones dragged against their wills, the tall men, bright-eyed and stocky, the young girls squeezed into their clothes so keen to be older. All of them.

I would be any one of them and not me.

In front of me they parade: they walk and drink and eat and laugh and watch and come and go and grin and jog off to make coffee and sit up straight and throw back their heads and hold hands and use the phone and sit down, stand up, stretch out, preen and play and *everything*. And they don't think – never – how good it is just to move without pain. To appreciate the simple power to walk quickly and surely across a room. To belong in a body that's strong and healthful.

Why should they appreciate things like that? They're not old and rotting. They are young and come and go as they please.

But I am not old either. I am only fifty-two. How can I be so brittle? I am the youngest in this ward of crones. I am the youngest by a long way. That is why they test the new drugs on me. They hope I will prove things for them.

I notice the old, watery crone eyes on me when the pinstripe men come to visit with their special tablets. I have never been envied in life, I'm quite sure, but these old bitches, gone in the tooth, seethe at the special attention I'm getting. They wish the pinstripes would crouch and bend about them.

But they don't wish they were me for one minute.

My moment of fervour passes and those who would woo me drift away with promises to return. Power returns to the rest of the ward, for while I lie here burning in my gut, I must watch the visitors bustle around the other beds while mine is silent. The pain makes me bold and I want to scream and scream from my bed and scare them all away. I want to bring down darkness so the visitors will leave. They will leave quickly, sprightly, knowing they can do everything again the next morning.

I will prove things to the pinstripes.

At night I close my eyes and glide through the dark wards and the corridors. My hair is short and grey or it would stream out behind me like a mermaid's in the sea. My eyes are shut so I can see better; if I opened them they would be big and wide and glittering green as I float this way and that.

No one sees me. I've been part of this place too long to be noticed. I follow my nose to the good wards in the new part of the building. There she is. Katrina with bad kidneys. She was here when I first arrived. Her children are young. They would crowd around her as soon as visiting started. I watched her being so strong for them; only at night would the truth crawl out. She could barely move and rocked with the pain.

Day after day the children made noise and rushed about. So much life and energy, spent so carelessly. I lay there and snapped at them if they came too near. They looked at me half-wondering, half in fear, this woman lying still like a reptile under lamps, drying out and exotic for a time in this, my new home. Unknown, not to be approached.

Katrina watched them play and rush with a mother's tender eye. She would never let her smile dip. I heard the nurses say of her, 'She's so strong.'

Why should some of us be strong and others weak?

When I go drifting, I reach into their mother getting better on the nice ward and I squeeze hidden handfuls of her. I numb Katrina's mouth so she can't scream. This is my strength and she shuts up soon enough. She wasn't so strong really. It's easy. The nurses will wonder whatever's happened to all that wonderful strength of hers, all that resolve to get well.

I must be careful not to overdo it, though, because if she gets really bad she will be brought back to the bed in the corner. And I don't want the children with their rushing about and shouting, or the *Ahhh, bless the kiddies, they bring life into the wards* and the whoops and shouts and *She's so strongs* she'll tug here with her.

There are others here, and my green eyes snap open to study their strength.

I see me. I'm in my bed, of course. The pills make you see things and feel funny. I'm scratching my stomach. There is a rash there. I tell a nurse twice.

It is sunset the next day before the specialists come and prod and pick at it. *It could be the new drug,* they say. *You could be having a reaction. Yes, we'll have to watch that.*

II

Between three and four o'clock in the morning is the closest it gets to dark. The black girls are clustered around an anglepoise at the nurses' station, laughing. Someone shuffles along from the wrong ward, looking for someone or something, he can't remember what.

He glances at me, then stops and looks back and stares like he recognises me and doesn't want to. He makes a mouse's noise and scuffles away.

On the walls, the shifting lights cast by the traffic thin and fade, the ceaseless drone of engines weakens. Shadows creep back into the ward. It's like the night is trying to let go of everything, to expire. But the dawn swabs it with white, wet clouds, shines the mean little light of the sun into its eyes – makes it run and hide before it can go through with things. Day has her say, and only when she is worn through and burnt out does the darkness come with its soothing promises, to smother her. She realises too late; sets and sinks, shuts her pink eye in sorrow as it takes everything from her.

I watch the two of them living and dying through the filmy curtains at the window. Never any change. Performing for the world, telling them when to stop and when to go. Pretending there's an order to anything.

This place should have been shut down years ago but it hangs on. There's talk of refurbishment sometimes; men in dark suits sweep in and speak of sweeping out all the old. Then they look at us and cringe and shoot idiot glances at one another and later they will snort about it. They think we're too far gone to notice their little gaffe.

But I am not old. I'm fifty-two, that isn't old. They lump me in with all the others because they think I look like all the others. It's because the doctors and nurses are all so young – barely out of school, some of them. Shaking heads and whispers at first, but as the process goes on and draws out, the voices grow louder. They talk about you like you can't hear or know.

Lymph fluid. Catabolic reactions. Mutation of the brain's natural catecholamines. Decline. The words are heavy and smother like the sheets. Comfortless as the pillows jammed under your head.

They say this drug could help me. It could get me up on my feet again. They say I could give hope to others. But I don't know. All my life I've been looking in at the windows wanting stuff. *Want, want, never have*, my mother used to say to me. Then she would turn to my little sister and say, *Yesssssssss*.

I see the grey-haired doctor in his dark suit and ruffles, by the nurses' station. He's looking at a folder. My notes are in the folder, and he rubs his nose. He turns to his dolly-bird in her powder-blue suede jacket and gauzy blouse and sees she's uncomfortable. He scratches the back of his neck, watching me from a distance.

I glance around at the crones. We're dolls in shoeboxes, plastic and lifeless; the children in the nurse uniforms dumped us here for inspection. The needles don't hurt, not after all this time. So why should words?

Even the big ones.

This doctor, who's grand and dandy enough for a big D – Doctor – he comes close to inspect me, his young secretary with him. His hair is nearly white. His lined face is kindly. His gaze is shrewd. His nose is big and so is his smile. The cloak he carries so well holds a blood-red lining. I always wanted a cloak like that. I catch myself wondering what it would feel like between my fingers.

'Hello,' he says; his voice is warm with a sandpaper edge. 'Mrs Marion Connors?'

That's what it says on the board above my head so I nod at him.

'I'm the Doctor, and this is Jo Grant. How are you feeling today?'

I don't know how to take that. I look at the girl, cute and small, smell the fizz and energy bundled up inside her. I feel nothing as my eyes narrow to slits.

'I'm dying,' I say.

Jo Grant cringes, looks crestfallen at the floor. But the Doctor is unfazed.

'Today you're alive,' he says calmly, and sits on the side of the bed. 'One today is worth a dozen tomorrows.'

'Depends what you do with it,' I say.

He raises an eyebrow like it's a language all by itself. 'True,' he concedes, having considered. 'And stuck in here, I don't suppose you can do much.'

I spy Sapphy over at the nurses' station. She has just come on shift. She is filing her long, elegant nails. They are pearls that gleam at the end of her black fingers.

'No. I can't do much.'

'You've been here for three months.'

It doesn't sound like much the way he says it, but think about it. Imagine what you did in the last three months. Not just the big stuff but all the little bits too. Imagine spending that same time in a little bed too frail to move, with no comfort, no visitors, no conversation that wasn't using words you couldn't grasp.

'This may sound a ridiculous question,' the Doctor warns me, 'but you're quite sure you haven't moved from this bed in the last week?'

I gesture to my wires and leads and bags and pipes. It's enough to stop that line of questioning.

'We were told you were responding to the treatment,' Jo Grant with the soft skin mutters from under her fringe. She's upset; perhaps because she thinks she's been misinformed. She's embarrassed. Uneasy. Jo Grant with the trendy clothes doesn't like hospitals. Jo bloody Grant is bobbing her head about like a baby bird wanting to be fed.

The Doctor's beak is big enough, I think, and I could smile if I wanted.

'But you *are* responding to the treatment, aren't you, Mrs Connors?' says the Doctor. 'We've seen the test results.'

He is poking his big beak into me.

'So she *is* getting better!' says his baby bird, hoping to nest in the cosy thought.

The Doctor keeps his eyes on me. 'Are you, Mrs Connors?'

Thump, thump, thump go the fat feet on the floorboards. The nurses are all plump and healthy. They talk about stockings and men and the telly and pop stars. I lie here all day and night and listen to the kind ones lie: *how much better you're looking* and *it's all down to the new drugs* and *you're responding really well*. And *one day, my love* – it's always my love in this forsaken place – *you'll be tap dancing your way out of here*. Elaine's like that, the ward manager. She and her kind think they're being cheery.

I was so polite to them, and grateful when I first got here. I felt embarrassed to bother them, a nuisance. Well, it's breeding, isn't it. Good manners.

The politeness doesn't last long on either side.

You hardly know these people and suddenly their fingers are everywhere and the things they hold are inside you or wrapped around you or pushing and poking about.

Intimate strangers, changing every few hours, taking you apart in shifts. They look at the bits of you that are secret and special and saved for just one, and their bored eyes dissolve that mystery with a glance. It's nothing to them.

I don't notice their interfering fingers any more, the little tugs and pulls that strip me away. I am an infant, dumb, no strength to cry. The filth comes out of me but it's their job to deal with it. Frank was one of those that if he blew his nose or went to the toilet, he'd always have a good peer at what he'd done.

He'd go over it and study it. I shied from it, that muck and filth inside us. I blew my nose when no one was about, scrunched up the tissue inside another tissue and tossed both in the kitchen bin. I flushed before I left the seat.

Now I don't even move unless they make me. I pass control to them. I can just lie here and let it out into tubes and bags. I don't have to touch or do anything.

I respond to the treatment but I'm not getting better.

I've taken my pill and I'm feeling the pull from down the corridor. I'm dancing out of here, Elaine. I'm hovering in the grimy service lift with its one working light, it's clanking me down a floor to where the men lie in a better ward than mine. I watch them lie, fitful and pained, all boys together. I wonder where Frank ended up. They have a TV in the corner. Their lights don't hum and whirr like bees are caught behind the glass.

I visit the men, I brush my stubby fingers against the stubble on their cheeks. I have spent a life longing for their roughness and strength, for their stride, their success. They stir softly like children under my touch. Men are just babies with tougher hides. They feel so little. I am stuffed like Sunday's bird with feelings. My heart is scaled with them.

But men, they just brush these things – these everythings – away. They can walk out and they can just leave and won't come back.

So now I float from bed to bed and when I find Jackie's dutiful son I press my soft, rotting lips against his, wishing that I could take as men do and not care. And with each viral kiss, I wonder what I give him.

The Doctor comes back the next day. Now he asks about the rashes on my stomach. He was playing it cool yesterday. But I suppose this is why he has come to see me. There are things he wants to know. Yes, I get that very clearly.

He asks if he can see them. His assistant pulls along the pink curtain. Frank's sister had something like it in her bath, to stop the shower attachment spitting water over the chipped porcelain sides. I can see the chips on the porcelain but I can't see her face any longer or remember her name.

He asks me gently to hitch up the material of my nightdress, he's sorry to ask. But they condition you, the pinstripes. My fingers are already twitching to obey. 'Property of Central Middlewich Hospital' is stamped on the fabric in the faded blue of an old vein.

He gives me a reassuring smile. It makes me uncomfortable. I have been a ghost, accepted and tolerated by those who must live here in my haunting. He makes me feel like I am real.

I like the girl better for looking away. There's nothing to see here. Nothing to see.

But the Doctor looks at my belly and then up at me, sharply.

He looks angry. No, it's more than that. There's fear in that look too.

I remember I have a spine when a shiver runs through it.

'Doctor, what's wrong?' asks Jo Grant. She does it well; it is her station in life.

'Mrs Connors, would you kindly explain to me the meaning of this?' he asks in a low, clear voice.

I look down at myself, at the red blisters. 'I don't know. You're the Doctor. Don't *you* know?'

'No, I don't,' he says hoarsely. A few minutes have passed. 'That's why I'm trapped here.'

Not all the nurses are kind. Kindness and patience are spread too thin here, like the butter on our hard, dry bread. Some you know have just drifted into the job; it's a lazy choice for a girl. Some think it's their calling. These are the wearying ones, because they try to care and make you see the good in things and you almost start to bother yourself about what will happen tomorrow, and how you will feel.

When the specialist told me I was going to die, there were two nurses with him. Skinny Elaine, all scruffy blonde hair and bad teeth, and Sapphy, the Caribbean girl. I know I should have been listening to the specialist with his special words and his explanations of why I was going to die. But just knowing was enough. I didn't care for the details and I had no one to tell about them anyway. I found myself looking at my nurses.

Elaine was staring at me, so sorry, big dopey eyes behind her round glasses. Broad, black Sapphy kept tapping her fingers against her hip, kept glancing out the window, quick and careful glances so she wouldn't be told off. She was thinking about her weekend, about escaping I suppose, and I almost said to her, *what do you see out there? Tell me what you see.*

I wouldn't want her to get into trouble.

I see the way Sapphy looks at some of her patients. It's the way I look at them.

She doesn't want to be here. Never wanted to be a nurse, I don't suppose. Kid to support. Or a man as useless and lazy as mine was. Some of them, they live and breathe it, like plain Elaine does. Winks and cheery banter for her loves. She thinks it helps us. Chivvies us along. She hopes we will care about her, perhaps.

But Sapphy works the night shift not from care, but because she just has to. She and I were both forced into our different positions here, no choice in the matter. She treats me like I'm not really here; takes my bloods and hands out the pills and yet, beyond the stranger's touch of her fingers on my skin, there's no contact. She's remote, removed, and I covet her strength so badly.

I can barely remember my eyes were green. I had a friend once and she asked Frank and he didn't know. I moaned at him, I suppose, and he looked into my eyes like a stage hypnotist, saying, 'Green, green,' over and over, making our table of friends laugh; and, though it was just for a few moments, that unsettling, silly look is the one that stays with me. Frank looks wrong to me, when I think of him in my head, saying 'green' like it's something he's been taught and he can't see it.

He was always wrong; I can see that looking back, jaded.

III

There was a new face in the ward that first time it happened. Jackie someone. The nurses thought it was funny as Jackie sounded like a young girl's name, but this woman was pushing seventy. She'd had something taken out of her, through the throat. There were leads and catheters and wires and God knows what. She was mad with the morphine. It often takes them like that.

They gave it to me, after the first few poke abouts. But I'm bad with it. I tried to stab a nurse with scissors. I thought they were all out to get me. The lumps in my brain swelled up and the pressure made me blind. The morphine made me think I could see. I thought the scissors were a gun and I was going to kill everyone before they could kill me.

I heard the porters laughing about it, once I'd been brought back under control. It's their way of coping, I've heard.

My troubles with morphine are one reason they decided to try new drugs on me. Brand new drugs. They knew: I had Nothing To Lose. They told me like I should feel special.

Now the Doctor's gone, I can see back there to that first time.

Jackie's looking at me. Aside from the plumbing in her throat, she looks normal and plausible. 'Don't move,' she says. 'There are wild animals under your bed.'

I used to talk to these fools, try to calm them, but I don't now. Sham sleep.

'Wild animals, hiding under the bed! It's not right. We should complain about it.'

I can't hear you. Sorry.

I listen to my heart and each thud is a footprint in the thick white juice of my disease. I see it furring my body like scale in the kettle. No, more like fresh snow blanketing your garden. Some people groan at the sight of it and the bother it will cause. Some want to trample through it, to muck it all up.

It's perfect, like icing on a cake. I traipse through the sucking stuff, step after step, compelled to.

'We can't tell the police,' says the old woman, 'because they're in on it. They wouldn't let my husband see me. They've got him.'

I ruck it all up, splash in it. And when there is no clean white to dirty, I shall be dead and all this shall stop. The thought doesn't scare me yet; these fields run on forever through me. There's always fresh, virginal muck I can stand on. I feel like a little girl again, and this would be a wonderland except I'm lost in this ageing shape that's frowned down on, lost in the rotten-meat shadows and creaking, condemned corridors of the hospital.

A moan and cuss from Jocelyn across the ward. Jackie beside me has yanked out the tubes from her neck. She's off to rescue her husband. And the blood's pouring from the bag and wetting the bed. She's making her way indignantly across the night ward, tubes splashing as she walks, but she doesn't feel a thing. And the nurses sigh and speak loudly at her in their colourful accents, get up and guide her back like she's a little girl.

But Sapphy hangs back and in her bulging eyes there's this mean little gleam and suddenly I know, I can tell what she's thinking: *I just changed that bed, you old cow. Look at this damned mess everywhere. Right. I'm giving you clumsy needles when you can feel them tomorrow. In the arm. In the behind.*

And maybe she'll mellow with the morning and forget the threat and maybe she won't.

I look at her and I feel sick-jealous for Sapphy's strength. Her power. Her two dark legs stretching up thickly into the dark blue tunnel of her starched skirt, dark bruiser arms folding across that perfect white apron. The dark bolster of her bust beneath her clothes and the eyes and the swell of her nose and cheeks: I look and I want, I am ditches and flat fields to be walked over and she is a dark mountain that I would kill to climb.

I watch Jackie closely next day when she is patched up. She blinks so slowly it is like the weight of the long hours is hooked to her wrinkled lids. The visitors come visiting and make noise, look polite but shifty. She has a devoted son who slouches in to bring Jackie a newspaper. Jackie reads her stars and sleeps a lot.

She recovers something of herself in the afternoon and uses her time to say sorry. Sorry to me, to the nurses, to the other ladies. Sorry for being trouble.

Jocelyn catches my eye. We nod like old lags. We know this behaviour.

Jackie is new. She will stop apologising.

I sit all day watching her and wondering when Sapphy starts and if she will make good on her promise.

I itch my belly. There's a rash. I peer down my hospital nightdress, the faded and raggedy fabric catching on my bitten fingernails. It almost seems to make a pattern. A dark red crab blooms from the blisters. Its pincers snake up fiercely from its body towards my breasts.

I look to my left, at the newspaper folded over on the bedside table, at the tubes poking through Jackie's neck (secured with sticking plaster) and it's quite funny because the chart above Jackie's head gives her surname as Crabbe.

I lie perfectly still as Sapphy takes the sharps and rolls Jackie over and gives her three – a needle in the behind and two in the arm. She says she can't find a vein, that rolling accent of hers making the words sound so jolly. She goes in clumsy and Jackie is crying by the end of it.

I lie perfectly still and wonder if people can see me shake with scandal and glee. My own pain is driving me out of my body and I want to be in beautiful Sapphy's dark skin, taking revenge and doing what I want, which is what she does while the others only wish they could.

The pattern on my belly doesn't go away the next day or the next so I buzz for a nurse and I get Elaine. She squeezes my hand and smiles all her bad teeth at me and won't blame it on a pinstripe's pills; she thinks perhaps I am allergic to a new soap powder. I would like to believe the silly miss, but my skin's not even itching. It's just hot and sticky, like a burn but with no pain.

On the fourth day, the crab on my stomach is brighter and redder and clearer, and pinstripes come to look at it, and they talk in the big words and say they will speak to reps and practitioners and experts and don't speak to me at all. There's humour in their eyes at the crab I have grown, it's diverting, and their pink, well-fed fat faces crease with smiles, their neatly combed heads shake from side to side with amazement.

Good son struts in, damn him, damn him moving so bloody freely, and damn his idiot mother who's bad every night, squeaking and wailing, telling us all she's surrounded, that they're closing in on her, that they want to hurt her. But in the morning, when the morphine's washing out with her piss, she can't remember what she was frightened of.

Son complains that whatever she's got, it's catching – or maybe it's hanging around this hospital, he doesn't know – but he has to see the doctor tomorrow. He seems slightly strained about this. His mother wonders what his stars will say about this. He is a Taurus. A typical Taurus, butting about in this china shop. His mother is a Cancer. Mrs Crabbe is the crab. A nurse overhears and she big-grins. A white one, a skinny white streak, red spots pocking her stupid face. She says it's not surprising I've got a crab on my stomach when I'm next to Crabbe who's the crab and I'm crabby as I am. The words slip out before she can stop them and a little chuckle zips around the ward and for a moment I've brought them all together, nurses and patients and visitors, all of them. Why can't I feel a part of it, even for only a few seconds?

The dutiful son keeps his appointment with a doctor. He is diagnosed as having cancer. He will maybe have to start by losing a leg. The crab on my belly starts to fade.

I don't speak for two days but, while Jackie sobs into her pillow through the night, I think about the marks and I grieve once there's only skin there, once the crab has gone. Perhaps the doctors, who are testing me daily, have scared it away with their pincers and prongs. Or perhaps it is simply hiding under a black rock inside me, minding its own, better alone.

The son will be placed in the ward downstairs. Tests and strategies will start.

I shall float through the grey seas that wash through our hospital and see her dutiful, strong and patient son there and I will clutch at the blackness in him and rub it into a bigger ball and I will test his strength.

'They have a better ward than us,' I tell him. 'This is the worst ward in the place. It's because we're none of us worth saving really.'

'Is that really what you believe?' The Doctor sits by my bedside, alone this time. It's the third time he's visited. No one else has come. No one knows I am here.

Friends walked out when Frank did.

I shrug. I'm not used to talking. I sound hollow, not all here. Only my head is visible above the sheets, and I feel hot and sore, like the rest of me is dribbling into the hard mattress.

I see the eyes of the others on me, hear them muttering. It's outside visiting hours, and the noisy yawn of the evening traffic is starting to die.

'Why are you bothering with me?'

He looks at me. 'The people I... associate with got to hear about you.'

'About my rash. About the pills they've got me on.'

'About you.' The Doctor smiles. 'They thought you might have been got at by an alien from another planet.'

I stare at him. I've never been good with jokes, but I know he must be making one.

'I don't think you have,' he assures me, with a charmer's smile. 'Just a routine check, you know.'

I know routine. This man breaks it.

'And is that why you're here?' I ask him. 'You're still checking?'

'Good grief, no.' He seems shifty. They often are in visiting time, not sure what to say next. 'But your affliction is very, very interesting.'

Interesting is a word that holds you by the throat at arm's length and studies you.

I look him in the eye and I move a creaking branch limb and pull back the covers and show him my stick-thin carcass is still here. He says nothing, but I know this is what he wants. The markings he saw before. I wriggle a bit and lift the nightdress a little to show him.

He sketches the shapes on to a napkin. His eyes scan over my thin belly like he's lost something there.

'Do you know what I'm showing you?' I whisper.

He looks at me gravely. 'I think it's part of a time equation.'

The words are meaningless to me. Time equates to different shades through the window, that's all, and night is gathering its strength here.

'It's what hurts you,' I say.

He stops, nods, and for a moment I am complete. I have guessed right. I have a power and Frank cannot sponge it and my sister cannot bleed it away and my mother need not know of it, because this tall, dandified man in his gorgeous cloak is looking at me like I have all the power in the world.

I can see something in his eyes, and it is how the crones look when the pinstripes come, except this is just for me.

'I know what it is like, Mrs Connors,' he says quietly, 'to be trapped in a tiny plot. Buried in a backwater. Left to rot, thrown to the mercy of others.'

'While others roam freely.'

'Yes,' he says. 'There is a man I know well, a man like me. He can come and go as he pleases, while I...'

I see a hard hurt in his eyes, it is harder than words. The distance in his eyes is so great, it's something he can't share with the likes of me.

'Please.' He leans into me. 'Please, you must show me more.'

I start hitching up the nightie, and he places a hand on my stick-arm. 'No, no, Mrs Connors, not your skin, I mean –'

'I'm Marion.' It's almost like this is news to myself. 'I don't know what I showed for Katrina,' I murmur, secretly, seriously, keen to impress. 'It was new to me then and I couldn't see what it was – it might have been a kidney, I suppose, because it was kidneys that almost did for her; but it might have been anything on my belly, just blotches.'

He's frowning. 'Katrina Fuller, the woman who was starting to get better, but –'

'Then I showed a crab for Jackie's boy. Cancer, see, I got the ideas from the stars in the paper she was always looking at. And I never really knew, not properly like I was told – but I showed he had cancer right enough, didn't I?' I sound almost petulant for his approval. 'And I'm showing these squiggles for you now though I don't even know what they mean.'

'Subconscious interpretation of energy waves,' the Doctor said. 'I don't understand it yet myself, but I'd like to perform some tests if that's all right.'

'You want to know more.'

'Yes. Yes, I do, very much.'

'Bloods?' I smile at him. I used to have a nice smile, Frank said. 'You can have bloods.'

He looks awkward. 'I need a little more.' He looks uncomfortable and I start to panic he will bite his tongue and not ask. 'Humoral extractions. The cyst matter in your brain may...' He lets the big words fall away, blows up a smile. 'According to your notes, the markings fade after a few days. And these markings, I believe they could be of great importance.'

'Who to?' I ask, cradling my stomach like something good grows there.

He smiles at me. 'Well, to science, my dear,' he says.

Over his shoulder, I see Jo Grant walk into the ward and hover meekly. She is done up in boots and blue tights and a purple skirt and a little blouse and clears her pink throat, big eyes grave and expectant. She knows something. And he sees me looking and turns and smiles at his little slip of a girlfriend.

And I see in a second that the smile he has given me is a weak imitation, is useless, is worth nothing.

'You can take what you like from me,' I tell him quickly, and my fingers crush against the rich black velvet of his cloak and the red, raw lining sewn so beautifully into it.

'I'll be back tomorrow,' he says, patting my hand. 'Goodbye.' He walks to the girl. She holds folders in her hands.

He walks across to her and places an arm around her shoulder and she walks away with him. Familiar. Easy.

As they move, they show Sapphy to me, yawning at her desk, looking around with big eyes like she wants a target.

That night, sleep won't come, though they have given me extra tablets and I am exhausted from not sleeping the night before.

I have not left this place for so long, but now I am drifting through the walls and stretching into the night sky beyond it, rising high above the city and there is a warm, well-fed feeling in my blistered stomach. Then I feel the weight of his eyes on me, seeing me somehow. His telescope eyes tug me down.

I am in lodgings beside a field, guarded by soldiers and trucks and I have never been out so far before but he is calling me and I creep through and see him pacing his room while the girl sleeps down the hallway, sleeps like a little girl. The folders are stacked untidily beside her bunk, I know the faces in there but it is him I watch: still dressed, his face sullen, muttering under his breath. Words and symbols and syllables there are no clue for in my brain.

My skin tingles with the sound of his tongue. I would kill to feel needed like the girl in the room down the way.

I reach into this Doctor and I squeeze the things that beat and pulse. He staggers, wants to shout but I have a little finger around his throat and my chewed thumbnail has pierced his tongue, hooked it to the roof of his mouth, he can't speak at all. He can't smile at anyone.

He has such strength about him though and I am sick. I cannot feed on this rich stuff. I press my lips against his pale cheek, let go and drift away through his walls, and as he collapses I am snatched away, dripping and blown into lovers' darkness.

IV

It is hard to wake the next day.

Sapphy takes my wrist and my eyes wrinkle open. She's not looking. She's staring at her watch, checking the second hand, doing her duty.

The crones seem to be sleeping, they notice nothing of course, their thoughts thick with who will come to see them today, counting away the hours and I want to scream, *I left here, I left you all last night.* I want them to look at me, wonderingly. I want them to stare hatefully at me, ask me how, ask me why not them, why couldn't they be the ones to be so free.

Jackie looks terrible. I see from her neck she was busy again while I was gone. Her eyes have opened and she is saying to me, 'They have my husband. They won't let him see me.'

'How is your son?' I ask her, though I know. I know how soft his skin feels against my cheek. 'How is he?'

'He'll be wanting his tea,' she says. 'I have to reach him. I have to tell the school.'

'Silly old trout,' sighs Sapphy, and my heart leaps because I think she is talking to me, but no. There's no one here to talk to.

I'm taken by orderlies to a new room. The Doctor is there on a hard chair. His velvet jacket is dark blue. His shirt is white, like the walls. He looks up as I'm wheeled in, and it's like he's been jolted from some faraway place.

He thanks the orderlies and invites them to leave. It is just me and him. He looks at me for an age.

Then he says, 'You came to me last night.'

'Yes,' I say. 'You were hurting. I was dragged to you.'

His eyes narrow dubiously. One seems bigger than the other. 'You were *dragged* to me?'

I nod, my chin scratching my itchy collarbone. I pull open the neck of the hospital slip. The red spills out bloodlike over the grey.

He rises from his chair, eyes hooded.

The lesions spell out numbers I don't know, solve sums I can't imagine. They sit on my shoulders, on my small breasts, lie like scree on my ribs.

'They came out for you,' I whisper.

His eyes sweep over me, they linger and I have not felt so bright before.

'But this is incredible,' he says. 'Phenomenal. I almost feel I can remember...'

And I close my eyes and I remember warm days out of doors, not pinned behind glass. How when I married Frank it was a beautiful warm day, how nothing could spoil that and I remember I thought then: whatever happens, I'll have today, in my lovely dress and Mum smiling and the blue sky at noon.

I thought it would be enough.

The Doctor looks at my arm. The shapes are wrong, not yet right. He stops, suddenly uneasy.

'I'll show you more,' I promise.

His eyes meet mine. Hesitate.

'Marion,' he says. 'I know what you can do to people. I know what you're doing to Katrina Fuller.'

I don't move a muscle.

'And what you're trying to do to me.'

'It's the new drugs,' I say quietly.

'No, it isn't,' the Doctor says. 'They haven't worked. I've checked.'

I look at him. 'I'm feeling better.'

'No. You're feeling stronger. But your body is close to collapse.' He shakes his head. 'And as your body weakens, so something else is getting loose. Something evil that thinks it can feed on others to make you stronger.'

I accept his words. I accept everything here. It's part of me, part of the shadows that whisper through this hospital at night. I took the old pills and new pills and did what I was told and I rested and ate the food and gave the bloods, and this thing in me grows.

'I can't explain what's happening to you,' he says, his lips moving like he's reading aloud. 'Not yet. But perhaps it's not too late to –'

'It's too late,' I tell him. I pull my sheets back over me, hiding the patterns.

'No.'

I don't answer.

'We'll start today.'

'I don't have a dozen tomorrows to balance it out. The nearer I get to dying, the stronger this becomes?'

'It would seem that way.'

'I can't wait on while you try to find out what's happening. Can't.'

He looks troubled, holds his head to one side. 'But if we can arrest the process –'

'I'm not stopping here.'

'Where are you going?' He's watching me closely, warningly. 'To hurt someone else?'

I sneer at him now. 'I left my little buried backwater last night. I'm not stuck in it like you are, not any more.'

'You were dragged to me, you said. You have no control.' His voice softens. 'The urticaria has spread over your body. You're weak, close to death, and yet the force within you grows stronger. It is feeding not from Katrina or Larry or me, but from you. And you are letting it.'

'I can give you the answers you want,' I tell him quickly, my voice is loud and high, it exhausts me. 'I can set you free. I can show it all to you, I know I can.'

He watches me. That fierce gaze, the nose, he should be like a hawk. But his anger is turned inward now, because he is listening to the devil at his bony elbow, though he knows it's wrong and bad.

'Help me to die,' I whisper.

He pretends he hasn't heard.

'Make it happen fast and I'll let you see it all. I can. I know I can.'

'No. No, you can't ask me –'

'I can make it do what I want it to.'

'You *can't*. It's been hurting people, it almost killed...'
I nod slowly. I show I know.
And he understands now that I don't care about that.
'You can make me stop.'
'Mrs Connors,' he says slowly, 'you must fight this sickness.'
'There's nothing to fight,' I tell him. All the brightness has gone except the glitter in my green eyes, looking at that strength in him, that self-restraint. Because what he needs is all over me, I am tattooed with it. I see the hunger in him, the dissatisfaction, the wanting. He wishes this dry, flaking skin was his, I know it.
'I'll come to you again,' I tell him.
He walks away from my skin. He hesitates more than once but he goes in the end and I know he shall not come back.

It's Sapphy they send to take me back with the orderlies. She is humming to herself, a tune I don't know. I don't care for anyone, I want to tell her, I want her to know. This is my only strength now.
My body is itching and sore. I rub my red ruby feet together, I tap them together, and there is no place like home anymore, no place at all.

Back in the ward and Sapphy plumps up my pillow when I tell her to. She does it unflinchingly. She does it like it's her place. Sapphy likes the other girls and she will do her job. It's the way to get on. You have to just get on with it.

The pinstripes stay away now. Jackie has been taken someplace else. At night I float hungrily and my form is frightening even to me, but the shapes and scribbles that so hurt him have left no space for anything new. I shift in the lift and glide out but the Doctor is waiting there with Larry, holding the man's hand as he sleeps, and he sees me as I come closer and he is a fire. He can warm me, light the way, or he can scare me off.
'I can only help you if you let me,' he says.
'I can only help you if you let me,' I say back.

It's day. I want to see Katrina again, to see what the shadow on my stomach might have spelled. I go there, tiptoe out through the doors, but the bright red brick of the new block makes my eyes hurt, and she's getting better again and she's still so strong.
He has been to see her. He has taught her something, some strength, something he wanted to teach me.

Sapphy leaves on time as the bare morning rubs against the windows, she changes her uniform, she puts on a pretty red dress and a shawl and heads out through the doors.

Elaine is feeling my wrist for a pulse, and her fingers snake down to join with my own. She squeezes my hand, squeezes out a fat tear.

But I can't feel that, I can only feel the whiteness of the morning as I drift outside, blown like a leaf, out into the air. And I was dragged out here once before, weeks ago, looking for him, but there is nothing to tug me down now. I look to feel that force, to find the eye trained on me, and soon I am soaring through the sky, past the white and into night where the struggle stops, and nothing is dragging me down. I am searching for him and perhaps I won't stop.

In the darkness, I can feel the patterns complicating my old skin. The Doctor watches the men open the drawer, sees my fifty-two years spill out into the light. He is unhappy.

He has seen death so many times; it is not that which scares him.

He does not want to see me like this.

He pulls a little way at the bag that holds me close. Sees the curl of an equation loop into others. Pauses.

'What a mess,' says one of the men. 'Lost the will, I shouldn't wonder.'

'The will?' he says.

'To carry on,' says the man. 'I mean, it gets to the stage where you think... what's the point?'

The Doctor looks at him, stony-faced for a time. Then he nearly smiles. 'That,' he says, 'that is the point where you start from.'

I suppose he has started away from me, but I'm too far distant to know for sure.

My old body blooms in the bag as he leaves, the patterns pressing up against the plastic. Patterns my Doctor will never see.

Lust

She had been aware of it almost since she arrived on the planet, had tried to shut it out, but it would no longer be denied.

Two hearts. A double pulse. *Thump thump. Thump thump.* Twin pathways leading around his body; a gush from one heart pumping hot red life through the spider's web of vessels, and a split second later its fellow chasing after. Some organs were fed by both hearts, made full to bursting with the sweetness. Others were the domain solely of the right, or the left.

It had been many years since she had needed air to survive, but she found herself drawing in great, gasping breaths.

It had been almost as long since she had wanted for anything. A desire had barely risen in her breast before it was fulfilled. On her planet, not a thing was denied to her. Because it was her planet, it belonged to her, as did all the people on it.

So long ago that it took an effort to summon it to mind, she had had to fight for what she wanted. A battle of wits; evading the sharpened stakes and the axe and the fire. Now it was handed to her on a plate. Young men, young, beautiful men, lining up for her pleasure; some scared, some unable to hide their desire for her, even though they knew what she was. Some she drank quick and some she drank slow. Some she would drain and others she would return to again and again. She tasted other pleasures with many, but without the blood they were nothing.

She was never denied, surely this man could not deny her...

She stretched out a hand, almost involuntarily, scarlet-tipped fingers brushing back his dark curls to expose the creamy softness of his neck.

His reflexes were almost as quick as her own, his hand suddenly circling her wrist in an iron grasp. For a second she thought she felt pain, then she realised it was the shock of her immediate desire being unexpectedly thwarted. It only made her want him more.

'No,' said the showman, staring at her with brilliant eyes that seemed to pulse from blue to grey to green in time with his beating hearts. He had to feel it too, that desire, that connection, he had to want her as much as she wanted him; she could not conceive that she could long for a man this much and he would not reciprocate.

She could hear the blood boiling inside him. She gasped, 'Please...' – then remembered who she was. Queen of a world. Supreme one. She must not plead like a servant girl with her master.

But, right now, he was her master. She knew nothing but him; cared about nothing but him. 'I could take you now,' she said, flexing her hand and breaking his hold on her wrist. 'I have strength such as you have never known.'

He smiled, his eyes never leaving hers. 'Even if that were true...' he said. 'I thought you came here because you wanted to feel again. When was the last time you felt as strongly as this? Have you forgotten the thrill of the chase? My blood will taste all the sweeter when – if – I submit.'

He reached out again and took her left hand in his, guiding it towards his other wrist. Gently, he straightened out her long, white index finger, and with a swift flick brushed its scarlet talon against his flesh. A bead of blood glistened on his wrist and she felt her own withered heart trying to beat with the passion it stirred within her.

The showman raised his wrist to her mouth.

She shuddered as the single drop hit her tongue.

She needed him then, not just wanted him but needed him, knew she couldn't exist if she didn't take every part of him into herself, knew that she would die if she didn't drink him. She grabbed for his wrist but it was gone. Gasping, she lunged forward, but now he was behind her. His hands landed on her shoulders, and the sound of the double pulse in each ear hypnotised her.

'Tell me how it happened,' he said softly. 'Tell me how you became like this.'

'I don't remember,' she said, lying. 'It is too long ago. Please. I need you.'

There was a laugh. 'Tell me,' he said. 'And then you may get a reward.'

She was humiliated now; a queen begging for favours. But she felt she had no choice. How long could she endure the burning desire within before the flames consumed her?

'I was a priestess in our village,' she told him, voicing a tale that no one left on her planet knew. 'I tended the shrines and communed with the gods. I belonged to the gods. No mortal man was allowed to touch me, because I belonged to the gods.' She smiled suddenly, and reached up a hand to her cheek. 'I was beautiful then.'

'You're beautiful now,' he said.

She nodded in agreement. 'Yes, I am. I have been beautiful for three hundred years. Three hundred years of youth. Yet no man desires me as strongly as they did then, when I was forbidden to them. When the blood was still pumping in my veins.' She looked down at the transparent whiteness of her hand, and sighed. The hand began creeping upwards, towards the wrist so close to her face, where the smell of blood mingling with the air of the room was intoxicating her. But the sudden pressure from his hands on her shoulders showed he was aware of her thoughts, and she forced herself back into the past.

'There were tales of dark princes who lived in distant castles, men who kept people like we kept sheep, but I paid no heed. All I cared for was tending my shrines, and communing with my gods. I talked to the gods. And then one day, a god talked to me.' She laughed. 'Oh, that I can remember as clearly as yesterday.' Clearer, for what was yesterday but another day of sated desires and endless existence? 'The voice spoke inside my head, telling me it had another purpose for me. Telling me it wanted me. That I had been chosen.'

'But it was not a god?' he prompted.

She shook her head. 'There are no gods, that I've learned. It was him. I... He told me – afterwards – that he had been riding through the village. That he saw me. I was alive then; oh, not just because I was not dead, but so full of life, hunger, passion, that it shone as bright as day. He wanted it so desperately, he wanted *me* so desperately. He drank from many of my people at that time – not that we knew then what caused the death that came in the night – he could have drunk from me just as easily. But he wanted more. He wanted to possess me utterly.' The words caught in her throat as she realised, perhaps for the first time, what it was to feel that way. Because she had to possess this man, this showman, whose life shone even brighter than hers had so long ago. It wasn't enough to drink him. If her soul had not withered and died long ago, he would be her soul mate.

'He had the power to put words into my head. While I was praying to the gods to stop the curse that had come upon our village, the curse that found its way into locked rooms and drained men of blood as they slept – why, the gods were telling me that I must give myself to them, give myself completely to a god made flesh. If I gave myself willingly, the curse would be lifted. The voices were so persuasive, they overcame my resistance. I went to him, fled to him. His voice inside my head had filled me with such passions, such desires...'

There was a silence.

'And?' the showman said at last.

She smiled. 'It is as you said,' she told him. 'The blood is all the sweeter through submission. Not submission through fear, or servitude. But when you submit because you want it as much as they do...' Her smile became sad. 'And so he took my life that shined so brightly, and I gave it willingly. And he gave me in its place this half-life. And I embraced that willingly, too, and joined with the dark princes as we grew and conquered and ruled. And I raised armies and conquered the conquerors, and became the greatest of them all.

'And for a hundred years, there has been no one to challenge me. I have power and wealth. I have everything and I want for nothing. I am... content.'

'If you were content,' he said, 'you would not be here.'

She nodded, conceding the point.

'I have no fear. No pain. No sorrow. I do not feel at all.' She paused. 'Except for hunger.'

'Except for the blood lust,' he said, and moved so slightly, his chest brushing against her back, his hearts so close she almost fainted with longing. 'There are some who say that lust is barely a sin at all. Certainly not a deadly one. A desire to gratify one's bodily senses – what could be more natural? How could it be wrong to pursue such a course?'

Without warning, he whipped her round to face him, and she gasped.

'Who knows what lusts created the vampire races, creatures with no thoughts but to take whatever they wanted? It was lust that created you – killed your friends and neighbours, took you from your true path, from your life. It was lust that reared its ugly head when you teased those village boys, toyed with them, knowing that you were a priestess and inviolate, and it was through the treachery of those village boys, driven mad with longing, that Prince Vrilac knew of you, knew how to reach you through your gods.'

She stared at him, the closest thing she had felt to fear for a long time, realising that he knew her story already, had known it long before she walked in this room, had been planning for this moment.

'Your blood lust has been strong and always sated for three hundred years, and yet it has never been as strong as it is tonight.'

He pulled her to him and kissed her full on the lips. She responded at once, pulling him closer, her teeth grazing his mouth, nipping at his tongue. The blood was so strong, so hot, she almost felt like she was alive again. There was nothing for her but the blood.

Now he had her head in his hands and was pulling her away. 'But this is not why you came here. This isn't what you came here to feel. And it's time for you to feel that now.'

She screamed as he turned from her. He wiped the blood from his mouth with one hand and held it out to her. With the other hand he pushed at a switch on the wall. And as strange images flooded into her mind, the blood lust overwhelmed her. Fangs bared and primitive, savage strength coursing through every limb, she threw herself at the showman.

Suitors, Inc.

Paul Magrs

Sex Symbol, Never
Over the years, he had spent a lot of time on Earth and he'd been many things to many people. To some he was the mysterious stranger who arrived out of nowhere to help out in their moment of desperate need. To others he was the old friend they thought they'd never see again, who would turn up in a flash one day, wearing a different face and ready to whisk them off, once more, into startling adventures. To others again he was the meddlesome fool who stymied their plans and schemes with an insouciance and irreverence that was all his own.

Here in England, through the many centuries, from the green days of Robin Hood to the dreadful Dalek invasion of Bedfordshire, he had adopted many, many roles.

But... sex symbol, never.

Yet, in the last days of summer, 1979, someone was working hard to change all that.

Suitors, Inc.
Romana was making the most of her afternoon off, having her hair done in a salon just off the high street. (She had no idea what city this was they'd arrived in. She was simply making the best of it. The Doctor was busy with something or other and he wanted her out of the way. So she was having a shampoo and trim and a nice old lady was chatting away to her from the next chair.)

'I was thinking of getting one myself. I was, dear. Really. You'll think I'm silly for saying it, won't you? That I'm too old or past it.' The old woman cackled from under the drier. 'But, you see, that's what they were designed for. Have you seen the adverts? They were invented especially for women of a certain age. Like me.'

Romana smiled and nodded into the mirror. She had lost the gist of what the old dear was on about. Luckily her hairdresser was keeping up.

'So, why didn't you buy one, Maude? What stopped you? I hear they're very expensive.'

Maude shrugged. 'The money isn't a problem. I'd be happy handing over my life savings for one of them things. I know a couple of women – older than me! – from bingo, who've splashed out on a Suitor, and they're *very* satisfied.'

A Suitor? thought Romana.

'Oh, very satisfied indeed. Suitors can do anything. They never tire, and they never give up, if you get my drift. They can do your housework for you, too! But mostly what they're programmed for is... well, you know... wooing and courting and... what not.'

Ah, thought Romana. Robots. Rather early, wasn't it? 1979? She closed her eyes and let her mind drift a little. She wasn't overkeen on uncovering some new mystery this afternoon, thank you very much.

'I know what it is that's put you off,' said her hairdresser all of a sudden. 'I've just realised! It's the shocking reports, isn't it?'

Shocking reports? wondered Romana vaguely.

'Hmm,' said the old lady. 'It was indeed. I saw it on the news. Sudden disappearances. Old lady's boudoirs being found abandoned, left in an uproar. And all of them owned a Suitor. The police have drawn the conclusion that all the missing pensioners are linked to the Erotic DoctorBots.'

The *what*? Romana's eyes flew open at this. 'The *what*?' she shouted at the old woman.

'The Erotic DoctorBots,' the old woman said. 'You've seen them, haven't you? They're everywhere this summer. Everyone wants one, don't they?'

Full Colour Spread

She found K9 flicking through magazines by the door. Well, not flicking exactly, but he was sucking up the contents in a very absorbed fashion. She'd never have thought he was that bothered about hair and shoes and fashion.

She was wrong.

'Mistress!' he yapped. 'I have found something very, very disturbing.'

She frowned, tapping her foot slightly.

'The mistress's hair looks very nice,' he said dutifully.

The other ladies, sitting close by, waiting their turns under Andre's skilled fingers, were very impressed at Romana's dog's solicitude.

'What have you found in *Cosmo*, K9?'

'This,' he said simply.

It was a two-page advert for a new brand of aftershave for men. Instead of the usual brawny hairy chest and denim shirt that one might reasonably expect in such a spread... Romana found herself staring at a photo of a model in rather scruffy tweeds and a singed-looking multi-coloured scarf.

'What I was starting to suspect is true, then,' Romana gasped. 'Like when we saw that billboard advertising, and the side of that bus stop. It's him! It's all him! Somehow – without even knowing it – the Doctor has gone and made himself into a sex symbol!'

Flattery

That vain and stupid man! she seethed. She knew very well how he would react when she and K9 returned to the ship and told him what was going on. He wouldn't be appalled and horrified like she was. He wouldn't think for a second about the implications for the web of time. He'd be flattered and pleased.

The men of Earth were aspiring to look just like him; to become exactly like him.

His reaction?

Good thing, too! I don't know why it took them so long. Hurray for good taste!

That was the thing with him, Romana thought grumpily, sitting on the bus with her robot dog. (Half fare for a robot dog!) The Doctor was a whole lot more superficial than anyone would think. Oh, to everyone else: there he goes, bounding about in eternity and forever seeing the bigger, multidimensional picture. But she lived with him on a daily basis and, really, he was pretty shallow and silly on the whole. And, of course, when she told him what was going on here in 1979, his eyes lit up.

'Oh!' he said beadily. 'Well, you know... I *do* have a certain bearing and charisma...'

So there was a spring in his step as he went flicking switches and yanking leads around on the control console.

Romana was furious! She went off to choose an outfit for going out to dinner. The old fool hadn't noticed her hair, either.

Dogging

K9 was watchdogging at home, though there wasn't much need. The TARDIS had materialised on a canal tow path at the edge of an industrial estate. No one would bother it.

He bid them farewell sadly. He wished he was going with them into town for an Italian.

Romana was still terribly miffed, even though the Doctor had praised her new frock. He was still in the same old ratty and tatty ensemble. K9 was very sanguine about the Doctor's whole look becoming trendy and sexy. It turned out that he'd always thought the Doctor–Master was an admirable-looking person. A well-turned out gentleman.

'Why, thank you, K9,' the Doctor had beamed, clapping on his hat. 'And so I am!'

Tête à Tête

Over Pinot Noir and deliciously sloppy pasta, Romana was becoming terse. She leaned across the red-and-white checked tablecloth and hissed, 'But doesn't it bother you? That someone knows you so well they can market your whole style?'

He stared back at her through the candlelight.

'You mean... the Black Guardian?' he gasped. 'Has gone into fashion? And fragrance?'

'Don't be ridiculous.' She shook out her napkin and gave her tagliatelle a desultory poke. 'You're so... glib.'

He considered this. 'Hmm. You're right. Glib. I'm glib. *And* sexy. Apparently!'

She rolled her eyes. 'Do you know, that aftershave... They claim it has an irresistible whiff of old tweed and jelly babies and a wistful undertone of burning circuitry...'

'Ha! That's good!' And he chuckled away to himself, twisting his pasta round his fork. 'Still, I suppose you're right. It sounds very much like someone is mucking around with time and everything and it'll be up to us to sort it out.'

'It's these robots I don't like the sound of,' she said.

'Hmmmm.' He nodded. 'Do they look very like me?'

'I haven't seen one yet.'

Still, he thought. The people they'd encountered so far on this evening out had been treating him very strangely. Warily, almost. Hushed respect. Restrained excitement. Awe. As if he was very famous indeed. As if he was very sexy indeed.

'I don't want to involve UNIT,' he said thoughtfully. 'Usually they'd be one of my first ports of call in this period, if I discovered something fishy. But on this occasion, I think not.'

'You're embarrassed,' she laughed. 'You think your military chums will laugh at you.'

He shrugged. And then they were interrupted by a young woman from the table across the way. She had sidled up nervously, with a napkin she said she'd like the Doctor to sign. For her gran.

'Oooh, she loves you, my gran,' said the young woman. 'She's saving up, you know. For one of your robots. One just like you. But to think... I can tell her... I've met the real thing!'

The young woman swallowed tremulously and stared at him. 'You are... the real thing, aren't you? You really are... him?'

The Doctor grinned broadly. 'I am! I am! I'm me!'

And afterwards, after they'd tried to pay the bill (the owner wouldn't let them! He wanted photos taking. Of the Doctor standing with him and all the waiters. To go up, pride of place, on the wall), the Doctor and Romana were walking off through the dark city streets and his mood was changing. It became pensive.

'You're right,' he said. 'Someone up to no good. Needs sorting.'

Romana took his arm. 'You're a bit tiddly,' she said fondly.

'Hurray!' he said. 'Hurray for good taste!'

Industrious

K9 plugged himself into the TARDIS's sensors while they were away. He bided the time drinking up all sorts of local data.

And that was how he picked up on the alarming power surges going on in the factory not two miles away from the TARDIS.

The factory was using technology that simply shouldn't exist on Earth in this period.

K9 felt very pleased with himself. He wagged his tail, eager for the Master and Mistress to return, so he could tell them.

The factory was emanating some very strange data. It would need investigating. And he would have to go with them, naturally.

To the factory called... what was it? Ah, yes.

Wildthyme Unlimited.

Investigators

Somebody already had this adventure well in hand. Somebody was already investigating the factory with its queer power surges and its robotic army that patrolled the perimeter fence and all the miles of corridors within.

So while the Doctor and Romana made their tipsy way back to the TARDIS, to sleep on their suspicions and misgivings, two rather more conscientious investigators of everything strange and untoward were using wire cutters and shimmying under electrified fences.

Excitement

He insisted on leading the way across the compound, from doorway to doorway, gallant as ever, and just as foolhardy. Sarah had no choice but to follow in his footsteps.

'It looks just like an ordinary factory to me, old girl.' He frowned, as they both huddled in the shadows.

'It's not,' she insisted. 'I had that private tour, remember. And I saw things I wasn't supposed to see. They're up to something here, Harry.'

'Hmm.'

'Don't you think it's weird? Those robots of theirs? The Suitors?'

'Robot Doctors. Who'd have thought it? But even if it's strange, I don't see what harm it's doing...'

'Oh, *Harry*,' she hissed. Sometimes he could be so obtuse. They'd only been reunited for about a day and a half and he was already driving her mad. Just as he had years ago.

'All right, old girl. We'll trust your instincts.' He grinned and brandished his wire cutters. 'Let's break in.'

It was the Doctor who connected them and it was with him they had shared some of the most terrifying moments of their lives. Neither had heard from him or of him in years. They had slipped back into their own relatively quiet lives and vaguely imagined him flying about in time and space, having a whale of a time without them.

Both secretly held out hopes that he'd land on their doorstep once more.

Occasionally Sarah and Harry would meet to have a drink and talk over their adventures. Living in the past. Nothing new to talk about. Nothing in their current lives to compare with what they'd experienced together, in the earlier part of that decade. That made them both feel sad. As if time travel had aged them prematurely.

So there was always something a bit upsetting about Sarah and Harry's reunions. Except now. Here was excitement. Here was something out of the ordinary.

These sinister androids flooding the domestic market! Old women snapping them up and hurrying them home and getting them to do their bidding! Gigolobots – also known as Erotic DoctorBots. And both Harry and Sarah had been appalled to see the shape these automatons had taken – with their disturbingly familiar shock of brown, curly hair, manic grin and ludicrously long scarf. Could this all be the Doctor's doing? Why had he made himself into an international sex symbol? Could it be the doing of one of his awful enemies?

And then came the disappearances. Wrecked bungalows and no sign of robots nor owners.

That's what brought Sarah and Harry tiptoeing through these factory corridors, penetrating deeper and deeper into the complex. She would never have admitted it, but Sarah found Harry's presence very reassuring.

'So, when you had your official tour of this place,' he said, 'when you told them you were writing a magazine story, how did they explain the DoctorBots? Did they say how they chose the... model?'

Sarah frowned, chewing her lower lip. 'They were evasive about that. They just said they'd hit upon a formula they knew lots of senior citizens would love. And how it was all the inspiration of the owner of Wildthyme Unlimited.'

'Did you meet this owner?'

'Not this time,' Sarah said, grimly. 'Not yet.'

'You know this person? You've met before?'

Sarah nodded. 'If it's who I think it is... Oh, yes.'

He jumped and seized her wrist. 'Listen! Footsteps!'

Sure enough, there came a tall, menacing figure sweeping towards them from around the next corner. His eyes were intent and his scarf was flailing out around him.

'Run!' Sarah screamed and it felt very odd to be running from the Doctor.

And more Doctors! They came out of the woodwork with plastic hands outstretched, pursuing them as they pelted ever deeper into the complex.

Fretting In Her Boudoir
After a while and just before the drear dawn, quiet and calm returned to the factory. The two intruders were captured almost effortlessly by the tireless 'Bots and they were slung in a cell deep underground.

The single shareholder of Wildthyme Unlimited sat in her heart of operations, sleepless all night, and mulled everything over.

Tomorrow was a hellishly busy day. The first of the new models would be rolling off the conveyor belt and would require testing out. She would need all of her strength for the test drive.

Yet she sat up all night in her boudoir, fretting.

In her new (rather delectable, she thought) incarnation and a blue silk nightie trimmed in mink.

In her new body she felt... rather sexy, actually. And just a bit naughty and evil.

So... they were on to her little game. All the meddlers and investigators and spoilers. Maybe they would put the kybosh on her intrigues.

She doubted it. She was doing nothing wrong. Not really.

She flicked a sensor pad on the arm of her chair. A door shot open and two identical DoctorBots came traipsing in, grinning.

'Feeling a bit tense, loveys,' she said, with a shrug. 'I could do with a good rub.'

Thank the Goddess she'd given them sensitive fingers.

Riled
What has got me so riled in the middle of the night? wondered Romana. She was sitting up in bed.

What's got my goat in the middle of the night?

Not that 'in the middle of the night' meant much, here aboard the TARDIS, which of course occupied some region – as the Doctor always put it – in which time and space were one. Like much of what he said, Romana found this statement of his almost completely nonsensical. He was always making high-flown, vaguely poetical, quite inaccurate statements and they were something else that got on Romana's wick.

She'd been travelling with him for a number of years now and there was always some novel irritation he could spring on her at any given moment.

She smiled.

The TARDIS was a good place to go wandering, stomping, traipsing, marching, gadding about through the sleepless night. Its corridors were infinite. It was like patrolling the pristine intestines of the biggest beast in the galaxy. It was cool and calm and the insomniac Romana found it useful to go pacing up and down and round and round and round and round all night and somehow she never got lost.

Why did he drive her mad?
Why did he?

Hours Later
When she had tired of wandering all the corridors – exhausted herself really,

like some fairy-tale princess dancing herself silly and wearing down the soles of her satin shoes – she found herself delivered to the bright, humming cavern of the console room.

Morning. Good morning! Artificial morning!

And the exterior doors were swishing open and here came the Doctor, striding in from outdoors. He was beaming and shabby and holding a half-eaten bacon sandwich and slurping tea out of a styrofoam cup. He had been out all night without her.

'Ah! There you are! I've been having a look round. Didn't want to wake you.'

She pursed her lips.

'This mysterious factory K9 was rabbiting on about. We went to have a look.'

The dog was at his heels – smug.

'It's the place where they manufacture my robot selves! My dubious duplicates! You must come and see, Romana. It's terribly interesting.'

'Hmm,' she said lightly.

'Just fancy! Someone going to all that trouble! Just to make lots and lots of me!'

Memory Bank

K9 went through his records. He was hunting out a likely suspect. His ears twiddled round thoughtfully as the following names occurred to him:

Sutekh the Destroyer. Blown to smithereens. Unlikely.

Davros. Unlikely. Not born yet. Shot to smithereens anyway.

Omega. No horrid sticky antimatter detected in the vicinity. In anti-smithereens.

Mehendri Solon. Not born yet. Unlikely.

Morbius. Smithereens. Unlikely.

The Black Guardian. Tends towards more cosmic predicaments.

The Master. Smithereens.

Azal the Daemon. Possibly. Most likely, smithereens.

Iris Wildthyme. Hmmmm.

K9 often checked through the database like this. And this time he had a brainwave. He printed off a set of handy pocket-sized cards. Each one featured one of the Doctor–Master's enemies. There was a picture of them at the top for ease of recognition in dicey situations, and there were written details underneath the picture, as to the enemy's past misdeeds, known whereabouts, super powers and fear rating.

'What are you up to over there?'

The Doctor thought K9's cards were marvellous.

'Why! They're like Top Trumps!' he cried, flicking through the pack. 'And so useful, too! Can I keep them?'

'Of course, Master,' K9 yapped. 'I made them especially for you. And the mistress. To help you in your adventures.'

'Will you print off a set for Romana, K9? She'll be needing them even more than I do. She's been in this job such a short time compared to me...'

Romana scowled. No doubt, she found K9's pack of Monstrous Enemy cards very embarrassing. There was no way she would bring herself to use them.

Sexy For Centuries

'It's still the same *her*,' Sarah said, with satisfaction. 'She's regenerated and she's lost a few stone and, by the looks of it, dyed her hair purple, but it's still the same woman. The same awful woman.'

This was the following morning, when Sarah and Harry were being led along by two impassive DoctorBots into the gilded and ornate secret chamber at the heart of the factory.

Harry was gazing around with some interest. 'So you say you and the Doctor met her before? Wasn't she supposed to be some kind of old friend of his?'

Sarah pulled a face. 'She was a little too friendly, for the Doctor's taste...' Frisky, he'd called it.

Then they were confronted by the triumphant and gleeful Ms Wildthyme: glorious in a lilac one-piece and svelte as a dumpling.

'My dears,' she said, grinning. 'Sarah! It has been simply ages. I'm not sure I've met your delectable man friend before. I must congratulate him on his sideburns...'

Harry blushed.

'Don't trust her, Harry,' Sarah hissed.

'Oh, she seems all right to me...'

'I'm sorry I didn't get to meet you when you made your first, official visit to my complex, Sarah. I was awfully tied up. Suitors, Inc. is incredibly time consuming and draining, as I'm sure you can imagine.'

'What do you think you're doing?' Sarah thundered. 'You know that the Doctor doesn't want attention drawn to his activities here on Earth. When he's here he has to keep a low profile. He can't go round being famous! And... he can't go round... being sexy. That just *isn't him*!'

Iris smirked. 'Isn't it?'

'Of course it isn't!' Sarah stammered. 'He's the Doctor!'

'Well, I've found him sexy for centuries,' said Iris. 'There must be something very strange about me.'

'Oh, I'm sure there isn't...' said Harry, and Sarah rolled her eyes at him.

Suddenly Iris was clapping her hands together. 'Let us see what you make of my newest invention. Let us examine the latest clockwork toy to roll off the production line here at Suitors, Inc.'

She was grinning with barely repressed joy and pressing her chubby hands together.

At the far end of the room, the doors swished open and a tall, rather elegant figure stepped through into the opulent chamber.

'Oh, my God.' Sarah choked.

He came, all in velvet and ruffles, with his bouffant blazing silver in the light from the chandeliers. He marched towards them with his cloak streaming behind him, shot his frilly cuffs, and bowed sharply as he stood before Iris's throne.

'Mistress,' he purred. 'I am here at your command.'

Fence

In the long grass on the inside of the perimeter fence, the Doctor had managed to wrestle one of his robotic selves to the ground and deactivate it. 'Fascinating piece of work,' he bellowed, prising at the thing's face with his sonic screwdriver. 'And – *goodness!* – he's anatomically correct in almost every detail!'

Romana, who was helping K9 to slip under the metal fence, had straightened up and just noticed the name of the factory's owner on the side of the building.

'*Her?*' she groaned. 'Why didn't you say?'

The Doctor shrugged, happily fiddling with his doppelgänger.

'I suppose it makes complete sense, though,' she went on. 'She's always had a very peculiar, obsessive relationship with you, hasn't she?'

'Why peculiar?'

'Oh, you know what I mean.'

'No, I don't. You think that, to be obsessed with me, someone would have to be very peculiar indeed.' He was frowning heavily. 'You know, I think I resent that.'

Romana was exasperated. 'Look at what she's done! She's flooded the market – the whole of your precious planet Earth, for all we know – with robotic facsimilies of you. Robot sex slaves who appear to kidnap their owners and whisk them off to nobody-knows-where! Are you telling me that this scheme is the work of someone wholly balanced and sane?'

He shrugged huffily, still poking at his robot double. 'I never said that much. But I don't think she has to be mad to... what's it called... *fancy* me.'

'*Fancy?*' Romana laughed out loud. '*Fancy!* Oh, Doctor... You just don't know the meaning of the word.' She was doubled up by now. '*Hahahahahahahahahahaha!*'

The Doctor glared at her furiously.

Then he swapped coats with his android self (because the one the android was wearing was of better quality and also because he had come up with one of his rather special plans).

Romana could stand around laughing like a crazy woman all day if she wanted to. He, meanwhile, had work to do.

Plans

There are a number of options available to us at this stage of an adventure such as this, mused K9. One obvious route is to destroy the whole factory complex. Perhaps the military could bomb it. The Doctor has friends like that, doesn't he? Or, perhaps, while he's inside the building, he could tamper with the machinery at the heart of the complex and set it to have a nervous breakdown or explode or something.

He needs, at some point, to come face to face with an army of himself. I imagine that's what he's doing in there now, don't you, Mistress? Now that he's inveigled himself into that industrial complex, he's most probably peering over a banister, down into some sinister concrete space... and there's a regiment of Doctors... all primed and hatted and scarfed... and ready to take over the world.

He's probably grinning down at them, and they're grinning back.

K9 was trundling alongside Romana, around the perimeter of the fence. 'We can't just blow the whole place up,' she sighed. 'Not with Iris there. No matter what she's done, the Doctor would never let us simply blow her up.'

'A pity,' sighed K9.

They were both doing a lot of sighing.

'Do you think he could have feelings for her?' Romana asked.

'Surely not,' the dog scoffed. Feelings? For her?

Romana shrugged. She felt around in her pockets for the brain of the robot Doctor. She'd confiscated it before the Doctor himself went running into the factory. 'If we could figure out exactly how these work... perhaps we could find some way of sabotaging them...'

K9 nodded. That was the other way of proceeding, and one he was just about to suggest to his mistress. Rather than wholesale bombing and destruction... the best way was to find some method of jamming the signals by which Iris was controlling the mechanical minds of her robotic Suitors.

Then, maybe they could build some hefty-looking, futuristic-looking weapon that could shoot out beams that would make all of their enemies simply collapse!

'Good plan.' Romana nodded tersely. 'Let's get back to the ship and get on with it.' She patted his nose. 'We're better off without him, really, aren't we?'

Marched About

They were used to being marched about by the Suitors by now. Sarah and Harry had become quite blasé about all of their enemies looking just like one of their dearest, most-missed old friends.

When they were marched back to their cell this time, they took hardly any notice of the DoctorBot that was leading them along.

That was, until they reached their cell and he grinned at them.

Sarah blinked. 'It's really you, isn't it?'

He gathered them up in an impulsive hug. 'It is! It is!' he bellowed. 'Fancy seeing you here!'

And, next thing they knew, they were running through the corridors again, away from their cell and deeper into the complex. Harry at Sarah's heels, Sarah at the Doctor's. Sarah's heart thudding madly so that her ears were ringing with... well, joy.

It's him! It's him! It's really him!

Binky

Of course, Iris was working for a higher power. She wasn't up to all this malarkey of her own volition. What had started out as a reasonably fun endeavour and wheeze had become something altogether deadlier because of the intercession of...

'Binky,' Iris said, giving an abrupt curtsy to the colossal viewscreen. 'Greetings from Earth. Greetings to all on the Pussyworld.'

Binky tutted. Binky was a Siamese, wearing a tiara. Binky was on a pile of satin cushions in a boudoir of her own, a million parsecs from Earth. And Binky wasn't altogether happy.

'Where are my old ladies?' thundered Binky. 'This scheme of yours started out well, Wildthyme. Then it started slowing down and down and now it's at a standstill. The supply has dried up.'

Iris shuddered. She hated being used as somebody's servant. 'We are trying to fulfil your deadlines, Madame Binky. We'll be sending more old ladies soon.'

'Good,' purred Binky, 'because I will not tolerate failure. You send enough old ladies here to the Pussyworld, or we keep your bus. And without it, you'll be stuck on that ghastly planet forever. Miaow!'

With that, Binky vanished.

Iris was left sitting slumped on her throne with her head in her hands. Oh, how had she ever become involved in this ridiculous scheme?

And – oh, Binky, how can you turn against me so? And how was I to know you were the powerful warrior queen of a world filled with evil cats?

And what the hell do you want with a million old ladies anyway?

Iris's mind boggled.

So solicitous and responsive were her marvellous DoctorBots, they picked up immediately on her disconsolate mood, and three of them hurried over to pet and primp and generally cheer her up.

'Ooooh,' she said. 'Loveys! Oooh, you *are* good to me! And really, you're the next best thing to the real thing, aren't you? And I'd imagine that it's worth it to those poor old ladies... just one hour of pleasure with you lot... and then to be whisked off through time and space... in a sexy shanghai to the Pussyworld... why, it's not such a terrible fate after all, is it, really? I've not really done anything bad at all, have I? Hmmmm?'

But she knew she had really. wartorn

Velvet and Tweed
The Doctor stopped abruptly, Sarah and Harry hot on his heels.

They'd come face to face with the newest of the Suitors. It was the more debonair, silverly patrician version. The expert-in-karate version.

'AAAIIIIIIYAAAA!' said this new one, flashing his hands like deadly blades.

'Ulp,' said the Doctor. 'I think he wants a fight.'

Sarah grabbed his elbow. 'Your previous self was quite nifty. Watch out, Doctor!'

Harry squared his jaw and put his dukes up. 'I'm here to help, Doctor!'

At that very second, the robot duplicate launched his attack.

'AAAAIIIIIIYYYYAAAA!'

News
K9 soldered wires on the large, silver, machine-gun-shaped device that Romana had lashed together. It hadn't taken her long. It was a very impressive piece of work.

Meanwhile, she was watching a news broadcast on the scanner screen.

'Mistress?' K9 asked. He hadn't really been listening.

'More bad news about the DoctorBots,' she said. 'They've been malfunctioning. Exploding at the most inopportune moments. With nasty results.'

'Exploding?'

She shook her head. 'Losing their temper. I didn't mean blowing up. Shouting. Being irritated. Being irritating. Being the very opposite of a gentleman. I should have known that anything made by Iris would go wrong...'

'The device is completed, Mistress,' he said. 'Let's call it the Kybosh Machine!'

Which Is What They Did
And, as Romana led the way determinedly from the TARDIS on the canal towpath back towards the evil industrial complex, she was reflecting that she found adventures quite easy, actually.

That is, she found them much easier to get on with and finished and sorted out than the Doctor did. She was even starting to suspect that he span the things out... Just for the fun of it. She wouldn't put it past him.

He loved all of it. All the getting captured/escaping/running away/putting on disguises/going back in, undercover/getting captured again...

He went in for all that with great gusto.

Romana tended to want to finish things off neatly. She found a certain satisfaction in the neatest and most efficient straight line between A and B.

So here she came, thumping through the long grass in her hunting boots, with the glitteringly proficient Kybosh Machine slung over her shoulder.

'It's an interesting question,' K9 mused. 'Why does he drag things out? Why does he make our adventures and missions more complicated and dangerous than they need to be? And why, do we let him?' K9 was finding the rough ground hard going, but he struggled on. 'Remember how long it took us to find all the components of the Key to Time?'

Romana shuddered. 'Don't remind me.'

She was determined to hurry the Doctor up. To stop him messing about.

He desired adventure. He desired complications. That's how it seemed to her. She couldn't see the point in any of that, and neither could their robot dog.

The kind of nonsense that both the Doctor and Iris went in for... that they were steeped in... it meant nothing to Romana and K9. It was all a bit immature.

'If we had adventures of our own, Mistress,' said K9 wistfully, as they slipped under the metal fence once more, 'I feel that they would be very sensible ones.'

And not ones in which a giant Siamese cat was glaring down from a giant viewscreen, hypnotising everyone present in Iris's centre of operations. Not adventures where this cat – their deadliest foe – was, it seemed, called Binky.

They arrived full of gumption and common-sensical determination. They set the Kybosh Machine to full and devastating power. DoctorBots came running out at them with scarves flailing and rubberised hands clawing at them.

Very coolly, Romana swished past her enemies, towards that central chamber.

It was time to put an end to it.

But a portal was open by now and all her compatriots on this adventure – Sarah, Harry, Iris, the Doctor himself... all were marching into the swirling vortex in time for a deadly audience with the crazed Binky and her hordes of kidnapped old ladies.

Romana howled with frustration. 'Not even the Kybosh Machine can get us out of this one!' she seethed. 'Can't you see, K9? It's not as easy as all that! We can't just put a stop to them!'

She felt herself and K9 being drawn into that vortex after the Doctor and Iris and the companions and the hordes of marching DoctorBots.

'Miaow,' said Binky, from across the other end of the universe.

They were being drawn into new adventures. Just as they always were.

Pride

As the showman entered, the room's occupant stood up stiffly and made a formal bow. He was tall and dignified, dressed in flowing silk robes of peacock blue. A long moustache drooped down to outline both sides of his mouth; it twitched as he said, 'Howdido.'

'Good afternoon,' replied the showman, pushing a blood-spotted handkerchief into his pocket, then bowing in return. 'Let me first say that it is very good of you, as a nobleman of the highest rank, to condescend to talk to me, a mere... travelling doctor.'

The man gave a slight sneer, but acknowledged the favour he was granting. 'It is undoubtedly my duty to so do. Although I do not usually condescend to say howdido to anyone under the rank of a stockbroker.'

'I appreciate that,' said the showman. 'In fact, you are well known as possibly the second most proud man of – of your type.'

'*Second* most proud man?' Elegant black eyebrows were raised at this assertion.

'Well, a certain nineteenth-century novel...'

The eyebrows did not descend. 'I think you will find that, despite the emotion being referenced in the title, it was little in evidence by the end of the novel – by which time the gentleman in question had taken a bride whose family was not only of a poor status, but had suffered considerable scandal. Whereas I, who can trace my ancestry back to a protoplasmal, primordial atomic globule, upheld my family pride – which is something inconceivable – to the very end. Not only do I have several songs referencing my pride, but my very name has become synonymous with a person of excessive haughtiness.' He whipped a small book from his pocket. 'Let me quote to you from the dictionary: "A pompous person of great influence. W.S. Gilbert, *The Mikado*, 1885."'

'You are quite correct,' said the showman, admitting defeat. 'Let us say that you are, instead, the most proud man of all. The pinnacle of pride. The epitome of ego.'

The man gave an appreciative bow. 'Indeed.'

'So,' said the showman, 'I wonder if you would be so good as to relate to me a little of your history.'

The man waved a manicured hand. 'That may come under the heading of a state secret.'

'Oh, what a shame,' said the showman. 'I was so looking forward to hearing the history of such a great man... Perhaps I should have gone for Mr Darcy after all...'

The other started slightly. 'I did not say I would not tell you.'

'Of course not. You would not be so ungracious. Perhaps you could start with your origins... A fascinating story, I have no doubt, that few could parallel.'

'It is as you say,' said the moustached man. 'Few can have their beginnings rooted in such technological splendour. In such a fervour of invention!'

'Well, apart from all the others engineered at the same time as you,' put in the showman, hastily adding, 'Sorry! Sorry!' when he saw the other's expression. 'I mean it was a time of, er... technological splendour, I've heard it said. I understand there was also a fervour of invention.'

'Indeed,' said the man, placated. 'We were... experimental. Originally we were engineered merely to function as players in a... dramatic production. A...' – he sneered – '... a theme park. They soon realised their mistake. We were perfect. I don't mean as persons,' he added hastily, 'only a few individuals, such as myself, could be so described. But in construction. We embodied our characters. How could a Mikado be content to enact a fragment of a story, when he should be ruling a country? How could a major general happily sing a few songs, instead of commanding an army? How could I, with my gifts for holding public office, endure a life as a comedy sidekick?'

'Distressing for you,' said the showman.

'Not entirely,' replied the man. 'In fact, not at all. I am incapable of feeling distress. It is not in my character. A small amount of fear may be in the script – the mention of being boiled in oil, you know – but being well aware that there was no possibility whatsoever of a tragic ending, it was never something I had to focus upon.'

'I see.'

'And so we went our separate ways.'

The showman leaned forward. 'But there was a tragic ending for some of you.'

The man's moustache flopped forward as he nodded. 'That is true. Human understanding had not moved at the same pace as technology. There were those who did not believe that engineered beings, such as ourselves, had the right to be classed as... as "people".'

'And those of you who are trying to integrate yourselves into society found it a challenge...'

'We did.'

'But you knew you were in the right. You were proud of your heritage. You, with your love of bureaucracy, and your self-importance, and a distinct flair for the ridiculous – you, who were the most human of the lot! You were a slave to your insatiable ambition, your belief in your own abilities. You thought you had the right not only to be accepted by humans, but revered by humans.' The showman shut his eyes for a moment, shaking his head. 'You should have known that the pride of the humans would never accept that.'

'But we were superior in every way!' cried the man.

'No,' said the showman. 'You were only engineered to believe that.'

'It is the truth! To start, our bodies are not only perfect externally, but also have an internal structure of such splendour that they do not age or deteriorate like those of non-engineered life forms.'

'I'm not denying that is very impressive,' said the showman. 'Of course, in your case, though, there is the slight matter of the facial expression...'

'I can't help it,' said the man, 'I was born sneering.'

'And it does you credit,' the showman said. 'It makes you look very... patrician. Nevertheless, humans could never believe in your superiority. And so what had become a fringe worry, a niggle from small-minded technophobes, became a bloody conflict. Your people were hunted down by humans.'

The other sneered. 'Barbarians! Philistines!'

'Pirates, fairies, yeomen of the guard, gondoliers, little maids from school, disassembled as if they were broken toasters,' said the showman.

The man inclined his head. 'It was as you say. And yet still I felt nothing.'

'Except pride,' the showman said. 'The pride that turned a disagreement into a slaughter. You are now the ruler of all your kind, of biologically engineered beings, of clones and constructs. And yet still the conflict rages. If you were to negotiate, be willing to see yourselves as equal partners with the humans...'

The man looked at the showman with contempt. 'But I am in the right! I cannot back down! I cannot admit the possibility that I might be wrong. In short, I am perfectly happy with my actions.'

The showman looked sorrowful for a moment. 'I wish I could say I didn't understand. But I do, only too well. As you'll see shortly.' He gave a rueful little laugh. 'I'm no one to judge you. There are – vices – that I judge others for. Sloth. Envy. Not vices I have tasted frequently. But this one – this touches a little close to home.'

The other looked confused. 'Vices?'

The showman seemed to pull himself together, collect his thoughts, then bowed slightly once more. 'Forgive me, I was distracted. Speaking gibberish. Not something that a... tremendous swell such as you would understand. I hope you have not construed any of my words as a criticism. I would not dream of questioning your decisions, which were undoubtedly the correct ones. If I did at times sound unsure of your policy, of your actions, it is obviously because my more humble understanding could not hope to comprehend the intricacies of your thoughts.'

The other drew himself up, preening. 'Of course. That is a very reasonable position.'

'But I do have to ask,' said the showman, spreading his hands, 'why are you doing this? Why are you here? I know you will have an excellent reason, it couldn't be otherwise – but what is that reason?'

The other was silent for a moment. 'You could not, perhaps, be expected to appreciate the delicacy of my unique situation.'

'No,' agreed the showman.

'I am entirely self-satisfied. I know no other state. Contentment is my lot. I have great wealth and – as the dictionary says – great influence.'

'And yet...' the showman prompted.

'I felt that to experience other emotions – negative emotions that I am incapable of feeling naturally – might make me into an even more perfect being, if that were possible.'

'I think it's possible,' said the showman, getting up and moving over to stand by a switch on the wall. 'Er, if anyone can improve on perfection, it's you. Is what I mean. By the way – what you said earlier about being superior to humans. First, the perfection of your bodies. What else? I am eager to know.'

'Another reason we are superior to humans,' explained the man, 'is that we are never confused. We know exactly what we think – and exactly who we are.'

'Ah,' said the showman. 'Then you might be in for a bit of a shock.' And he pulled the switch.

The 57th

John Binns

Part One

The research team was comprised of three people, two men and one woman. They had worked together on the head station that orbited Fraternity for six months before arriving on the planet itself, just over three years ago. In those days, there was an expectation that the most senior scientists would be the ones chosen to staff the sixty-four research stations on the surface; but the way it actually worked was that the teams were chosen on the basis of how they worked together. This was a long assignment, which would require each small team to live in each other's pockets for a period of years. It would be no use choosing three very senior professors who were used to working alone and would fight each other like cats and dogs.

Professor Sarah Emmins was thirty-two years old, and she was in charge of the project. The head station bosses had been impressed both by her intellect and her tough approach to defending ethical standards in research. She had jumped at the chance to lead the fifty-seventh research station, relishing the prospect of finding out how such a rich diversity of basic life forms had managed to evolve on such an inhospitable world.

Dr Stuart Gorey had been Emmins's husband for just six months before the recruitment decisions were made, and had been reluctant at first to join her on the station. It wasn't that he didn't want to undertake the project, he was keen to protest, and at that stage of his career (a few years behind his wife), there was no sense in turning it down. It was just that he worried about the dynamics of that relationship: he and his partner, newly-weds, him working for her, with a gooseberry tagging along for good measure.

He needn't have worried. Ian Bird, at twenty-four the most junior member of the team, turned out to be more than capable of relating to the couple on both a professional and a personal basis. He was quiet and studious, occasionally nervous, but exceptionally easy to get on with. Over the last few years, the three of them had become an inseparable team, their shared work and emotional investment in the project like an invisible umbilical cord.

Their lives on the station had been less than eventful before the duplicate arrived. The area of the planet that they were tasked with researching (roughly five-hundred square kilometres at the main continent's southern tip) was frequently hit by chemical storms, which the scout robots had assured them would prove fatal to humans in an instant. So their samples had to be collected in the brief periods – days or weeks, many months apart – during which it was safe to go outside. Just twelve times so far they'd been able to open the huge, heavy bulkhead doors of the warehouse they called the collection room, donned their protective suits and gone out with their buggies and their large red crates. It had become almost like a ritual or a festive celebration – like the Christmases from their childhood, except with red crates packed full of algae, mould and fragments of quartz instead of gift-wrapped presents.

It was on the last day of June that the duplicate arrived, just over three weeks ago. They were near the end of the collection period, and all three of the team had been out collecting samples. Gorey and Emmins returned together in the buggy, and were sealing up some of the large red crates in the collection room. Bird, who had been scouting around the environs of the station on foot, was late coming back. This was not unusual.

What was unusual was the fact that not just one Bird returned: there were two. They arrived within moments of each other, both apparently from the same direction. The first Bird was carrying a red crate, peeling off his green plastic bio-suit, offering a tired-looking smile to his colleagues. The second Bird was carrying nothing, and kept his suit on; he walked right into the collection room as if there was nothing unusual about it.

Gorey, typically, pulled out a gun. It was an old model that hadn't been used in three years and stood very little chance of working, but the duplicate didn't know that. It put its hands up. After some prompting from Gorey, and with Emmins and Bird looking on anxiously, it took off the top part of the bio-suit and showed its face. Bird, understandably, swore loudly and repeatedly in shock and disbelief, while Gorey demanded that the duplicate tell them what was going on.

'I really don't have a clue,' the duplicate said. 'I know it doesn't make sense, but I don't know how I got here.' And then: 'Please, for heaven's sake, put the gun away. I'm not going to harm you.'

That was how it started. The duplicate Bird, as the team soon found, wasn't just an exact copy in physical appearance. It also sounded like Bird, it talked like Bird, and it even had some of Bird's habits and characteristics. It coughed and sniffed a little when it was nervous; it narrowed its eyes when it didn't understand what was going on; it shared Bird's tastes for jazz and Spanish omelettes. Once they'd got past the three days of quarantine, and the inevitable early stage of inspecting its body and testing its blood, the scientists started to ease off and to treat the duplicate just like it was a member of the team. Of course, it was hardest for the original Bird to adjust to the idea. In the end, though, even he agreed that accepting and even welcoming their new team member was the right way forward. It just seemed easier.

For some reason, the head station didn't quite have the same perspective. They sealed off the fifty-seventh station from the rest of the network instantly, and stopped the other stations from conducting any more collection exercises – even with robots – until they could be sure it was safe. The head of Fraternity insisted he be kept informed of all tests and interrogations that were conducted on the duplicate, and made clear his frustration when they failed to reveal anything useful. 'I want answers,' he told them. 'I don't care how you get them, but I want them quickly.'

This was a politician's take on science, of course. To the head of Fraternity, research findings were something that could be constructed out of thin air if required. Professor Emmins duly took no notice.

She was concerned, though. This was something different, something unknown. She wasn't afraid as such – not for herself, anyway – but she was frustrated. She wanted to know what the duplicate was, and all it could tell her was that it shared her curiosity.

Then, out of nowhere, the head of Fraternity announced that he had engaged an independent investigator and his assistant, who had apparently arrived unannounced on the head station that day, to find out what the duplicate was and decide what should be done about it. Just where they had come from and why they should be trusted were not matters for debate, and so the researchers were forced to accept that they would have to cooperate with their investigation – and, with luck, persuade them to share their view that the duplicate was essentially non-hostile. The threat of an investigation assuming the worst or somehow threatening the duplicate helped to bring the three members of the research team together in support of the duplicate. On the morning that the Doctor and Nyssa were due to arrive, the four of them sat on the sofas in the recreation area, discussing tactics. They felt like four corners of a structure that was vulnerable, uncertain, and wide open to attack.

The Doctor watched as Nyssa came to the end of the researchers' report, and set the thin electronic pad down on the seat next to her. She frowned a little, rested her hands in her lap and then looked brightly up at him, every inch the attentive student.

'So what do you think?' he asked her.

'The evidence seems to suggest a clone,' she said carefully. 'Identical genetic structure, identical appearance and behaviour, bar a few exceptions. The fact that it speaks the researcher's language implies it was brought up in this culture somewhere. Do we have to keep calling it "it"?'

The Doctor smiled. He could always trust Nyssa to apply compassion as well as logic. 'It's what the research team seems to be happy with,' he said, 'although, from the sound of it, they've started accepting it as a person.'

'Well, again,' Nyssa offered reasonably, 'that's what the evidence seems to suggest.'

'I'm not so sure,' the Doctor said. He leaned over, across the aisle of the train carriage, resting his forearms on his knees and clasping his hands together. Despite the fact that there was no one else in the carriage with them, he felt a need to convey a sense of secrecy. There wasn't any sign of security cameras in the carriage, but it couldn't hurt to err on the side of caution. 'It's come out of nowhere,' he said softly, hoping to convey a sense of apprehension and danger. 'They don't know what it is, and it claims to have no memory of anything before it came aboard. You can see why the research heads are suspicious.'

'Of course,' Nyssa said. She sat back a little, as if unwilling to be complicit in the Doctor's play at secrecy. 'But there have been no signs that it might be hostile.'

She held his gaze for a moment, determined in her innocence.

'Not yet,' he said.

They sat in silence for a moment. Apart from the faint sound of the engine, there was hardly a clue they were even moving through the pitch black of the tunnel, at what the head of research had told them was over two-hundred kilometres an hour. The Doctor had chosen not to activate the television screens placed above their heads, which no doubt would have just provided more promotional films of the Fraternity research project. Instead he had read through the research team's report some three or four times, and tried briefly to lie down across the four green faux-leather chairs on his side of the carriage (they were surprisingly uncomfortable). Now Nyssa had turned her attention back to the report, he found himself distinctly bored.

He looked absently at his reflection in one of the tall mirrors that lined the carriage, and considered that he looked pretty tired as well. He found it a uniquely disappointing feature of his fifth incarnation that its apparent youth didn't seem to have given him any extra vim or vitality.

'We should be arriving in a minute,' Nyssa said. She'd clearly been keeping an eye on the time. 'How are we going to do this?'

The Doctor hadn't thought about it. 'We'll improvise,' he told her. He attempted a reassuring smile.

'You did say we weren't going to interfere.'

He raised his eyebrows. 'We're investigating, not interfering.' He smiled again. 'Unless we really have to.'

The carriage doors opened smoothly and silently. The Doctor stepped through them and then through the small airlock space, into the recreation area.

It was a spacious, comfortable-looking lounge, with bright lights set into a high ceiling. Three sofas, with the same green covering as the seats in the train carriage, were arranged in a U-shape in the centre of the room. The bare light grey of the walls was offset by various shelves, desks and tables in shades of deep brown and blue. Almost every visible surface was piled high with papers, small exotic plants, framed photographs and hard-backed books.

There was a strong sense of functionally designed living quarters, customised by years of use; in other words, it looked lived-in.

The Doctor quickly registered the positions of the four people in the room. There were two men on the sofas, sitting opposite each other: one tall with long brown hair and a half-grown beard, the other a much younger and shorter man, blond, his expression reserved and impassive. A third man, standing to greet them, was identical to the blond man on the sofa – except that he was making a nervous effort to smile. The Doctor hazarded a wild guess that this was the original Ian Bird.

The young woman who came to shake the Doctor's hand was not exactly what he had expected of Professor Emmins. She was petite and sharp-featured, with shoulder-length brown hair in somewhat half-hearted curls. Her clear, green eyes fixed the Doctor's gaze and held it, as she announced, 'I'm Sarah Emmins. Pleased to meet you, Doctor. And Nyssa, I assume.'

There was a brief round of handshakes and pleasantries. Gorey and the duplicate stood after a while: they seemed reluctant to accept the travellers' presence. The duplicate, in particular, kept his eyes down throughout the encounter, as if to acknowledge its role as the object of discussion rather than a participant in it. The Doctor fancied he saw Nyssa staring just a moment too long at the duplicate as she shook its hand, and he gave her a reproving glance.

Professor Emmins invited them to take a seat on the sofas, and told them Bird was going to fetch them some cups of coffee. While he did this, there was an awkward moment while everyone waited to see who would speak first. Eventually it was the Doctor who broke the silence.

'Look, I know this must be a daunting process for you,' he told them, 'but the important thing is that we're not coming here with any preconceptions. The idea is simply to try and find out just what our friend here is, and what the implications are for the project.'

'That's what we've been trying to do,' Emmins said, a little impatiently. 'I can't see that there are any tests you can run here that we haven't run already. And, to be frank, the brief I was given said next to nothing about your qualifications or experience.'

'A-ha.' The Doctor flashed what he hoped was a charming smile, and tried a diffident scratch of the head. 'Well, I realise it's a lot to take on trust,' he said. 'Let's just say that odd and unexplained events are more or less my area.'

'We do have a lot of experience of that sort of thing,' Nyssa contributed.

Emmins didn't seem convinced. 'Even taking that as granted,' she said, 'I want to be kept informed of exactly what you're doing and what evidence, if any, you manage to find.'

'Of course.'

At this point, Bird was handing around coffee. The Doctor accepted the small brown plastic cup, and looked forlornly at the mouthful of espresso sitting at the bottom. He put it to one side.

'So, how do you want to do this?' Gorey asked. It was the first thing he'd said. His voice was gruff and deep.

The Doctor looked briefly at Nyssa, hoping to imply that they'd discussed it beforehand. 'We thought we'd start by interviewing each of you in turn,' he said. 'I thought Professor Emmins and I could have a chat first, while Nyssa here speaks to Mr Bird.'

'Perhaps you could speak with me after that,' the duplicate offered. 'Let me in on any thoughts you might have.' His voice sounded measured, calm on the surface, but with a subtext of anxiety. Not at all surprising, in the circumstances. 'Professor Emmins and I have broken down the theories into two broad strands, broadly that I'm human – a clone or a twin, in which case the circumstances need explaining – or that somehow or other, I'm a product of this planet.'

Nyssa spoke up just then. 'It seems incredible that you have no knowledge of this yourself,' she said.

The duplicate shrugged, as if the point were trivial or irrelevant. 'I'd have to agree,' he said.

The Doctor stared at him for a moment. 'Come on,' he said, addressing everyone in the room. 'I think it's high time we got started, don't you?'

Part Two

Emmins showed the Doctor through the station's primary lab first. There were two labs, she explained, but they had had to move a lot of the specimens out of the secondary lab when they had used it as a quarantine space for the duplicate. As a result, the primary lab was almost overflowing with specimen jars and research equipment. The two of them walked through a narrow corridor that had been cleared of clutter, right through the middle of the room; there was hardly any space to move on either side.

'This planet is absolutely amazing for sheer diversity,' she was saying. 'Over half of the samples we've collected in this area seem to be completely unique to it, and the same goes for most of the other research stations. I dare say if we could afford to set up some more here we'd find even more to look at, but that's assuming we'll even have time to catalogue what we've got.'

The Doctor absently cast his eye over some of the labels on the specimen jars around him. There was nothing particularly interesting, to him at least, but it wasn't hard to see how it could get a twenty-second-century Earth project a little hot under the collar. Of course, if they'd been able to use some of the equipment that would become widely available a hundred or so years from now, they might have been able to catalogue those specimens rather more quickly.

He decided to change tack. 'But what you haven't found is any advanced form of life,' he said.

'We've got an incredible variety of plant life, bacteria teeming just under the surface, and about a thousand different species of slime mould. But as for anything above that...' She shrugged her shoulders. 'Not so much as an insect, let alone a vertebrate. We'd all but ruled out the possibility of sentient life here.'

'Until three weeks ago,' the Doctor pointed out.

'Well,' she said, noncommittally.

They reached a heavy, wide door at this point, which Emmins opened with the use of a primitive-looking keypad. She led him through into an exceptionally large room, more of a warehouse, piled high with more specimen jars and a large number of red crates. Two rather ramshackle exploration buggies – not so different from those used by the early UNASA missions in Earth's own solar system, the Doctor noted – sat in the centre of the room, looking distinctly unloved. A pair of gigantic bulkhead doors dominated the far wall.

'And this is the collection room,' Emmins explained. 'Apart from being the place where we store our specimens immediately after their collected – and you'll see there are some that haven't yet been moved to the labs – this is also the place where the duplicate first arrived.'

The Doctor nodded. 'As if it had followed you in.'

'That's how it looked.'

He turned to face her. 'What I'd really like,' he said blithely, 'is to have a look around outside.'

Emmins actually laughed for a moment, before realising he was serious. 'There's no way,' she told him firmly, 'at least for the next few weeks. The atmosphere's highly acidic, and dangerous enough at normal times: you have to wear a suit if you're out for more than a few minutes. But when there are storms around, even the suits are no good. You'd be dead in seconds.'

'Well, my constitution is stronger than most,' he confided, and found himself enjoying her incredulity. He smiled as, as if on instinct, she took a step sideways so as to block his way to a large grey lever – which presumably operated the doors.

'Perhaps I'd better not,' he reassured her. He made a mental note to find out more about the atmosphere and the chemical storms, and wondered if he could get away with sneaking out that evening for a look around.

'I'd be prepared to bet that it's something from the planet that has created the duplicate,' Emmins was saying, 'although, of course, I've no clear idea of exactly what could do it.' The Doctor began pacing along the side of the room, peering at the specimen jars. 'My only thought so far is that there's some substance on the planet that can copy organic material exactly. But for it do that in such detail that it could copy his brain as well as his body – even down to the patterns of speech in his long-term memory – is just incredible. I've been looking at...'

A few seconds passed before the Doctor realised she had stopped speaking. 'Go on,' he said. He turned to look at her for a second.

'You're not interested in what I think,' she said then, matter-of-fact. 'You think you can work it out all on your own.'

The Doctor frowned. 'That's not fair,' he said, a little taken aback. 'Of course I want to know...'

'Yes, all right.' She didn't seem remotely convinced. She sat down on one of the red crates, looking tired. 'I'm sorry,' she said, not looking up at him. 'This has all been very difficult.'

He looked around for another crate, but there wasn't one, so he stayed standing.

'The way Stuart sees it, this thing is a sure sign of something intelligent here, something that might not want us around. When he hears the duplicate say it doesn't know where it came from, he takes that as proof it must be lying to him.' She sighed. 'And the problem is, I've just got no rational basis for saying he's wrong. I just trust it – these last few weeks, we've spent a lot of time together. Working as a pair to try and find out the truth: if it wanted something else, I'd have known it by now.'

The Doctor's first instinct was to point out that this was not necessarily true, that the duplicate might simply have very good skills of deception. But he managed to hold back against it. 'What about Bird?' he said.

'Bird is scared too,' she answered. 'I think Stuart's attitude rubs off on him. And more to the point, I think it rubs off on the duplicate as well.' She frowned, seeming to realise something. 'If your friend is seeing Bird now, then this is the first time Stuart and the duplicate have been alone together.' She gave a rather weak laugh. 'He'll be giving it paranoid delusions within the hour.'

'Then I think perhaps it's time for me to speak to it myself,' said the Doctor.

The Doctor's session with the duplicate didn't go well at all. They were in the secondary lab, which as Emmins had implied had been largely cleared of specimens and equipment. It was virtually a bare room, with two very functional chairs in the middle of it, where the Doctor and the duplicate sat, and a makeshift bed in the corner. The Doctor tried to imagine what it would have been like for the duplicate to spend three days quarantined in here. The duplicate alluded to it almost straightaway.

'I couldn't blame them for being cautious, of course,' he said. He gave the impression of someone striving to be scrupulously fair. 'I could have been carrying any kind of infection, quite apart from the risk that I had any hostile intent. I just would have preferred it if I'd had slightly more interesting surroundings: it's hardly a positive introduction.' He smiled broadly, as if to show that there were no hard feelings.

'You mean an introduction to the Fraternity settlement,' the Doctor ventured, 'or to the human race?'

'I wish I knew,' the duplicate answered at length. It held his gaze for a moment. 'I look and sound like them, and so it's easy for them to relate to me as a human being,' it said. 'And the thing is, the fact that they relate to me that way makes it easy for me to think of myself as human. I don't think of myself as separate or distinct, although obviously I am somewhat in a unique position. The bottom line is that I'm happy to stand alongside human beings, even if I don't know whether I'd call myself one of them. Does that make sense?'

The Doctor found himself smiling at that despite himself. 'Yes, it does,' he said. They sat in silence for a moment.

'I'm as keen as anyone to find out what I am,' the duplicate said. 'Of course, there are practical questions to consider – whether my constitution and my diet is normal, for instance, what my life expectancy is – but I'm actually more concerned about finding out how I could be connected with the planet. Sarah's been looking at this from a biodiversity perspective, and the fact is that we just don't know what properties the chemical compounds around here might have. She's doing the right thing, following the evidence, looking for the bigger picture. From a purely objective point of view, it raises fascinating questions.'

'But no one here can be objective,' the Doctor offered. This is where things started to go badly.

'I'm starting to think that no matter how much I cooperate, no matter how much I share in the project to find out what I am, there's always going to be someone who'll be suspicious of my motives,' the duplicate said. 'That may be Gorey, the research bosses on the head station, or a couple of mysterious investigators who just turn up out of nowhere. There's an agenda here,' it went on, 'to start from the assumption that I'm an alien life form, and that I'm hostile. The irony is that you're not even interested in using proper scientific methods, and in the name of defending your settlement you're prepared to break some of your most cherished rules.

'What about my rights,' it said, jabbing a finger in the Doctor's direction, 'while I'm being experimented on, what about my say in what happens to me? Whatever else you might think, there's at least a strong case to assume that I'm sentient, and capable of experiencing pain and fear. What about "first, do no harm"?'

The Doctor sat back in his chair, hoping a more relaxed stance might not inflame the situation. 'No one's going to harm you,' he told the duplicate.

It laughed hollowly in response.

The rest of the afternoon passed uneventfully. The Doctor spent some time with Bird and Gorey, hearing the latter's theories on how the duplicate could be a clone developed by enemies of the Fraternity settlement, perhaps with the aim of disrupting the project and driving them out of this system. The

Doctor's recollection of this period of Earth's history was a little sketchy, but more than enough to tell him that Gorey's ideas were less than plausible. Even if one of Earth's major power blocs had been able to develop such advanced technology and were inclined to disrupt the European bloc's ambitions in this sector, this would surely not have been the most logical or cost-effective method of doing it. The Doctor was starting to realise that Emmins's light-hearted comment about her husband's paranoia had perhaps held more truth than she'd intended. But the sad truth was that, to an extent, Gorey's perspective was typical, both of the likely response from Fraternity's political masters, and of the human race in general.

Bird, meanwhile, seemed keen to stress just how intellectually strong and clear-sighted Sarah Emmins was, and how her approach to the question of the duplicate – calm, open-minded, compassionate – was not to be dismissed. The Doctor listened and nodded, thinking that it was interesting that such passionate advocacy for the professor was coming from her research assistant and not her husband.

He didn't have very much to say on the subject of what the duplicate was. 'I'm less interested in what it's made of, and more interested in what it does,' he said. 'It copies us, not just physically but behaviourally as well. Perhaps it latches on to whatever's around it: it found me outside the station, and so I became its template.'

'Like a newly hatched chick, you mean,' the Doctor said. 'It identifies the first thing it sees as its mother.'

Bird frowned at that, and gave a non-committal grunt. The Doctor wasn't at all sure that was what he had meant, but the idea was an interesting one nevertheless.

At the same time, in the collection room the duplicate was talking to Nyssa. The Doctor's doubts about trusting it in such a situation were assuaged by Emmins's idea of setting up a video link from the collection room into the recreation area, so that she could keep an eye on what was going on. It seemed to be important to Nyssa that she get the chance to talk to the duplicate alone, and the Doctor was glad to be able to accommodate it while minimising any risk to her safety.

By the time she had finished her interview, Nyssa was just as firm an advocate of the duplicate's rights as Emmins. She told the Doctor that it deserved a chance to take part in the project and prove itself as a person. The Doctor didn't disagree with her point at all, but he chose to take it with a pinch of salt. Whatever the duplicate was, it clearly possessed powers of persuasion (more so, it seemed, than the original Bird), and there was a naive element of empathy in it as well. Nyssa, after all, was also the only one of her kind, left without a home or a family. Perhaps she spoke up for the duplicate because she empathised with its uniqueness and its rootlessness. These were uncomfortable truths the Doctor couldn't afford to ignore.

He called for a break in the early evening, so that the six of them could take some time to relax and he could think about the next steps from here. If he was honest, the Doctor wasn't sure exactly how they were going to proceed, short of a nagging feeling that he'd be better off with the TARDIS's lab facilities to call on. Nevertheless, he was sure he could determine the truth and deal with it before another day was out. It wasn't as if he hadn't dealt with hundreds of more serious and more complicated situations than this before, after all.

The Doctor, Nyssa and Bird were in the recreation area when the long, loud tone of the alarm started blaring out. Bird reacted with a start, going to one of the computer consoles to check the source of the trouble. 'Gorey's quarters,' he said, his voice rising in panic. He ran from the room, with the Doctor and Nyssa following.

They had to run through the secondary lab to get there. There was no sign of Emmins, Gorey or the duplicate. When they got to the door of Gorey's room, Bird hesitated for a second before pushing it open.

Gorey was lying on the floor of his room, struggling to get up. His face was streaked with blood; it looked like he'd been struck on the back of his head. He let out a moan of pain.

'What happened?' Bird said.

With an effort, Gorey managed to raise himself up from the floor. 'It came out of nowhere,' he said. And then: 'The duplicate: it's got Sarah. I don't know what for.' He put his hand to his face and scowled as he saw the blood. 'And it's got my gun.'

Part Three

They tried Emmins's quarters at first, but there was no one there. There was furniture overturned and a smashed glass on the floor, clear signs of a struggle. Gorey swore loudly when he saw it.

'Where would he have taken her?' the Doctor said aloud. The secondary lab was his first idea. The duplicate would associate that with captivity, with imprisonment. If its goal was to make some point about the way it had been treated, then that would be a logical place.

He ran there quickly, the others in tow, but there was no one there. It was as bare and as quiet as it had been earlier in the day.

'I was sure it would have come here,' the Doctor said. He managed to spot Gorey out of the corner of his eye, about to make off in the opposite direction. He called his name, which succeeded in stopping him for a second. 'I think we should stick together at this point, don't you?' he suggested lightly.

'I don't want to waste any more time,' he said. 'We should try the collection room.'

'All right. Come on.' The Doctor led them back through the accommodation block and they managed to squeeze through the primary lab in single file.

The door at the other end, the door to the collection room, was shut. 'What's the combination?' he shouted out to Bird. He gave it to him, and the Doctor tried it three times, but there was no effect.

'Blast it.' He gave the door a useless thump. 'The duplicate must have changed the code. Hold on a minute.' He started searching through his pockets, on the off chance that he'd brought something that could help him open the door. He was constantly finding himself in situations that demonstrated a need to replace the sonic screwdriver, and yet somehow he'd never managed to get around to it. Not for the first time, he silently cursed his own incompetence.

'We'll never get through the door,' Bird lamented.

'But we can see in there,' Nyssa contributed. 'We can use the video link you set up for me earlier.'

'That's a very good idea,' said the Doctor. 'Good thinking, Nyssa.'

'The audio system is a two-way link,' Bird said. 'We can use it to talk to them as well.'

'I think we should find out what the situation is first,' the Doctor told him. 'Gorey, I think you and I should go back to the recreation area, see what we can find out about what the duplicate wants. Bird, Nyssa, I want you two to stay here in case they come out. And while you're at it, see if there isn't any way to get that door open.'

Bird looked about to protest, but seemed to accept the idea after a nod from Gorey.

Nyssa nodded too, and gave him an attempt at a brave smile. A wave of guilt washed over the Doctor as he contemplated everything she'd been through lately. It was probably about time he treated her to a holiday, when all this was over.

'It's all right,' he told her. 'I'll see you later.' And then, quietly, as an afterthought: 'Keep an eye on Bird.'

Gorey was wincing and worrying at the cut on his head all the way back to the recreation area, and eventually the Doctor managed to persuade him it needed some treatment. He opened the first-aid kit in the lounge and dabbed the wound briefly with antiseptic. Gorey insisted on applying some dressings to it himself while the Doctor went to the control panel, and switched on the video link.

It was difficult at first to see what was going on. The camera had been mounted quite a long way up the wall, and the room was frustratingly dark. The Doctor fiddled with the controls and found a zoom function. After a second or two, the machine itself adjusted the picture brightness to compensate for the gloom.

It was a depressing sight. Emmins was seated in the far corner of the room, her arms and legs apparently bound to the chair with tape. She seemed to be conscious and her eyes and mouth were uncovered, but she wasn't saying anything. The expression on her face betrayed extreme exhaustion and fear.

She was looking at the duplicate, who appeared to be pacing along the width of the room. It had Gorey's gun in his hand, an unwieldy and archaic staser pistol. It held it awkwardly, passing it from hand to hand in what looked like an unconscious sign of nerves. If it had been telling the truth earlier, of course, then this was the first time it had handled a gun. It would have had to improvise the use of the duct tape, not knowing it was almost a cliché for the experienced kidnapper.

With a sickening suddenness, it occurred to the Doctor then that there were two reasons why the duplicate might have chosen the collection room. One was that it was effectively sealed off from the rest of the station; there was no way they could stop it doing anything unless it let them. The other was that whatever advantage it got from the gun, or whatever else could be adapted into a weapon on this station, there was nothing more potentially devastating here than the prospect of those bulkhead doors opening and the chemical storm finding its way in. He was going to have to work hard to make sure the duplicate was either persuaded not to employ that particular tactic, or that it didn't get the opportunity.

'Oh, my God,' Gorey was saying, as he looked up at the screen. The Doctor couldn't tell whether the threat of the storm had occurred to him too, and he thought it best not to mention it just for now. The young scientist had been volatile enough before this had happened; now was not the time to panic him further.

'I knew there was something like this coming,' Gorey muttered bitterly. 'We should never have let it loose in the first place. We should never have trusted it.'

Still looking at the screen, the Doctor saw the duplicate briefly look up towards the camera, then resume walking. So, it had been waiting for them, the Doctor surmised. It had known the video link was there; this had been its plan.

The Doctor decided it was about time he took charge of this situation himself. He turned on the audio link.

'Well, you've got our attention,' he said. There was a faint echo as he heard his own voice coming through in the collection room. 'Do you want to tell us what it is you think you're doing?'

Gorey walked over to the mike, his face like thunder. 'You'd better let her go now, you wretched –' he started to say. The Doctor waved a dismissive hand in his direction, and he seemed to get the message. He literally took a step away, seeming to realise that, in this situation, it was better for him to take a back seat.

'I'm all right, Stuart,' Emmins spoke up.

'We'll get you out of there,' Gorey told her. He sounded less than confident.

The duplicate coughed loudly then, as if to remind them who was in charge. For something that had only had three weeks to pick up human mannerisms and behaviours, the Doctor thought, it had become adept at using them surprisingly quickly.

'I really do regret having to do this, believe me,' the duplicate said. It was looking directly at the camera, playing to its audience. 'I don't want to harm any of you. But you've got to understand. There's only so long this situation can go on; that you can treat me like you have. It's time you listened to me.'

The Doctor waited for a second before responding; he didn't want to risk antagonising it. 'We're listening,' he said through clenched teeth.

'I'm glad. All right.' It moved the gun to its right hand, pointing it away from Emmins as if to signify a lessened threat. But it was still holding it. 'I'm not a laboratory specimen,' it said. 'I'm not an object, or a piece of research. I've been thinking that perhaps we've got it all wrong: perhaps I'm here to study you. I'm here for the planet, sent in to find out about the human race and then somehow report back. Perhaps we all need to get used to the fact that I'm not going to remember anything, because there's nothing to remember. I was made out of nothing, out of the raw stuff of the planet outside. That makes me an alien life form, and that means what we've been doing for the last three weeks is first contact between your race and mine. And how have you behaved? With suspicion. With fear.'

It seemed to remember Emmins's presence at this point. 'I don't count the professor in this,' it added. 'I'm sorry it had to be her in this situation, but the fact is I don't blame her for a moment. Perhaps it's my fault. If I'm right, I'm an ambassador. I should have behaved like one from the start, instead of waiting for you to realise it.'

The Doctor frowned. 'I'm sure we can talk about this in a civilised way,' he said. 'We don't have to do it like this.'

'I want to be sure you're going to do what I want,' it said. 'This is important. I hadn't realised this before today, but there's no way I want to go on in this situation. Whatever the reason, I'm something unique, extraordinary. If I can't get the answers I want here, then I need to find them elsewhere, and if I can't trust you to find the answers, I have to go out and find them myself.

'I very much doubt you've considered it,' it went on, 'but, at the moment, I'm totally alone. There's nothing else in existence that shares my background, that I can truly connect with. If I'm ever going to change that, to find someone or something else I can be a part of, then I have to do it myself. The only alternative is that I stay like I am, a one-off, with a little respect from someone like the professor being the absolute best I can hope for.'

'Perhaps you could spell it out for us,' the Doctor interrupted. 'What exactly is it that you want?'

The duplicate stared directly into the camera. There was a fiery expression on its face that the Doctor took to be deep resentment, possibly hatred. He held that expression for a couple of seconds. Again, the Doctor had the distinct impression that it was intended to convey a message of defiance.

'I want to have free passage to the head station. I want to be able to speak directly with the heads of research, and to have a say in what happens next with the project. What's clear to me is that there's more on this planet than you ever expected, and that means either you accept that there's something sentient here and treat it with some respect, or you start accepting that this isn't your territory any more, and you damn well leave it alone.'

The Doctor had had enough. He caught a glance from Gorey, who was stepping forward as if to say something more. But the Doctor shook his head, and he stepped back again.

'Even if we agreed that any of this was reasonable,' the Doctor said, 'you must see that we can't let you dictate terms. Let the professor go, and then we can talk.'

'That's not the idea,' said the duplicate. It had started swapping the gun between its hands again, either through nervousness or to draw attention to it. The Doctor decided to call its bluff.

'You're not going to use that,' he said.

'We're not even sure it works,' Gorey added, his voice raised so he could be heard. 'It's not been used in months. Those things jam easily, and the power on that one was low even when it was issued.'

The Doctor saw Emmins nod quite vigorously, and was convinced that she at least believed him. But the duplicate shook its head. 'That may have been true three weeks ago, Gorey, but you'll have checked it out since then. In case you needed to use it on me.'

There was no response from Gorey, which the Doctor took as confirmation that the gun was live.

'And besides, there's something else I can do in this room.' It headed over to the large grey lever that operated the doors. The Doctor winced as Emmins let out an involuntary yelp and fixed the duplicate with a stare.

'Don't do that. Please, don't do that.'

'You're bluffing,' the Doctor said. But now he wasn't so sure.

'Am I?' said the duplicate. It raised the gun then, and pointed it at the camera. Before the Doctor could get a chance to shout out, the duplicate had fired a shot directly at it, and the screen went blank.

Part Four

Gorey and the Doctor rushed into the primary lab just as Nyssa and Bird were finding a way to open the door. Their expressions as they saw Gorey and the Doctor running towards them went quickly from pride to alarm. Bird's face in particular was a mask of panic.

'What happened?' he asked Gorey.

'He shot down the video link,' Gorey said. 'He's threatening to open the exterior doors.'

'Oh – my...'

'It's turned completely psychotic. I don't know what it's doing any more.'

'I wouldn't say psychotic,' the Doctor corrected him. 'It's still basically rational; I'm not convinced it's actually prepared to hurt the professor. What it does have,' he went on, gently staying Bird's hand as he went to open the door, 'is a highly exaggerated sense of its own importance and status. It wants to be an ambassador.'

'We're still taking a risk, though,' said Bird. 'While it's got Sarah captive, aren't we better off just giving it whatever it wants?'

The Doctor smiled. 'That's the last thing we should do,' he said. 'I think you should leave this to me.'

'It's my wife in there,' Gorey cut in. 'I can't just sit here –'

'Look, we're wasting time,' the Doctor snapped. 'The fact is, it doesn't see you as equals any more. Like it keeps saying, it's unique, extraordinary; an alien visitor making first contact with your species. This needs someone who's not intimidated by that sort of thing.'

He put his hand on the door. Bird and Gorey looked sceptical, but not about to challenge him. He shot Nyssa a look.

'The Doctor's right,' she said.

And besides, he thought, if those doors do open, I'm the only one here who stands the remotest chance of surviving it. He didn't relish the thought of having to say that out loud, and was relieved when both Bird and Gorey nodded slowly. He waited a couple of seconds, until he was sure they weren't going to follow him. Then he stepped through the door into the collection room, and closed it behind him before he even had time to register what was there.

As he walked in, the Doctor saw the duplicate hunched over next to the professor; he seemed to be talking to her intently. The Doctor almost felt as if he were interrupting.

'This has gone on long enough,' he said eventually.

The duplicate stared at him. It was surreally uncomfortable how similar he looked to Bird, and yet how different. The expression in his eyes was something it would be difficult to imagine in Bird, something hurt and feral, frightened and yet proud. Liked a caged animal, perhaps; forced to let its prey be brought to it.

'Don't take any risks, Doctor,' Emmins urged him. 'He says he won't hurt me, but I just can't tell any more. There's something different about him.'

The Doctor took a step or two forwards, just to see if it would have an effect. The duplicate, still a good ten feet or so away, reacted with alarm.

'Don't come any closer,' it said. 'I know what you're here to do.'

The Doctor was wrong-footed for a second. 'And what's that?' he managed.

'You're here to kill me.' The duplicate raised the gun, narrowed its eyes. It seemed to be terrified. 'Unless I kill you first.'

'All right. I want you to calm down.' The Doctor stepped back, raised his hands. 'You can see I'm not armed. I'm not here to kill you at all; I'm here to help.'

'You expect me to believe that?'

'You can believe what you like. But that's what I do. These are risky situations, where one sentient species meets another. They can go spectacularly wrong, or spectacularly right. I tend to get involved whichever happens, but I rather prefer it when they end up happily.'

'I'm sure you do,' the duplicate said. It kept its gun trained on the Doctor. 'But I'm not sure I trust your motives, Doctor, or even that I'd want you in my corner. What makes you think you should be involved here anyway?'

'Let's just say, I have a knack for being in the wrong place at the wrong time,' the Doctor said.

The duplicate lowered its gun a little. But it was walking towards the grey lever, slowly but intently.

'We really have to work together to put this situation right,' the Doctor offered.

'But on your terms, I suppose,' the duplicate replied. 'I don't know if that's really the point any more. You know, I thought if I could leave this station, perhaps even the planet, that I could be part of the project up there. Not just any old researcher, you understand, but someone who could help direct things, help to discover what this planet's secrets are. But you know, I doubt they'd even listen.'

'They might,' the Doctor said. He'd at least stopped him moving for a moment. He wondered how long he could keep him talking. 'Human beings are stubborn, you know,' he went on. 'They won't listen to reason until they absolutely have to. They'd prefer to find facts to fit their theories, rather than the other way around. You just have to learn how to deal with them.'

'I'm not sure I want to.'

'I think you do.'

'I can see what you're doing here,' the duplicate said. He took a step towards the Doctor, raised himself up to his full height. Another gesture of defiance. 'But you shouldn't make assumptions about what it is I want, or what you can do to placate me. The fact is that you don't know what I am, any better than I do.'

The Doctor thought about denying it, but decided to try honesty. 'No, I don't,' he admitted. 'But what you're made of isn't the point. It's how you behave that interests me.'

The duplicate smiled. 'And what do you mean by that?' it said.

'I can see you're afraid,' the Doctor said. 'You're one of a kind here; you feel alone, and you want answers. But the thing is, there's no one around here who can give them to you. You're bound to feel powerless, to want to strike out at anything in the hope that it can make you feel in control.'

The duplicate seemed lost in thought for a moment. The Doctor was alarmed to see Emmins lean back in her chair suddenly; he couldn't tell if the discomfort was psychological or physical, but there were tears welling in her eyes.

'You're wrong,' the duplicate said. He took another two steps towards the lever, so that he was standing right next to it. 'You don't know anything. Not a thing.'

'If you pull that lever –'

'Yes?'

'Then you'll kill her. You'll kill the professor. I don't think you're going to do that.'

'I know. You're banking on it.' That smile again.

'Well?' the Doctor demanded.

'Well, perhaps I want to prove you wrong,' the duplicate said. 'I want to show you why you shouldn't interfere. I want to prove to you that you'll never understand what I am, that you can't predict what I'll do.'

The Doctor took a breath. 'This isn't about me,' he said.

'We're quite similar, you and I,' the duplicate said. 'We're both alone in this world, we both stand apart. Neither of us has a name, although for opposite reasons. I've never been given one, because no one's convinced that I'm a person worth naming. Whereas you, I assume, have one, but won't tell anyone what it is. It gives you power over someone, to know their name; only a small amount, but it's something you won't give up. Not to anyone.'

'I want you to stay away from that lever.' The Doctor was almost yelling.

The duplicate stared at him. Very slowly, very deliberately, he placed his left hand on the top of the lever. The right hand still held the gun, still pointed towards the Doctor.

'I wanted us to talk to each other as equals,' the duplicate said, 'but you won't even tell me your name.'

'Please, don't do this,' Emmins was screaming.

The Doctor considered bolting right then, making a quick calculation that he could at least reach Emmins before the duplicate pulled the lever. He'd at least have the element of surprise, and he assumed the duplicate's reaction time wouldn't be as fast as his.

But there had to be a way round this, he thought. He couldn't let the duplicate pull the lever; there had to be a way to stop it. If only he could think...

'I'm not your problem, Doctor; I won't be reasoned out or resolved. I won't let you control me. I won't let you win.'

And almost before he could see what had happened, the lever was down. The bulkhead doors began to open, alarmingly quickly. Already there was thick red smoke rushing in through the widening gap; the noise of the storm whipping and kicking through the air was sudden and deafening.

Emmins screamed, a long, shrill note. In a desperate, panicked thrust she thrust herself sideways in the chair, and it jolted to the floor. But her bonds were tight, and she couldn't pull herself free.

The Doctor took his eyes off the duplicate and ran towards Emmins then, but he fell almost instantly, hit by a shot from the duplicate's gun. His legs fell away from under him, and he felt a searing pain in his left thigh.

He'd fallen facing the doors, and he could only watch hopelessly as they continued to open. The smoke looked more solid now, like a torrent of dust and thick, deep-red snow. There was an unbearable heat to it as well, clutching and pawing at them, reaching in like the claws of some ethereal predator.

It was hard to see anything now. But, from somewhere behind him, he could hear heavy footsteps rushing in, and he saw Gorey and Bird racing up towards Emmins.

The duplicate's arm was just about visible through the smoke. The Doctor tried to shout out, but it was too late to stop Gorey being felled by a blast to the shoulder. Bird managed to reach the professor though, and with a massive effort he hauled both her and the chair back towards the door.

The Doctor struggled to get up. He could hardly make out the figure of the duplicate in the distance, but he was closer to Gorey. He too was struggling, and yelling in pain. The storm was ripping right through the centre of the collection room now, and knocking some of its contents to the floor. A large red crate clattered to the ground between the Doctor and Gorey, before careering off into the distance.

The Doctor could feel the effects of the storm on his own skin, even now. He would have to act quickly. He looked towards the door to the lab, and saw Nyssa about to come in. He yelled at her to shut the door, but she shouted no. The Doctor was thankful, however, that she didn't try to come inside.

He turned back towards Gorey, but he'd fallen to the ground. The Doctor limped up towards him, turning him over gently. The storm had already ravaged his skin; his face was a mass of bare flesh.

The Doctor winced. He tried to find a pulse, but it was clear that Gorey was dead.

He had to get out quickly. He ran for the door, the storm whipping around his body, and slipped through. Nyssa slammed it shut behind him.

The secondary lab had escaped the effects of the storm. The Doctor saw Bird helping Emmins out of her bonds. She was shaken, but unharmed.

'I'm sorry,' he told Bird breathlessly. 'Gorey's dead. I couldn't save him.'

'I know,' Bird said. He hugged Emmins to his chest. She buried her face in her hands.

'There was no other way,' Bird said. Then: 'I didn't see what happened to the duplicate. I assume –'

'I don't know,' the Doctor said honestly. 'I don't know.'

'Are you all right?' Nyssa asked him.

He inspected the skin on his own hands. They looked sore, but there was no lasting damage. He had been lucky.

'I'm all right,' he said.

An hour or so later, the Doctor and Nyssa were back aboard the train carriage. There didn't seem to be anything else they could do.

The report back to the head station had been depressing. The head of research was inclined to recommend to the board that the project be scaled back, even to the extent of leaving the planet well alone. The Doctor had briefly protested, but it was hard to fault his logic.

Nyssa had told the Doctor a couple of times that she felt they had done all they could. He imagined it was an attempt to console him, for which he was grateful. But the truth was, it was precisely that thought that made him most depressed. They *had* done all they could, and failed nevertheless: it was somehow worse that way. It offended his sense of optimism, his love of a challenge. And he wasn't used to it.

He'd hoped that Nyssa would be able to sleep through the journey, but instead she was staring into space. He asked her what was wrong.

'I was thinking about the duplicate,' she said. 'I know we've every reason to be angry with it, and there's no excusing what it did. But I can't help feeling sorry for it as well.'

This was typical of her, the Doctor thought. 'Why?' he asked her.

'Well.' She seemed lost for words, for a moment, and then she said simply, 'It was lonely.'

He looked at her sadly. A sudden sensation hit him then, a potent blend of deep affection and concern. Not for the first time, he had to remind himself that Nyssa was still very young, and very vulnerable; beneath all her dignity and restraint, she was a frightened child. He wanted to hug her, but it didn't seem right.

'We did all we could,' he told her gently. 'I wish we could have found a way to save it, believe me.'

She gave him another of her brave smiles. 'I know,' she said. And then she looked at him strangely, an expression he hadn't seen before. She seemed to hesitate before saying, 'Things have been difficult lately. Do you think it would be a good idea to... I don't know, to stop for a while?'

He grinned broadly at her, his spirits lightened. 'I was going to suggest a break,' he said lightly. 'It's exactly what we need.'

Nyssa was frowning. 'No, I was thinking more...' she started to say. And again, that odd look. 'No. Never mind.'

He peered at her closely, trying to work out what she was thinking. 'You're sure?' he said eventually.

'Yes,' she said. 'Let's take a holiday.'

'Excellent,' the Doctor said. 'I think we deserve it.'

Avarice

The showman took a moment to straighten his cravat before opening the door to the next room. Once inside, its occupant – the severely dressed, dumpy woman – looked at him impatiently. 'Time is money, time is money,' she announced, not bothering with, or waiting for, a greeting.

'I apologise for keeping you,' said the man. 'Although I must say I disagree with you. Time is far more important than that.'

'More important? Than money? Never!' The woman's head twitched as she spoke, scarcely able to believe someone could voice such heresy.

The showman flung himself on a chair facing her. 'I bet you were one of those children who insisted on playing Monopoly right to the very end, even though everyone else had got bored long ago. And I bet you were always the banker, too. And took backhanders from the other players for fixing the beauty contest.'

'Don't bet,' said the woman. 'Betting's wrong. Investments can go up as well as down.'

'A bird in the hand is worth two in the bush?' suggested the showman. 'But what's life without a bit of risk? You sit there waiting for guaranteed returns, you'll never move at all!'

'Secure,' she said. 'Risk-free.'

'And boring,' said the showman. 'Surely there are some risks worth taking? The nascent economies of developing worlds that come to your attention, desperate for your help, in order to survive. I would have thought it would make financial sense to risk an investment, for the possibility of large future returns. But no. You love money too much to consider losing even a penny. Better for whole civilisations to crash and burn than your shares go down a hundredth of a point.' He sighed. 'But perhaps I'm confusing life with finance. I've never had much of a head for economics. Don't really understand these things.'

He dug into his pockets and pulled out a handful of coins and notes. The woman's eyes lit up as he sorted through the pile, eventually coming up with a coin smaller than his fingernail, an imperfect circle of dull yellow metal.

'Now this I can understand,' he said. 'This gold coin is worth exactly the same amount as... as this amount of gold. But this –' he selected a rectangle of paper '– this piece of paper is just the representation of –' he examined it '– nine hundred Altivian Lorrets. A promise to pay the bearer on demand. Except they'd be pretty surprised if anyone did demand it – I don't expect there are nine hundred Altivian Lorrets left on the planet. They were a kind of large water vole, much in demand in ancient times. Nowadays no one would know what to do with them.'

His hand went back in his pocket again, and the woman watched eagerly for its reappearance. Her face fell when he produced a tiny carving. It was of a woman with long straight hair and a flowing gown. Her stone eyes gazed starwards. 'Beautiful, isn't it?' said the showman. The woman did not respond.

He swept the money off the table and put it back in his pockets, all apart from the last note. He placed that on the table, next to the miniature statuette.

'This is a piece of paper of no intrinsic worth,' he said. 'It is not created from rare or expensive materials. It has no artistic merit. But it promises to pay the bearer nine hundred Altivian Lorrets.'

He turned to the carving. 'This is a thing of beauty. It takes my breath away when I see it; there is grace in every line. However, a market valuation would place its worth at eight hundred Altivian Lorrets.'

He grinned suddenly. 'Pop quiz! There's a fire in the room, and you've got time to save only one of these two things. Which is it?'

She didn't seem to understand how that could be a question. 'Most value! Save thing of most value!'

The showman spelled it out further. 'Yes. But what is the thing of most value?'

She pointed to the bank note.

He sighed. 'Yes, I had no doubt you'd say that.' He picked up the statuette. 'But I'd save this any day. Even though I lied to you. It's not worth eight hundred Lorrets; it's probably not even worth eighty. Even though I could buy another ten or more of them if I had the cash, I'd still make the same choice.'

'Mad!' said the woman. 'Mad, mad! Loss! Profit!'

'I see,' said the showman, 'that you just really, really like money. Now me, my favourite kind of money is the chocolate sort. You know, like you get at Christmas.'

She glanced at her watch. 'Time! Wasting! Time is money!'

He jumped up. 'I apologise!' Then he sat down again. 'I owe you more than an apology. Time is money! I'm losing you money!'

She nodded eagerly.

The showman went back to his coat pockets once more. This time he pulled a piece of paper out of one coat pocket – a plain sheet, no bank note – and after a few minutes rooting around, pulled an orange crayon out of another. On the paper he wrote, 'I', then left a space, followed it with a 'U', and then underneath wrote 'a trillion dollars'. He finished it off with a drawing of a smiley face, and an unreadable squiggle that may have passed for his signature.

'Look at this,' he said, holding it up. 'One more letter and you could take this paper and claim a fortune from me. As it is, worthless.' He pulled the paper closer to him, and poised the crayon above the space. The woman leaned forward expectantly. The crayon touched the paper. He wrote a single letter: 'N'. 'Now it stands for: "I need urgently a trillion dollars",' he said. 'Could have been worth a fortune, now it's just a plea for cash from you.'

He handed the paper to her. She held it with the very tips of her fingers, not soiling her hands, and tore it in two.

The showman slapped his forehead. 'Oh, no! Shame you did that. I was just about to tell you. There's this planet – they don't know much about art but they know what they like – and I'm this really hot property there. Bigger than Leonardo. They'd kill to get something crayoned with my very own hands, and with the signature... priceless. A million, at least.'

Her eyes darted from side to side, a hunted look in them. Frantically she clutched at the two paper halves, trying to fix them back together through sheer will-power. The showman took them from her, gently, kindly. 'Sorry. Worthless now. Won't go for damaged goods, you know, even from me.

'But you needn't be concerned. Perhaps I was lying again. Perhaps it was really worthless all the time. After all, it was a bit rubbish. I could do better, with more time and a full set of felt-tips. Perhaps people weren't really willing to pay any money for it at all. Or perhaps next week I'll do a million sketches and scatter them across the planet, and my art will be instantly devalued through availability. Perhaps you didn't just destroy a million dollars. Nothing to keep you awake at night. Although you probably never sleep. Time being money, and all that.'

She nodded vigorously.

'Which leads me to the question... why in the name of goodness are you here? I can't believe it's for any form of gratification, however twisted. You – or your company – has paid a fortune for you to be here. And as you keep emphasising, the more time you're here, the more money you're losing elsewhere. So... why?'

'Diversity. Better client relations through understanding. Means greater profitability. Also, all tax deductible.'

He gaped. 'You're treating this exploitation of extreme suffering as a *management training course*? Wouldn't paintball have served your purpose just as well?'

The showman got up and walked over to the wall. 'You know, out of all the people I've seen today, I think you're the one who'll really blend well with this experience. It could have been made for you.' And he pushed the switch.

A klaxon sounded, a triumphant roar circling overhead. The woman looked above her for the source. Balloons and streamers fell from the ceiling on to her upturned face. A screen on the wall began to flash: 'Congratulations! Congratulations!'

'Well, what do you know?!' exclaimed the showman. 'You're our millionth customer.'

The woman put her head on one side like an enquiring bird as he bent down to examine the screen.

'All you have to do is answer a few simple questions, and you could win a huge cash prize!'

She squeaked in excitement. 'Cash! Prize! Cash! Prize!'

'Yes indeed,' said the showman, producing a set of flimsy white cards from nowhere. 'Just give me your answers, and that mountain of moolah will be coming your way. Question one: what's the name for a country's most important city?'

She jumped up and down. 'Capital! Capital!'

He threw the first card over his shoulder. 'Correct! Question two: what do you call someone who predicts the future?'

She drew in a breath, and then called out, 'Prophet!'

Another card went flying. 'That's the one! Question three: what's another way of referring to a hidden store of things?'

'Oh, oh!' Her eyes were wild. 'Cache! Cache!'

A card fell to the floor. 'Absolutely correct. Question four: what's a verb meaning to create a new word or phrase?'

'Coin!' She could hardly contain her excitement. 'Coin!'

All the remaining cards were tossed into the air. 'It is indeed! And now tell me, what do all those words have in common?'

The woman danced round the room, her attitude quite at odds with her soberly suited appearance, squealing, 'Money! Money!', and streamers and balloons and pound notes began to fall from the ceiling. The screen flashed, and triumphant music played.

And the showman pushed another switch.

Telling Tales

David Bailey

I keep finding dead ladybirds in the flat. Yesterday, while I was dusting the bottom bookshelf, one fell to the floor. Today, on the bedroom window sill, as I opened the window, to let the room breathe again. How they're getting in, I've no idea. And it's February, for Pete's sake... Aren't they like wasps? Should they be around in winter? Ellen would have known. Ellen would have spotted them sooner, too, probably.

Still, I brushed today's ladybird out of the window, sent its dried husk of a shell – two dots, I noticed, red on black, one on each side; one of the boring ones – dancing away on the cold breeze outside. I hope the downstairs neighbour – Peter, was it? Ellen would have known – doesn't mind. It landed on his patio furniture.

Maybe he'll start wondering tomorrow, 'Where has this dead ladybird come from? I've never seen one in February before...'

Or maybe it's just me.

And maybe they've just come to visit me. Crawling into my flat, through the too-wide hole where the aerial wire comes in, or the gap in the rotten putty in the sitting room window. Crawling in, looking around and adjudging this flat the perfect place to die. People in India or something, they probably have a myth about the ladybirds' graveyard, a fabled place where all ladybirds, red or yellow, from two spots to sixty-two (are there sixty-two-spot ladybirds? I'll ask Ellen. No. Wait), go to breathe their last. The two-piece jewels flicking closed for the last time, their black pin legs folding in like deactivated machinery. Piles upon piles of them. Except maybe it's not a myth, maybe it's now true, and soon I'll have to crunch through a knee-deep sea of carapaces just to get to my front door.

Although that's unlikely.

I don't move to the front door much, only when Ellen took me out. She had her own keys, and I'd hear them jingle, Monday, Thursday and Friday mornings at five to eleven. In she'd come, breezing round me and the flat, making everything better, making everything right. Then, after she'd cooked us lunch, out the front door we'd go. Down the ramp the council put in, and out the communal hall, leaving the car park and heading up the road, to the park.

Even when it was rainy and blowing a gale, out we'd go – like it was that day in November, the last time Ellen took me out. Ellen knew I didn't mind a bit of weather.

I could barely hear her say it, when she told me. At the top of the hill in the park, we were. Bits of Kent peeping through the sheets of rain that blurred the usually vast view, but only bits. That might have been Bromley, I suppose, but mostly all I could see was grey claustrophobia. It *was* nice to get out on days like this, but it was better when there was a view.

I was trying to make one, squinting to push aside the layers of drizzle, hoping to piece together the vista, when she told me. So, not only had I not been paying attention, but the wind was also whipping up, blowing her words away. I asked her to please repeat herself. I think I even may have been that formal, so shocked and unsure was I about the truth of what I thought I'd heard her say.

'Please repeat yourself.'

It sounds silly now, I know, but that was it, if memory serves.

'Please repeat yourself, Ellen.'

Oh, now it sounds like a job interview. That wasn't it. I didn't add her name.

Anyway, before she could repeat herself, I suddenly found myself thinking about the flat. All the injury-in-service insurance had made sure the place had been perfectly tailored to me after the accident. The wider doors, the lower worktops, the new bathroom. All done, just so I could stay there. I'd nearly paid the mortgage off when it happened, and the pay-out had been more than enough to cover the remainder, pay for the work on the flat *and* keep me in the manner to which I blah-de-blah for a few years yet. But without Ellen... I couldn't stay there, surely. I didn't know if I'd want to. The money had changed the world around me, but I suddenly realised I didn't connect with it any more – Ellen did, and I connected with her.

'They're finding a new carer for you. I'm moving to Wolverhampton.'

There. That time, I was listening, and that's what I heard.

She went on to explain but, as she talked, my attention drifted back to the non-existent view, for which I now found myself grateful. I didn't particularly want to see anything at the moment, much less hear her tell me about Damon, and the house they'd bought together in Tettenhall, and how they were going to get married, and she'd work at a hospital in Birmingham, work with 'people like you, Laurence', while he'd follow posting after posting, with the Fifth Scots Dragoon Massed Pipers Guard Artillery Watch Regiment or whatever the hell it was. She'd sit at home, smiling, job done, people helped, lives changed, while he'd rip the world from its axis, leaping and running and fighting and killing and *screaming and shouting and tearing me apart.*

'So, Laurence, what do you think?'

I pulled myself round in my chair, best as I was able, and smiled up at her. She leant to one side and over, like it was a pram she was pushing, not the sorry remains of my life.

'I'm so happy for you,' I said, my teeth aching with the lie.

★ ★ ★

The Doctor was shouting Peri's name again, and she really wished he'd learn to chill out sometimes. While she was reasonably certain he was no longer unhinged and out to kill her, she still felt like it would be a long time before her jumpiness subsided.

She didn't exactly enjoy his company at the moment. She felt uncomfortable around him, like he thought she was in some way responsible for all the little things that niggled him or sent him flying into his mini-rages. Like he thought she could do or say something to make it all better. When she was feeling well disposed towards him, she supposed that it was his way of making her feel involved, that his constant aggravated chant of 'Well, Peri? Hmm?' was her way in, her chance to agree and tut and shake her head and huff and puff and blow away the lack of zeiton 7, or the malfunctioning chameleon circuit, or the post-regenerative stress.

But really all she wanted to do was lie on her bed and read a book, and wait for him to get back to some sort of normality. To just *calm down* a little, for pity's sake.

'Peri!'

That, she realised, was going to have to wait.

'Peri!'

He was getting louder, and now she could just make out the thump-thump-thump of his angry footsteps along the corridor outside her room.

She sighed, folded her book closed, using a finger as a temporary bookmark, and sat up, putting her feet flat and neat on the smooth, white floor of the TARDIS. 'I'm in here, Doctor,' she said.

A muffled 'Ah!' from outside heralded the – polite knock-free – entrance of the Doctor. A whirl of colour spilt through the door, slamming it carelessly shut behind it. Peri winced a little: half at the noise of the door being rammed back into its frame, and half at the sight of that blessed outfit.

'Peri, we've got a problem,' the Doctor cried, striking a pose on her bedside rug. He looked down at her and noticed the book she was holding in her lap. 'Jeffrey Archer?' he spat.

'What is it, Doctor?'

'Hmm?' He dragged his disgusted gaze away from the book, and momentarily had trouble focusing on Peri. His eyebrows were high, surprised and questioning. 'Oh, yes.' He coughed, clearing his throat, then, like he was standing in the pulpit of some weird church of doomsaying, announced, 'We're being followed. Something is riding the TARDIS's coat-tails. Come on.' He walked to the door, opened it and looked back, expectantly.

Peri shrugged, put her book on the bedside table and went to follow.

The Doctor strode down the corridor, back to the control room, talking as he went. Peri caught most of it, as she jogged to keep pace. 'I detected it as we were leaving Varos, but I think whatever it is might have been there for longer than that.'

'Why do you say that?'

'The people of Varos don't have the technology to send something into the vortex like this, so it can't have come from them. Plus, it's leaking something, some sort of energy – and its signature is hanging round the TARDIS like a bad smell. It must have been leaking for a while.'

Suddenly, Peri remembered her book. 'Oh, nuts. I've lost my place.'

'The control room's just along here,' the Doctor said, his pace not wavering, a hand held out to a door not many yards ahead.

'No, my place in my book,' she explained. 'I just put it down, and forgot to mark where I was up to.'

'Does it matter?' the Doctor hissed. See? The tiniest thing exasperated him nowadays. 'You can just flick through and find it later.'

'I can never do that, I always get lost in the story again. I can never remember which bits I've read, who's done what, which things have and haven't happened.'

The Doctor stopped. They'd arrived at the control room and he stood, one hand resting on the door handle, ready to pull it open. 'Peri, I hardly think you should be worrying about that at a time like this.'

His raised eyebrow told her everything she needed to know about exactly what the Doctor thought of her being inconvenienced. He opened the door and disappeared inside.

'Well,' she said as she followed him into the control room, to find him already beavering away at the console, 'when exactly should I worry about it? If it weren't for you, barging in and –'

'Oh, so now it's *my* fault? I *barged in* to let you know of a potential danger to your own safety!'

'Whose fault is it, then? I don't remember anyone else *barging in*!'

'Heaven forbid!' the Doctor boomed, a brief scoffing laugh closing the sentence. 'You've been stuck in that room for hours, hiding away from the world.'

'Can you blame me? I step outside, and all I get is yelled at!'

'Peri, I... Hold on a minute.' The Doctor suddenly bent over a screen on the console. Glancing over his shoulder, Peri could see a long string of numbers, bright orange figures against black, pouring down the screen.

'What is it?'

'It's their wake.'

'What?'

'It's what whoever's following us is leaving behind. A trail.'

'Can you follow it?'

'That's just what I was trying to... Ah.'

'Ah? Good ah or bad ah?'

'Good ah. I think. Looking back at our own trail, I can see that it *did* follow us to Varos. And it's been there for a good while longer than that.'

'So, not that good a good ah.'

'Here,' said the Doctor, urgently, stepping aside to show Peri the screen. The numbers had gone, replaced by a much more abstract image. Orange lines and blurs of red swirled about, a confusing mess of information.

'What's that?'

'The vortex, Peri. And that –' his fingertip followed a darker line across the screen, the thread shimmering, broken briefly here and there '– is whatever is following us.'

Branching off from that line were a myriad of smaller ones, all tracking away palely to the edges of the screen. 'What are they?' Peri asked, pointing them out.

'That's the leakage, the energy it's giving out.'

'But they're lines,' Peri said, peering more closely at the screen. The glowing image shifted a little, turning on an invisible axis, showing a minutely different aspect.

'Hmm?' said the Doctor. By this point, he had wandered over to work on another panel of the console.

'The leaks. They're lines.'

The Doctor slowly came back to her side. 'What do you mean?'

'Well, if it were some sort of constant escape of energy, coming from something that was constantly moving, wouldn't it be evenly spread about the vortex? Something like that.' She pointed at a smear of dark red that wended its way hazily across the whole screen. 'I mean I'm no temporary engineer –'

'Temporal.'

'– but would a steady leak, if that's what you think it is, produce little targeted streams like that?'

'Targeted?' whispered the Doctor.

'Well, I don't know, I mean, they're obviously not just smudged across the continuum, I didn't mean...'

'No, Peri,' the Doctor said, his fingers skipping across a keypad below the screen. 'No, that could be it.'

The picture of twisted orange lines spun and whirled on the screen. It looked like the Doctor was zooming the image out, turning it, following the pale red lines. Until, suddenly, Peri saw the lines begin to converge, tracking together towards one corner of the image.

'Here we go,' said the Doctor. He pulled the image further along, the lines meeting and threading themselves into a thicker rope of trails, leading on across the screen.

Finally, the Doctor stood bolt upright. 'A-ha!' he cried, turning to Peri. 'You're a genius. There it is.'

He pointed at the screen, and Peri saw a small sphere of red blinking in the centre, the tight cord of lines leading straight to it. Next to the sphere, a string of numbers was slowly resolving itself. Coordinates, she quickly realised.

'So,' she hazarded, 'whatever is following us has been sending something back to that place?'

'Signals. The energy signature is unmistakable, once you know what to look for. We're being spied upon.'

There was a problem. On his screen, the red lines were peeling back, folding in on themselves, shrivelling. They'd been discovered, his worms, and they were retreating, taking cover.

Lotu patted a few keys on a pad next to the screen, and it was confirmed. The Doctor had detected the worms, and tracked their source. They were trying to hide, to protect him, but it was too late. He could see the TARDIS's sensor code running wild through his system, taking the worms apart, dissecting them for clues.

It wouldn't be long before he arrived, he knew that. How could he not know that? Sometimes, it felt like the Doctor was his oldest friend in the universe. But he was sure that Time Lord wouldn't see it like that.

He huffed a quiet laugh to himself. Ah, well. He had known the game couldn't last for ever – in some ways, that was part of the fun. He sent a message to Monitor Kall, and asked him to inform the Overseers. Then he reached for the controls to destroy the evidence, to deactivate and blank the whole system.

Lotu hit the key, and watched as his worms faded on the screen, burning into blackness and taking every scrap of the altered data with them.

I figured that it was just first-day nerves or, maybe, he'd forgotten about me. He's probably a very busy man, this Terry. 'He's like a locum,' Ellen had said on the phone. 'He'll just be standing in, till they find someone permanent to help you out.'

What, permanent like you?

'He's filling in with the other people in the area I used to look after, too.'

Infidelity. Oh, make it worse, why don't you?

'He'll be rushed off his feet! And he's having to look after the Sydenham area, too. I...'

Ah, a guilty pause, at last.

'I don't suppose he'll be able to give you as much time as I did, Laurence, but when they find someone full time, they'll be around as much as I was. I'm sure everything will work out fine.'

Yes, I'm sure too.

His first-day nerves lasted a week.

I tried phoning social services twice a day for seven days. Fourteen times, I left a message. Fourteen times, no one called me back.

Still, there was always, 'Ring me whenever. I'd love to hear how you're getting on.'

And the number she left?

'The number you have dialled has not been recognised. Please check and try again.'

'The number you have dialled has not been recognised. Please check and try again.'

'The number you have dialled has not been recognised. Please check and try again.'

Another lie.

Monitor Kall was striding down a corridor. Given the situation, it was all he could do not to run pell-mell along it, screaming with rage and confusion. But it always paid to make a good impression.

He was having to push through the throng, a mass of stumbling, dizzy people, drunk on their new experiences. Some were crying openly, gasping for air, holding on to their companions for support. Between the wracking sobs, they would stare, wide-eyed, at the ceiling, like they were seeing the world for the first time. And many of them were, Kall knew.

These clumsy figures were ranged everywhere, knotted around the long line of semicircular alcoves in the corridor's walls. All of these inconvenient people, he knew, paid his wages – were, in fact, making him as rich as they each were – but he wished to the Third Moon that they'd pull themselves together and get out of his way.

There was Lilandra Mase, Regent Divine of Pendendra, mouth agape, shock draining the colour from her face. She was staring at the floor, shaking her head. Her four attendants – bald-headed, possibly female clones – were scurrying around her, pulling the connection pads from her temples, offering water, bowing, scraping. But she couldn't see them, wouldn't respond.

One of her attendants suddenly wailed and, dropping the bowl of warm water she had been holding ever-ready for her mistress to wash her hands, took Lilandra's shoulders and shook them. The poor young woman was screaming, tears strangling the sound, 'Regent, my Regent! Please, no! Please!'

The attendants had never seen anything like this before: the sight of their normally implacable ruler shaken to the core was sending them into a fearful panic. But Kall decided quickly not to intervene and explain the situation to the women. Lilandra should have warned them – this was precisely why she had come here, after all.

Kall took a quick glance at the monitor above her alcove as he passed. On the screen, four-limbed, furry creatures were lumbering out of the mist, spitting with fury at the viewer, bubbling slaver flying from their yellowed teeth. Someone – some primitive human, his rusty, dented sword raised – was cowering from it. A very old tale. Always popular.

He nodded to Desire's-Birth Tenfemalesbeauty, Darling Crown of The

Bounty of Seeds. She nodded politely back, a stern look on her face reminding him that he should cast his eyes to the ground in her presence and blush. Instead, he hurried on. He was richer than her. Richer even than her entire Sphere of Devotion! And he just didn't have the time.

As Kall passed her, he saw her turn and connect herself to a console, and he quickly realised it was one that others had complained about before, some sort of glitch, apparently. A quick glance up at the screen confirmed that the weird flickering still hadn't been seen to. He really must have a word with the manager of that story – who was it now? Barnan? – and have it fixed. Last time, there'd been some excuse about the source material being significantly removed from the usual sources, something about the particular subject's unusual time distortion, but he hadn't really been paying attention. Considering he had been trusted with some of the racier stories on sale here, Barnan really was one of the most boring souls Kall had ever met. Never had such a grey man been connected with a more red-hot line of work.

Kall shook his head and, for a split second, closed his eyes. Then – thump! – he collided with... *Oh, dear me, no.*

'Monitor Kall?'

How did he know his name? That blessed receptionist! Kall spluttered something in reply. It might have been 'yes', but it lost any semblance to a word when it met the shock that had tightened his throat and slackened his jaw.

This is what Kall had feared, this is what he'd been rushing to the Overseers to discuss. The subject – *the* subject – had found out, and he was on his way. But Kall hadn't been quick enough, hadn't had time to warn anyone.

The Doctor had already arrived.

'Monitor Kall,' he said, breathing deeply, puffing out his plumage, drawing one or two odd looks from Kall's patrons, odd looks of recognition. This wouldn't do. This wouldn't do at all. 'I think we need to have a word, don't you?'

The Doctor was fuming. This wasn't a situation Peri was entirely unfamiliar with, but it still made her skin itch with the discomfort. This Monitor Kall at least had the good grace to remain silent, not to try to explain himself to the Doctor, as they strode down this brightly lit corridor.

Peri could no longer tell who was leading whom. Sure, the Doctor didn't exactly know his way around this place, but the way he purposefully stayed just a yard or so behind the Monitor, his eyes boring either into his back or the stretch of the hallway ahead, smacked of a teacher herding a troublesome boy to the headmaster's office.

The Monitor, meanwhile, scuttled ahead, occasionally glancing fearfully back, to make sure Peri and the Doctor were still following him. Every time he did, he caught the Doctor's fierce gaze, then winced and quickened his pace.

He was a strange-looking alien, Peri thought. He was bowed over, but she sensed it was from a life of grovelling and to-and-froing, not merely a reaction to the Doctor's ire. But the slouch to his shoulder, the downward crane of his neck, was a perversion of quite a beautiful form – slender, with pale, almost silvery skin, and dazzling white eyes. His neat grey hair was worn buzz-cut short, and he was dressed in a smart black smock and trousers. Businesslike.

Peri, meanwhile, was acutely aware of her own place; she walked quickly behind the other two, occasionally skipping awkwardly to keep up. She glanced around as she went, desperate to get some sense of what kind of trouble the Doctor had landed them in this time. But her surroundings gave her no clue at all as to the kind of place they were in.

This corridor was all there was, it seemed. And there weren't even any doors leading off it, just a long, long line of alcoves down either side, but these were plain, unadorned and empty. Curious, Peri thought, and she realised her interest must have shown on her face when she heard Monitor Kall say, 'This is all ready for the expansion. The Doctor's stories turned out to be more popular that we could have ever... Um.'

He had trailed off and Peri broke her gaze away from the walls to see that he had stopped outside a door – the first she'd seen so far – and was cowering under the Doctor's scornful glare.

'I *beg* your pardon?' he spat.

Kall flinched. 'I really should let the Overseers explain, Doctor.'

With that, he stepped forward and pressed his hand to a slim panel next to the door's frame. With a short, quiet beep, the door slid aside and Kall held out a hand. 'Ah, after you,' he stammered, hazarding a quick smile at Peri.

The Doctor swept past, chin boldly set to face the horrors within. With an apologetic shrug to Kall, Peri followed.

Peri looked about the vast space she found herself in, dwarfed by the five galleries projecting from the wall facing her, a giant window set behind them. They dominated the room, looming large over the two-dozen tables neatly arranged across the floor below them. Around these tables, more of Kall's people moved – talking, laughing, reading, arguing, sharing, clearly at work. Waves of these pale people, all dressed in the same neat, black clothes, washing around pile after pile of books and papers scattered across the tables. It was the busiest library Peri had ever seen, and these people, the noisiest librarians.

The sound of their voices echoed everywhere, bouncing off the metal mesh of the galleries, making a kind of shimmering white noise that Peri very quickly began to find a little overwhelming.

Her eyes were instinctively drawn to the window, perhaps hoping that the view might give her the sense of openness and freedom she was suddenly missing. But, beyond the glass, all she could see was jagged grey rocks, little whips of dust flicked this way and that by a vicious wind, and a cloud-filled sky. There was no sign of a sun, just a strange blue glow from the other side of the thick clouds.

It felt almost cruel, the sight and sound of the room noticing her, finding her, crushing in on her, a fist around her body, tightening, tightening...

'Doctor,' she said, and heard her voice, tiny and weak.

'I feel it too, Peri,' he replied, quietly and seriously. 'What is this place, Kall?'

'The main library, where the stories are held, catalogued, and vetted.' Kall had joined them and, noting their reaction to the room, was slyly smiling to himself, clearly pleased that he momentarily had the upper hand. 'Those galleries –' he waved a hand at the five great balconies in front of the window '– hold all the tales that we tell here.'

He walked to the nearest table and picked up a small black box, no bigger than a packet of cigarettes. 'This,' he held it up, turning it from side to side, 'holds a whole world's worth of stories. The true-life sagas from every person on a single planet.'

He then pointed back up to the balconies. Peri looked up and saw that each balcony was ranged with shelf after shelf of these little capsules, and that each gallery had to hold at least a hundred sets of shelves. She reached out to the table for support, feeling dizzier as every second crept by. 'I don't understand,' she said, unable to tear her gaze away from the shelves.

'I'm beginning to,' the Doctor muttered.

'The Overseers will explain everything fully, Doctor. If you'll excuse me?' Kall placed the box back on the table and walked away, quickly disappearing in the waves of people washing this way and that between the people.

'Doctor,' Peri began, 'what on earth is going on?'

'I've a feeling there's a box here with all my life in it, Peri,' the Doctor replied. 'I'm not sure why but, if what Kall says is true and we accept the fact that his people have been spying on me, it looks like they have been collecting... *stories* from my life, and putting them to some sort of use here.' The Doctor looked about the room, and Peri was sure she saw him shudder. 'Some nefarious purpose, no doubt.'

'Why does it feel like that in here?'

He turned to her, his eyes empty of the warmth she had always associated with *her* Doctor. 'Doom-laden?'

Peri nodded, then shivered. Stop *looking* at me like that! she thought.

The Doctor turned his gaze back up to the galleries. 'Oppressive, full of terror.'

'Yes, Doctor. I get the point.'

He shrugged, whipped back to face her and Peri watched as a thunderous shadow crossed his face. 'You must be the Overseers,' he whispered.

Peri was momentarily confused, before she heard the deep voice from behind her. 'Doctor. Peri. Welcome to our library.'

She turned to find the source of the voice, and saw four men just like Kall. Pale, tall, almost ethereal, neat and impeccable. On the right-hand shoulders of their identical black smocks, they each wore a strange gold epaulette, metal and finely filigreed. Peri peered at one, and she could swear she saw some sort of motion within its twisted pathways, almost like the cog-and-ratchet innards of a clock.

As she watched, one of the men reached up to his epaulette, touched it gently and closed his eyes. A second later, he smiled and opened his eyes again, glancing at Peri. His smile widened to a grin and Peri saw something unexpected cross his face – a familiarity, almost like she was staring into the eyes of an old friend. But she had never met him before.

'Could we,' she stammered, 'could we go somewhere else to do this?' She stepped forward and tugged the Doctor's sleeve gently.

'Yes, my friend and I... We find this place –'

One of the Overseers – the head of the party, Peri supposed – raised his hand and smiled. 'Of course. The library can be a little... disturbing.'

Two of the other Overseers chuckled.

'Please,' he continued, 'follow me.'

Thinking back – I'd found myself with an awful lot of time for thinking back recently – I suppose it was when Ellen and I met the Doctor that it all started to go wrong. I mean right. No. No, I mean wrong.

Holed up in that factory for nearly forty-eight hours, we were. Ellen had taken me back to see my old workmates, have a laugh. Good day out, it was, until those... things had arrived. But, hot on their heels came the Doctor, ill-advised scarf whirling, and that pretty girl, what was her name? Same as that girl on Blue Peter. Something Russian-sounding. Anyway.

The Doctor had bundled us into the manager's office, while he and the girl set about fighting them off. There wasn't much left of the factory when they were all finished, but at least he'd kept us safe.

Ellen had spent the better part of two days looking after me, staying with me, making sure I was all right. It wasn't like she had much choice, not like she could make a run for it – not with those things outside, the Doctor had made that abundantly clear. But still, we spent all that time together, just her and I, getting to know each other properly.

The Doctor's friend would put her head round the door now and again – more often than he did, anyway. Just to make sure we were all okay. She always paid particular attention to me, which people tended to do in most situations like this. (Not that I'd been in many situations like this, but you know what I mean.)

But she could see that Ellen was taking care of things, keeping an eye on me, making sure I was fine. A look, sympathetic, passed between them. They told each other, 'I know what it's like, looking after people, caring. I share your joyous burden.' They said it, silently, with smiles, content with their lot.

And it was then that I knew, then that I saw just how horribly painful it was going to be from that moment on. I hadn't felt like this about someone since school; a burning, thoroughly teenage lust. (Even Mary hadn't stirred anything like this intense a feeling. And she'd scarpered – politely, apologetically, but like the Road Runner – the minute they put me in this chair. No great loss.) There were times when Ellen would lean over me, tucking a blanket around my legs – Ellen cared whether I was warm, while the Doctor just made sure everyone stayed alive – when I hoped beyond hope that she wouldn't lean *too far*, and see or (heaven forbid!) feel what her closeness caused in me.

Either she didn't notice or she didn't care. Whichever it was, that was when it all changed, for the better or worse.

And now? Now she's God-knows-where, living it up with Damon, forgetting all about me. Just like the rest of the world.

I saw a neighbour walk past the window this morning. I didn't recognise him. First human being I've seen – without the aid of the cathode ray tube, anyway – in three days. Last one was the postman. He'd wanted next door.

Terry never turned up.

I gave up phoning.

I'm getting by; I've been through worse.

It was quite a story, Peri had to admit. Quite an audacious secret that they'd uncovered this time.

The Overseers had begun to tell their tale the minute they had been led into a small, quiet, blessedly warm and well-lit room. Peri had relaxed almost immediately and, as she sat and the last Overseer through closed the door behind them, she was immediately aware of just how oppressive the library had been. Here, though the room was no more than twelve feet along any side, she felt a real sense of space at last.

Their leader, Penser, had started talking before anyone had made it to any of the chairs ranged around the long wooden table in the centre of the room, and he had been quick to admit what the Doctor had suspected. The Overseers had indeed been spying on him, sending what they called 'worms' through the space/time vortex, following the TARDIS and relaying its tales of adventure back to this facility.

What the Doctor hadn't suspected was what Penser said next.

'I feel it only fair to tell you, now that you have exposed our little scheme, that we have been watching you for some time.' The Overseer rested his hands on the table, palms flat, fingers neatly spread. He looked down at them, clearly reticent.

The Doctor picked up on his reluctance to continue. 'What do you mean?' Peri had never heard the Doctor speak so quietly, and the cold softness of his voice shocked her.

'What you need to understand...' Penser ran out of words, and gave a long sigh.

One of the others leant forward and interjected. 'Sir, if you want to –'

Penser had silenced him with a raised hand. 'It's all right, Greth.' He looked up and held the Doctor's gaze, and Peri found it hard to read his expression. There was no guilt, but there was an awareness that the game was up. There was fear, but not of reprisal – Penser seemed sure of himself, just frightened of continuing.

'What do I need to understand?' The Doctor's voice was louder now, harder and sharper. 'Penser, what is this place? What is happening here?'

'Let me start there, then,' Penser said at last, his voice steady, comfortable. 'This planet once had a name, but no one can now remember it. This world fell out of the universe many, many aeons ago – no one knows how it happened, but it did. And the planet fell far, and it stayed hidden where it lay for millennia. It took us a long time to find it, to unpick the seam and open the fold that hides it.

'Because the world was still part of the universe, but also apart from it, we discovered that every journey to or from it – once you knew where it was – was instantaneous and direct. You can get here from anywhere, and you can get to – or *see* – anywhere from here. So, we looked, and listened, and the universe showed itself to us in the form of a glorious fiction. And that's when we realised that every story in the universe crosses this point, winds up and unwinds here.

'Since our people have always been great lovers of stories, we started to listen. For many years – many more than you can imagine, let alone live – we just listened, drinking in the fables, being swept away on the romances, getting tied up in yarns. But, after a while, we grew bored, utterly bored. Do you know how many stories there truly are in the universe? How many *different* stories make up the lives of everyone out there?

'Everyone is the same. For every man crying into his hands that his woman has left him, torn with a pain he thinks unique and new-born and totally his own... there are a billion more like him. It's like looking at a night sky. You may be able to think that every star is different, individual, but from where you are... Just white dot after dot after dot.

'And that's when Lotu had his idea. On the world we came from, Lotu had been a great businessman, chairman of a thousand boards, with more money at his command than our government had ever seen. He had been put in charge of the expedition to find the world, our leaders believing that he could bring it in under budget – which he did – and that he would be able to find some sort of commercial benefit. It took him some time, which was surprising as the means of money making had been staring him in the face for a long time.

'For years, we had been sending information back to our government from this world, the greatest source of information ever found. Some was used to ease trade relations with other worlds, some was used to ensure the security of our homelands, some was used to make giant scientific leaps forward. But, when it was all used up, when all practical use was wrung out of it, there was nothing left... Nothing except the stories.

'Our people, by this point, were rich, safe, happy. Coddled, pampered. No disease could touch us. Neither poverty nor famine nor war shook us. We were immortal, we knew the dimensions of the universe. We were bored.

'And Lotu could see what was happening. Everything was grinding to a sludgy standstill, our world was stuttering to a halt. So, he did what our kind has always been best at: he told a story. Plucking one thread at random, as it drifted past this planet, he spun it into a yarn unlike any other. A terrible tale, full of misery and woe, the likes of which no one on our world had seen for centuries. He sent the story back to our homelands, and watched as people wept, wretched and appalled, reminded how far they had strayed from their true, mortal selves.

'And then, they begged for more.

'Lotu had done it, he had shaken up our population again, made them feel alive again. And they fell in line like that –' Penser snapped his fingers '– desperate to remember what it felt like to actually *feel*.

'So Lotu put plans into action, had this facility built. He constructed a library where every scrap of misery, every tale of anguish and despair, could be safely stored and catalogued. And then he made a machine, a great storytelling machine, which he used to tell these tales again and again, to any who would pay to hear them.

'He sold the tales on, tempting in every member of the idle rich across the whole of the universe, selling them these stories so they could remember what it was like before their wealth anaesthetised them from reality. So they could feel misery, so they could experience sadness, hopelessness and desolation. Alien things, long-forgotten feelings.

'And so it was that the wheels of our society began to turn again, as Lotu amassed for us a fortune the likes of which no single planet had ever before attained, and never will. And we know this to be true, for we can see the balance sheets of everyone in the history of the universe. The rich men would come, and throw their money at us in the millions, the billions, just so they could feel alive once more.

'And so it goes. Still they come – these many years later, from every corner of space and time – and still they pay their pointless money, to know life. And still we run this facility, run the machine, just as we have since the day it was built.'

Penser's eyes had glazed over, Peri noticed. He had slipped away as he had told his story. If it were true, he was travelling back a long time in his mind's eye. She shivered slightly at the thought of what the people round this table had seen. Even the Doctor – though he apparently had nothing on these new men – had lived many more lifetimes than she could ever hope to. She felt suddenly, terribly, small.

'And where do I come in?' The Doctor seemed less affected by Penser's story. He still had a serious look on his face, obviously keen to get straight to the point.

'You have long been of interest to us,' Penser said. 'Your departure from Gallifrey churned up a huge swathe of misery, and our filters had long ago brought the beginning of your tale to our attention.'

The Doctor shifted in his chair slightly, and Peri found herself wondering why he was always so reluctant to talk about his life on the run. She didn't like that Penser obviously knew more about the reasons for his fugitive state than she did.

Penser continued: 'It didn't take much more investigation to see that misery always seemed to cross your path – sometimes you found and remedied it, and sometimes it followed in your wake. Whichever, it didn't really matter. You were clearly a rich seam of material, and we would have been fools not to mine it.'

'This is outrageous.' Still the Doctor's voice was level, calm.

'Not really. Everything that happens in the entirety of space and time – *everything* – causes an echo that passes through this world. It's just that, long ago, we decided to be more selective about which echoes we listen to. You should be flattered.'

'Flattered?' The Doctor's voice wavered slightly. Here we go, thought Peri. '*Flattered?* I have been spied upon, and the story of *my* life sold to millionaire idiots just so they can salve their festering consciences, so they *think* that they know what it's like to have to struggle. Flattered? I am *insulted* that what I work so hard to change is used in this sickening manner!'

Penser shrugged. 'I'm sorry you feel that way, but there really is nothing –'

'Nothing you can do?' the Doctor yelped. 'Of course there is! You can *stop*!'

'It's complicated,' Penser said, casting his eyes down and shaking his head.

'I'm worth too much to you, aren't I?' The Doctor was breathing hard through his nose, anger flaring out his nostrils. A fierce red blush was colouring his neck. 'What on earth do you need the money for, anyway? Look at yourselves! Your people have everything, *everything*! What difference does a few million more credits make?'

'Protection, Doctor.' Penser still stared at the table. 'Security.'

'But all the knowledge of this world – surely that is enough to guarantee your safety?'

'We tell all sorts of tales here, many of them involving the most powerful beings in history. Most don't yet know we are using their lives in this way. If they come here themselves, we are, of course, very careful to keep the fact secret from them. But if they were to find out...'

'You're afraid of reprisal, and yet you happily admit everything you've done to *me*?' The Doctor puffed his chest out a little.

Penser just laughed, once, mockingly. 'There are many, many more powerful threats in the universe than you, Doctor.'

'Well,' he replied, a little deflated. 'That's as maybe...'

'The kind of people we deal with, Doctor, they have a very different way of thinking than the ordinary man. They are scared of almost nothing; most have entire armies at their beck and call, ready to destroy whole worlds in answer to the merest slight. They believe themselves more powerful than anyone they might come across. And it is money that gives them this power, this belief. So, the only thing they *are* afraid of is a *richer* man, a man with greater resources.'

'And so you...'

'We keep them poor. Oh, yes, they're still sickeningly rich in the eyes of their people, but they know that we are richer still. And that will always be the case, since they *have* to keep visiting us, desperate to taste the pain of living again and again.' A little smile flicked round the corners of Penser's lips, and Peri felt her stomach lurch. 'And every time they return, the price is that little bit higher.'

'This is disgusting, Penser. And I am going to stop it, whether you like it or not.' The Doctor stood up from the table, and added, 'Come on, Peri.'

She went to join him as he walked back to the door. The Overseers just stayed seated, smiling. Their calmness caught the Doctor off guard.

'Well,' he said, 'aren't you going to try to stop me, or tell me that you will destroy me or something?'

'You still haven't heard the whole story, Doctor,' Penser replied, his smile growing wider. 'And you haven't heard our offer.'

When the Doctor had listened to what Penser had to say, he agreed to the offer. He made them a promise, and the Overseers let him go. It twisted his stomach into knots, he said, but it really was the only thing he could have done.

Filled with sadness, he came straight here. I expect he did it to make himself feel better. I hope it worked for him.

I asked him to explain the kinds of stories these men had harvested from his life, and he told me tales of the bloated English aristocracy, European tribesmen and their ancient magicks, broken old women hidden away in hospital, crazy old women at the edges of the universe, mistakes and promises. Good stories, sad stories mostly, and I was made happy by them. There *were* people worse off than me.

And then I asked him to explain why he was here, and he told me the story of Lotu. Turned out he was still working at the facility, and this is where the Overseers had the Doctor over the ropes. As time drew on, these rich people from around the universe were demanding more and more miserable stories, more and more depravity. But the cupboards were running bare – until Lotu had the bright idea of getting in there and *making* some misery, some tailor-made fairy tales to sully up the lives of the über-rich. He would build a machine that rewrote history wherever – and whenever – he wanted, sending stories *back out* into the universe.

And who better to star in them than... ta-da! That bright coat swirling through a galaxy of specially engineered, carefully plotted gloom. Lotu twisted the Doctor's life time and again, making every situation he found himself in a thousand times worse. The villain wasn't just out to destroy a city, he was out to destroy a world. The damsel in distress wasn't just thrown into prison, she was tied to a train track, gagged and blindfolded, and strapped with explosives.

Lotu was careful. He didn't make it obvious, nor did he change history everywhere the Doctor went. He just tweaked and twiddled, gilded the rotten lilies that fell in the Doctor's path. Put the players and plots in place, to make sure his viewers got the very best entertainment. And that's where me and Ellen come in.

Turns out, I was never meant to be in the factory that day. I was never meant to meet the Doctor. Ellen shouldn't have been there either, and she shouldn't have met UNIT Corporal Damon Burton. She shouldn't have run off to Tettenhall. She shouldn't have left me.

Lotu put me there as 'colour', it turns out. Like some twisted TV executive or something – 'Quick! Make sure there's a man in a wheelchair in there! Make the people feel sorry for him!' And then, Lotu took an interest in this new little pet, and started playing with my life, pushing me here, pulling Ellen there...

But it was worse even than that. When Lotu had panicked at the Doctor's arrival, he shut down the machine – with my story in it. He was fiddling with my history again at the time. 'I don't know... Should it be suitably drizzly or ironically sunny when Ellen tells Laurence she's leaving him?' Something like that, probably. But, when he shut down the machine, he left me inside. Which is why it's always night here, and why I'm all alone. It's why I haven't had to eat in weeks, and why the phone never rings.

And, the Doctor said, that was why he promised to take over the story-telling machine – or, at least, one of the reasons. Once the Overseers had explained that they'd been tampering with the Doctor's life, and the subject of me had been uncovered, the Doctor had been outraged – both for himself, and for little old me, bless him.

He told me that one day, when he has control over the story-telling machine, he can use it to fix my life again, make it better. That's what he said: 'I promise you I will make it all better. Undo it. Put it right again. But... But I can't do it yet. One day, but not yet.' He looked awfully sorry that he couldn't help me right then and there, but I took it in my stride.

Next, the Doctor told me about the promise he had made to the Overseers. They had explained to him exactly how their story-telling machine worked. It wasn't like a telly or a radio, it was much more powerful than that. You didn't just see and hear the stories unfolding, you *felt* them. This was, after all, why it was such a hit with the rich kids.

The only problem was, for the machine to have this incredible empathic ability, it needed to feed off the mind of a living being. Bravely, Lotu's little brother (probably stupid and picked-on, and willing to do anything to make big bro proud of him) had volunteered to be plugged into the machine when it was built, his immortal mind given over to making the machine work in the way his brother had imagined.

But, despite his immortality, despite his omnipotence and omniscience, Shen was dying. The machine was slowly – oh, so slowly – killing him, leeching off little bits of his not-so-infinite life to feed into the minds of those who experienced the stories.

So Overseer Penser... Well, he saw the chance to kill two birds with one stone and, hopefully, immeasurably increase the popularity of his sick little facility.

'We need you to give your word, Doctor,' Overseer Penser had said. 'We need you to come back and run the machine when Shen has died. Tell the stories, ensure that our work is carried on.'

'What?'

'It will be magnificent,' Penser had said. 'Your own view on all these tales, given to all our clients. Our star attraction, in residence at last. You would become story and storyteller as one: narrative perfection. The popularity, the income...'

'And if I refuse?'

'You don't know, Doctor, how popular your stories have become. If you don't do as we ask, Lotu will continue to twist reality around you, making you a magnet for misery. Everywhere you tread, sadness will follow. We will make you wear grief as a cloak, we will dress your feet in sorrow. Every step you take will make the universe a worse place, and we will revel in it.'

(Something like that, anyway. I might be exaggerating.)

'I could just destroy the machine.'

'The sciences that built the machine are beyond even the knowledge of the Time Lords. It is indestructible, eternal.'

'Just like yourselves?'

'More so.'

'So,' the Doctor had said (with a heavy heart, he'd explained), 'if I do this, you will leave me alone. Stay out of my life, and those of the people around me – whoever they are?'

'We promise.'

'I will be able to detect you, you know, if you try anything.'

'I know.'

'Fine.'

And so that was it, the promise. And that was why, he had explained, he couldn't just put my life back as it was right now – I had to wait until he took control of the machine.

But he had made me the further promise that he would return to do just that, when he had the ability. Strange as it sounded, the story he told me explained an awful lot and, even if it didn't solve my problems straight away, it at least took my mind off them.

'One last thing, Doctor,' I said, as he finished his mug of tea. (I hadn't bothered making one for myself. It would just have sat on the table and gone cold, unwanted.) 'It's been a while since I've had any company, and it's been really nice to hear some news of the outside world – even if it's as weird as all that you've just told me. I just wondered if you could stay a little longer, tell me another story? Please?'

The Doctor sat back in the armchair and crossed his legs. A smile, warm and open, crossed his face. 'It's a little hard to explain, but... well, it wasn't just my past that Lotu had been drawing stories from. It was all my lives, so what I'm about to tell you... It's a bit naughty, it breaks a few rules even to know this. But...

'Tell me, Laurence,' he sighed, leaning forward, eyes twinkling, 'are you a gambling man?'

Gluttony

The showman was swinging a plastic carrier bag against his leg as he entered the next – and last – room. Inside sat the tall, slim man. Almost everything about him spoke of health, from his sleek hair to his smooth, glowing skin. He stood up to shake the showman's hand, and the showman returned the grip enthusiastically. 'I'm a huge fan of yours,' the showman said. 'Never miss a programme, if I can help it.'

'You're too kind,' said the other.

'I've got several of your cookbooks too,' said the showman. 'Picked them up an incarnation or two ago. Funnily enough, I was sometimes accused of gluttony back then – but, without wanting to get all self-defensive, it simply wasn't true. Love of cake does not a glutton make, as you might say. A fondness for pie needn't make you sigh. Et cetera, et cetera. A healthy appetite is not something one needs to be ashamed of – as probably the most celebrated chef in the galaxy, I'm sure you will agree.'

'Absolutely,' the man agreed. 'Appetite is a thing to be embraced, not denied.'

'Indeed!' said the showman. 'Whatever the cost!'

A frown flickered across the other's face. 'The cost?'

'Yes, but you're quite right not to concern yourself with it. When you made that programme exhorting the delights of the Gervola Eel, sautéed in butter and rum, for example, and there was such consumer demand for it that the poor little creature became extinct. Sad for the disappointed gourmets, but just an unfortunate side effect of embracing one's appetite, and that's what was important.'

'These things happen,' said the chef.

'They do,' agreed the showman. 'At least the ducks and geese are still alive – well, for a short time, and if you can call it life.'

The chef looked puzzled. 'Ducks and geese?'

'Yes,' said the showman. 'The ones being force fed through pipes shoved down their oesophagi till their livers are so swollen the birds can't stand up and can hardly breathe, to produce the so-called delicacy you called in your last book "foie gras, a taste not to be missed". It had been banned on a number of civilised worlds, until your viewers offered suppliers so much money production was started again. And then there was your championing of veal, boiling lobsters alive, shooting fish in a barrel. Of kangaroo burgers and bushmeat pizza and panda tikka masala. Your many advocacies of cruelty in order to bring a few moments unearned pleasure on the palate.'

'Animals are there for man to use,' said the chef. 'Lesser creatures exist only for our benefit.'

The showman looked slightly sickened. 'Personally, I think the mark of a civilised society is how it treats its "lesser" creatures,' he said. 'But perhaps that's a discussion for another day. Let's talk about your effect on people, then. How about all those planets, millions dying from hunger, because you've persuaded them that a diet reliant on cattle is the way to go, when they could feed their world many times over by devoting the same resources to production of grain. Not to mention the pressure on the environment: the unsustainable use of water that will eventually lead to dry and diseased planets, all of which could be avoided if different diets were adopted. But appetite must be revered above all things.

'And let's look at individuals. Not whole planets swallowed up by your methods, but each member of your misinformed audience. You've suppressed scientific research that shows the terrible effects following your recommended diet would have on human beings.'

The chef waved a hand in the air. 'Needless scaremongering. Sheer piffle!'

The showman raised his eyebrows. 'Piffle? Following a diet consisting solely of your recipes, of the foods you recommend, of the lifestyle you suggest, is universally harmful to the human body.'

'Not so.' The chef shook his head. 'It is impossible for anyone to claim that such a diet is universally harmful. Because there is at least one proponent who is the very picture of health.' He gestured to himself. 'Me.'

'Oh, yes,' said the showman. 'The picture of health. Talking of pictures…' He walked over to the wall, and brought up a screen. 'I had an artistic – but scientific – friend run up this little impression of what you should look like by now.' The showman touched a key, and on the screen appeared an image of human wreckage. There was something about the eyes, something about the set of the mouth that showed it to be a picture of the same man sitting there in the room, but little else. The figure on the screen was not svelte but grotesquely overweight. Its hair was lank and its skin blotchy; its eyes dull and pained. Cutaways began to appear of clogged arteries and fatty, weakened organs.

'On second thoughts, I don't think that's really a very accurate picture,' confessed the showman.

'I should think not!' said the chef.

The showman smiled. 'No, an accurate picture would be more like this.' Another press of a key. Another image. The image of a coffin.

The chef laughed, derisively. 'But that is quite clearly not true! Look at me! I am alive, I am fit, I am in the peak of health! And my millions of viewers can testify to that. The public would hardly eat so much as a sandwich recommended by –' he shuddered as he pointed at the first image '– *that*.'

'True,' said the showman. 'Which is why they must never know the truth…'

The chef looked momentarily scared. 'The truth? Are you suggesting that I don't eat my own recipes?'

The other laughed heartily. 'Oh, no, no, no. No, no, no, no, no.'

The chef joined in the laughter. 'Well, that's all right, then!'

'I'm suggesting you secretly have extensive surgery. I'm suggesting your face is injected with so many chemicals to give it that healthy glow that just your nose could open a branch of Boots. I'm suggesting that your smooth, shiny hair is the best fake on the market, that you have your arteries hoovered and polished once a week in an experimental process that might have been of enormous benefit to medical science, if you hadn't hijacked the research for your own ends and insisted on secrecy so your little deception would never be found out. And your organs... your fatty, weakened, degenerating organs...' The showman's voice dripped with pain. 'I'm suggesting that your organs are replaced whenever they wear out. Replaced by the specially selected organs of men who have been kept fit and healthy, fed on grains and pulses and vegetables, exercised and cared for until the time when they are needed.'

His hands clenched involuntarily. 'And I am hoping – hoping against hope – that you are party to these terrible, terrible things because you are ruled, every part of you, by this terrible vice. That you can see no other way; that you have been forced into a corner by your greed. Because this is The Purgatoria Experience, and I have to believe that there is no vice from which people cannot be redeemed.'

The showman pressed another key. The image of the coffin on the screen became a hundred coffins, a thousand, a million, more, streaming off into the distance. 'And those men aren't your only victims.' He waved at the symbols of death, streaming off into the distance. 'That is what's happened to people who've listened to you, revered you, been misled by you.'

'But perhaps, at least, they die happy,' said the showman. 'Drowned in cream and suffocated in steak. Gorged on gorgonzola and choked on chocolate. Buried by the pleasures of the flesh.

'And I can sympathise,' he said. 'I'm not immune. In fact, I can't resist any longer.' He reached out an arm and grabbed hold of the plastic carrier bag he had brought in with him. He opened it slowly, carefully, not revealing the contents, then took a deep sniff. 'Aaah!'

A hand delved into the bag, rooted around, brought out a small, greeny-white globe. He held it up with a look of triumph, as the chef's eyes expanded in astonishment and longing. 'Is that... is that...?'

The showman popped the globe into his mouth, and shut his eyes as he chewed, once, twice. His face was serene; an ecstatic trance. Finally, blissfully, he swallowed. 'Yes,' he said. 'A moon truffle. Only found deep beneath the ground in one tiny region of Hyfes Eight's most inaccessible satellite. Takes a decade to grow to the size of a walnut.' He opened his eyes and smiled. 'And quite yummy, too.'

He walked over to the table where the chef sat. 'Oh, despite everything I've just said, I really am a huge fan of yours, you know. Not quite as huge as I might be if I ate all your recipes –' a friendly chuckle '– but a fan nonetheless.

You know the show of yours that I like best? The one where you get ordinary members of the public to bring you a bag of mismatched ingredients, and you create a gourmet masterpiece out of them.' He placed the plastic bag on the table, one hand clutching it protectively. 'I was wondering if there was any chance you could possibly do the same for me.'

The chef had almost stopped breathing. His hands crept towards the carrier bag. 'Are there more moon truffles in there?'

The showman pulled the bag closer and peeked inside. 'Ah. Only a couple. I'm afraid I've been snacking. But I hope you'll be able to do something with what's left.'

He took out two more of the tiny greenish spheres and placed them on the table, just out of reach of the chef. Then he looked back in the bag, drew out a package of an oozy, cream-coloured substance surrounded by a yellow rind. A pungent odour seeped almost visibly through its wrapping.

'Junfoot albino goat's cheese. Made from the milk of the one-in-ten-thousand Junfoot goat who is born an albino, revered as a sign from God, and hand-fed on clover picked by virgin priestesses. The cheese is churned beneath a blue moon, and left to mature for sixty years.'

The chef seemed hypnotised by the block of cheese, unable to take his eyes from it. The showman placed it carefully next to the truffles, and reached into the bag again. But something seemed to distract him, and he brought out his hand again, empty. The chef made a whimpering sound.

'There's just one thing I don't understand,' said the showman. 'Why are you here? What can this experience possibly bring to someone who exists solely for the pleasures of the flesh?'

It seemed for a minute or two that the other man wouldn't answer, that he couldn't tear his attention away from the flimsy plastic sack for long enough. But eventually he spoke. 'My appetite never grows less. Yet it is not as sharp as once it was. In my youth, before I was successful, I would seek solace in food after each setback, and it never tasted so good. Misery honed it to a fine point, the keenest of blades. I want to find that sensation again.'

The showman laughed softly. 'Grief as an appetiser. No, I don't think I'd ever have thought of that.'

He put his hand back in the bag, and this time he brought out a jar that sparkled and shone, refracting rainbow colours from the sunlight streaming in at the window. Deep inside the jar, a spoonful of a dull golden substance could be discerned. 'Honey,' said the showman. 'Honey made by the killer bees of Kawniker, where thirty suns shine on a lush paradise of petal and pollen. It's so potent that this amount –' he held up the diamond jar '– could sustain a family of four for a month. But the bees defend it with such vigour that eighty men die to harvest each jarful.' The jar went on the table. The chef was drooling now, his eyes glazed and disbelieving, as if he were receiving a vision from heaven.

Another thing from the bag: a plain stone pot wrapped in reeds. Nothing could be seen of the contents. The showman placed it reverently on the table. 'Unicorn liver pate,' he said. 'Made from a creature so rare, it doesn't even exist.'

The showman stood up. 'I'll just be over there,' he said casually. 'Feel free to help yourself.'

And as the chef lunged, the showman walked over to the wall and pulled a switch.

Too Rich for My Blood

Rebecca Levene

Bernice looked round at the cityscape, wavering under a heat so intense it seemed to suck the breath right out of her. Even in the glaring midday sun, the lights of the neon signs shone out, brash and intrusive.

She turned to Chris and smiled. 'Las Vegas: built by gangsters and populated by suckers.'

Chris frowned. 'I heard they tested nuclear bombs in the desert near here. Built a fake house full of fake people to drop them on.'

'I know. What a great place.' Bernice turned to the Doctor and held out her hand. 'So – give.'

The Doctor looked puzzled, and a little alarmed. 'Give what?'

'Money,' Bernice said. 'Two thousand and ten legal tender American dollars.'

'Whatever for?' the Doctor asked.

Bernice shook her head at him. 'For what everyone's here for, Doctor. Gambling.'

The small tributary road had joined the Strip now, and they were suddenly surrounded by throngs of people: locals, heads down, rushing to jobs and family; tourists, heads up, gawping at the great nodding cowboy hanging over the street and at the neon-lit outlines of the giant casinos around them.

'The house always wins, you know,' the Doctor told her.

'Not when you're playing poker,' Bernice said.

The Doctor looked at her consideringly for a moment longer, then dipped a hand in his pocket and pulled out a fat roll of notes which looked far too large to have been hidden in there. 'Don't spend it all at once.'

'But that's the whole point,' Bernice said, grinning and pocketing the cash.

'Don't I get any?' Chris asked.

The Doctor darted a sideways glance at him. 'I thought you were here to watch the competition.'

'Well, yes...'

Bernice slipped a handful of notes from the top of her stack, enjoying the slick, slightly greasy feel of the old-fashioned paper money, and handed them over to Chris.

'Thanks,' Chris said seriously. Then he smiled, that wide, carefree smile. It amazed Bernice he could still smile like that after all this time with the Doctor. 'I'm really looking forward to this. A proper holiday.'

The Doctor had halted in front of them and was staring up at the monumental building towering above them. Its shadow was so sharp on the ground it seemed to be cutting a slice through the street.

'Well, here we are,' he said. 'Las Vegas's newest addition – The Purloined Letter.'

Bernice scanned the building. Huge, red and bulbous, it looked like a giant concrete model of the sort of spaceship that used to have sparks fizzing out the back of it in early black-and-white B-movies.

'I thought it was called the Intergalactic,' Chris said, puzzled.

The Doctor shrugged. 'Same difference.'

The competition was being held in the casino's vast central atrium, the only room in the whole place – Bernice told Chris – where real daylight was allowed in. Everywhere else, any sign of the natural twenty-four-hour cycle was banned, clocks included. The bosses didn't want punters to know how long they'd been gambling, or that their bodies might be in need of some sleep. Chris thought it was a dirty trick, but Bernice seemed to think the guests at the casino knew the game and chose to play it anyway.

He hadn't expected the event to be so well attended. Every available space was crammed with wooden benches, and every inch of them was crammed with the bottoms of the thousands of spectators who'd come to see the main event.

The competitors themselves were sitting on high wooden stools in the centre of the hall, dappled yellow-green by the light filtering down through the carefully manicured tangle of vegetation above them. Chris pushed his way towards the stage, ignoring the grunts of protests from people feeling the sharp edge of his elbows. By his reckoning, he must have come further to see this thing, both temporally and physically, than anyone else. He was entitled to a front-row seat.

It was a competitive eating contest. When Chris had first read about them in the TARDIS data banks, he'd been amazed, then disgusted – but in an intrigued sort of way. People from the past were so *odd*. Sometimes he felt like a pith-helmeted explorer peering through the undergrowth at a bunch of tribesmen dancing round a fire and assuming they must be celebrating the roasting of some missionary when really they were just having a party. Maybe the people here had a good reason for seeing who could stuff the most hot dogs down his neck in the shortest space of time. Maybe it served some socially redeeming purpose. All he knew was, he had to see it for himself.

Up close, the contestants weren't much to look at. They were fat, sure, but they weren't grotesque. They looked like half the people Chris had seen wandering outside, taking in the sights with placid, bovine eyes. But these people had something else in their eyes, some fire that burned brighter than the sunlight streaming down on them. They wanted to win. They really wanted to win. And they knew that they could.

And then Chris spotted him, in the middle of all the other contestants. There was a good six foot of him, but he couldn't have weighed more than eight stone. He looked all the thinner for being surrounded by so much excess flesh. At first, Chris assumed he was one of the judges, but when he took his place on one of the stools, and stared intently into the distance, that same fire burning in his eyes, Chris realised that he must be one of the contestants.

What was the guy thinking? Chris had read up on the competition as soon as he knew the Doctor would bring him here. The record hot-dog eater had consumed fifty in twelve minutes. This guy didn't look like he could physically fit half that inside him.

Chris stared at him, fascinated. Maybe he had a death wish, maybe it was a dare.

As if he felt Chris's eyes on him, the skinny guy looked over, sharp brown eyes beneath shaggy black hair catching Chris's for a moment. They weren't just filled with fire, Chris realised, they were feverish. The man's mind not quite there behind them.

As if trying to quench that internal fire, the skinny man raised a glass of water to his lips and took a sip. But his hand was shaking, and a drop of water splashed out on to his hand.

As it hit, Chris could almost swear he heard it sizzle. And a small puff of steam seemed to come from where the drop of water had once been.

Chris was still staring at this, baffled, when the big, unshaven man beside him nudged him in the ribs.

'Smart money's on the little guy,' he said.

Bernice tipped her green visor down lower over her eyes, squeezed up the bottom of her two hole cards, and frowned at them. They hadn't changed: still the ace and eight of clubs. Halfway to the Dead Man's Hand, she thought, the hand Wild Bill Hickock was holding when he was shot in the back during a poker game in Deadwood.

The hand which, with the two and nine of clubs sitting on the table alongside an ace of diamonds, gave her top pair *and* the nut flush draw. She tried to look as miserable as possible and checked when the bet came round to her. There were only two other players left in the game, but if she didn't give away her hand she stood to win a pretty reasonable sum of money.

One of the other players, a woman in her mid fifties with blue-rinsed hair and raisin-wrinkled eyes stared gloomily at her small stack of chips. To stay in the game, she'd have to go all-in, risk losing all the money she had left. She looked up at Bernice, consideringly, searching for tells, the little physical ticks that let good poker players read bad ones like a book.

Bernice was pretty confident she didn't have any. Travelling with the Doctor taught you to lie well, if nothing else. She looked at the other woman under the brim of her visor and willed her to take that risk.

As soon as she thought that, Bernice experienced a moment of self-knowledge accompanied by biting self-disgust. The money she was playing with meant nothing to her. It wasn't even hers. If she lost every penny of it, it would have no impact on her life whatsoever. But for all Bernice knew, this woman was playing with her life's savings. She could walk away from the table with literally nothing.

Still, when the woman sighed and pushed her stack of chips into the middle, Bernice felt a surge of elation she couldn't deny. Then the woman hesitated a moment, and pulled something else out of her pocket, a coin-sized lump of purple plastic that glimmered with engraved micro-circuitry. With a flick of her wrist she tossed it on to the pile of chips in the centre of the table.

One of the other players gasped.

'Winner can take that too,' the woman said.

Bernice studied it, but the little purple token gave nothing away. 'What is it?' she asked eventually.

The woman looked Bernice in the eye, suddenly seeming a lot calmer. 'Entry ticket to the Big Game Upstairs,' she said.

'What big game?' Bernice asked.

The woman smiled, showing perfect white teeth that looked at least thirty years younger than she was. 'Win, and you'll find out,' she said.

The Doctor stood on a balcony and looked down at the seething mass of people below. In his mind were equations that described completely the motion of these atomised individuals, that predicted where they would meet, merge, part.

The equations were nonsense. You couldn't understand people from a distance, the Doctor had learnt that long ago. You had to be up close, close enough to smell and taste them. And even then you wouldn't understand them – but at least you'd have learnt to like them, and that was far more important.

Shifting his hat to a more comfortable position on his head, the Doctor trotted down the stairs, following a discreet distance behind the two leggy cocktail waitresses who were circulating among the many guests, passing out free drinks, smiling, laughing – doing anything the guests wanted, just as long as they kept gambling.

The Doctor saw some of the gamblers reach out hands to grope and fondle the waitresses as they passed. They seemed oblivious to the fact that the women's faces were covered in large grey masks with huge almond-shaped black eyes. Aliens out of recurring nightmares and bad sci-fi. Or maybe the men did notice and didn't care. Maybe that was part of the appeal. This was an area of human interaction that no one claimed to have an equation to explain.

The waitresses bore the fondling with the patience of people who had been through it many times before and could comfort themselves with the thought that they would end the night richer, and the men would end the night bankrupt.

After a while, the waitresses began to drift towards a small door marked 'STAFF ONLY'. The Doctor drifted along after them. The door was key-coded, and the waitresses kept their back turned to the main chamber as they typed in their access number. The Doctor hung back as they slipped through and let the door thud shut behind them.

Then, when he was sure they would be out of sight, he typed in the same code and slipped in after them. Musical door keys, always a bad idea. Maybe they'd thought the ceaseless ringing and shouting and clattering and chatter of the casino floor would render the key presses inaudible. Maybe it did. The Doctor sometimes had a hard time remembering how blunt human senses were. No wonder they filled their lives with such a grand panoply of sensations, pleasant and unpleasant. So little time to squeeze so much in, and not even the sensory apparatus to appreciate what was there.

He ghosted along the corridor, footfalls smothered in thick carpet, softer than a whisper. There was a different smell here from the sweat-and-desperation miasma of the main floor. It was bitter, almost acrid – like the hint of an atmosphere that humans weren't meant to breathe.

It seemed to be coming from the door up ahead. The door was shut, but not fully. The Doctor crept forward, sticking to the wall, until his head was flush against the door and he could peer into the room through the open crack.

It was immediately apparent that this was a changing room. The waitresses he had seen earlier were here, leaning against the counter in a relaxed attitude, freed of the pressures of service. One of them turned to the other and said something in a language the Doctor couldn't understand. The other one threw back her head and laughed as she reached around herself to unzip her costume.

Somewhere, a catch in her neck was released, and the whole thing fell to the floor. The legs and body and pink curves that had so attracted the men on the casino floor fell away in a loose heap, exposing a skeletal grey body on which the great almond-eyed head clearly belonged.

'So,' the Doctor said softly to himself.

The purple token, Bernice discovered, gave her access to a lift tucked away at the back of the building. She pressed the token against the security panel in the door and when a voice blurted out of the speaker beside it, asking her to identify herself, she told it she was Vivienne Jones and that she was here for the Big Game Upstairs.

She hardly expected it to work but, after a moment, the lift doors slid open with the kind of quiet whoosh only something really expensive can manage, and she found herself stepping into a lift that was as large as most people's living rooms and far better decorated. Only the lurching sensation in her stomach told her when it was moving upwards. She stared at her feet, to avoid having to stare at herself in the gilded mirrors that lined all four of the walls. All the same, she couldn't help noticing the extra lines that had deepened at each side of her mouth and around her eyes. It's not the big troubles that get you, she thought, travelling with the Doctor. It's the drip-drip-drip of it all that wears you down.

Outside the lift were two black-suited men who could only be described as goons. By the look of it, they were carrying large semi-automatics under their jackets.

'Mrs Jones?' the larger one said, scratching a hand back through the wiry brown stubble on his head.

'Yep, that's me,' Bernice said. She smiled, hopefully winningly.

The two goons eyed her up and down for a moment, then turned their backs and walked away down the red-lined corridor. She assumed she was supposed to follow.

As she went, she became aware of cameras tucked into each corner, swivelling softly to follow as she moved. Eventually the goons reached a large brown door and took up guard positions on either side of it. When they saw her hesitate, one of them opened the door for her and gestured inside. This, she was beginning to realise, might not have been the world's best idea.

Still, too late to back out now, so she marched confidently in with her head held high in an attitude that she hoped conveyed the fact that she had every right to be there and was exactly who she said she was.

There was dead silence as she entered. It wasn't the sort of silence that had been there a long time. It was the sort that happened right after everyone stopped talking and turned to stare at the person who'd just walked into the room. It went on so long she had time to study each of the twelve people in the room twice.

Four, one in each corner, were like sleeker, more high-tech and definitely scarier versions of the goons outside. One was a dealer, a sharp-faced young woman wearing scraps of sequined clothing. The remaining seven were the other players. They were a mixed bunch but it was clear they all had one thing in common. Money.

'Thought you weren't coming,' one of them said, a lean, leathery man in his seventies. 'Thought you'd lost your nerve.'

She sat at the table in the one empty seat, and the man pushed a big stack of chips towards her. The highest denomination was marked with a hundred, which didn't seem right. She'd expected a game like this to be playing for far higher stakes. 'Hundred thousand, right?' she said, holding up a chip.

The man shrugged. 'Whatever.'

Bernice's throat dried till it felt like her tongue was welded to the roof of her mouth. She looked at the door, but it had been firmly shut behind her, and one of the four goons had moved to stand in front of it.

The man swept his eyes round the table. 'Well, shall we play?' he asked.

Bernice saw several of the other players swallow, but they all nodded. She hesitated a moment, then nodded too. What choice did she have?

Very soon after the competition began, Chris was wishing that he had put some money on the little guy. Each contestant started with a stack of ten hot dogs in front of them, and the whistle had barely blown before the man – whom Chris had discovered was called Jimmy Lilly, of all things – had polished them off. He didn't even seem to be pausing to chew.

'More,' he grunted to the judge beside him. Remarkably, there didn't seem to be a scrap of food left in his mouth when he said it.

His plate was piled high again, and again he polished it off. By Chris's reckoning, only two minutes had passed by this point and Jimmy didn't show any signs of slowing down. To either side of him, his fellow contestants were still struggling to finish their first plate. The air was heavy with the smell of sausage meat, mustard and vomit from one guy who hadn't been able to stand the pace.

'Told you so,' said the unshaven man, who'd introduced himself as Tom.

'How did you know?' Chris asked. In the time it took him to get out these words, Jimmy polished off two more sausages.

Tom smiled and tapped the side of his nose. 'Insider information.'

'What, you've been doping the other horses?' Chris joked.

Tom looked at him sharply, then grinned when he realised Chris was joking. 'Exact opposite, buddy.'

Chris would have asked what he meant but on stage, Jimmy had now polished off what must have been his fourth plate. 'More,' he said again. It was almost a snarl.

The judges looked helplessly at each other. They'd clearly run out. But the contestant beside Jimmy still had half a plate left, and after a moment Jimmy snatched the plate away and stuffed the sausages inside his mouth. They were gone in an instant.

Chris began to feel a tingle of unease. 'There's something wrong,' he said. 'That isn't natural.'

'He's just hyped up, got his eye on the prize,' Tom replied, but he didn't sound convinced.

Chris was half turned to listen to him, so he didn't get a close-up look at what happened next. All he got was an impression of sudden movement, a horrible choked scream, then a spray of warm, coppery blood in his face.

He had to wipe his eyes clean to see what had caused it: Jimmy's jaws clamped viciously around the hand of the contestant beside him. As Chris watched in horror, Jimmy's jaws tightened and he bit the hand clean off.

Bernice was losing – badly. This wasn't like the game downstairs at all. These were great players, every one of them, and they were playing like it was the most important game of their lives. Maybe it was. It was only because she'd been playing cautiously that she hadn't lost more, but every ante and every blind and double-blind ate away at her stack, and she knew that the only way to get money back was to play aggressively. Can't win if you don't take a risk, she thought.

At the moment, she was sitting on paired eights, while the flop was showing paired sevens and a jack. Two others were still in the pot, the leathery old-timer the others called Slim, and a twenty-something man who'd introduced himself as Chuck with flat, blue eyes and something unnatural about his face. Plastic surgery, she decided, and wondered if he was an actor. The others certainly seemed to defer to him in some strange way. Though maybe that was just because he was such a great player. She was pretty certain he was sitting on another jack right now.

She could try a bluff, of course, frighten the others out of the pot. She looked round, at the four goons with their expensive suits and suspicious bulges, and at the other players, tension written in the stiff lines of their bodies. She could risk all her chips – but would that be all she was risking?

The betting had come round to her. Five thousand to stay in. She could see Chuck staring intently at her, a small frown marring the smoothness of his forehead. He was impossible to read.

'Too rich for my blood,' she said, throwing her cards to the dealer.

The word 'blood' seemed to hang in the air, resonating slightly.

The scene in the atrium now resembled something out of a medieval painting of hell. There was blood *everywhere*. Not that Chris was sticking around to get a close look. When Jimmy had attacked the guy beside him, Chris's first instinct had been to run forward, save the man and get Jimmy under control.

But when he was still three feet from the stage, the man Jimmy was chomping on had suddenly stopped screaming. His face had slackened and his eyes had blanked out till his shape was the only human thing left about him. And then he'd shaken Jimmy casually away from the spurting stump of his arm, turned to the man beside him and taken a bite out of *him*. At that point, Chris decided to run.

So did every single other member of the ten-thousand-strong audience. Chris saw a woman trip as she joined the rush for the exit. She disappeared under a heaving mass of bodies and didn't reappear. Chris tried to go back and help her, he really did, but the press of bodies had an inertia and a will no one individual could resist, and its single-minded purpose was to get the hell out of there. Despite his best efforts, Chris was pushed inexorably away from the woman and towards the exit.

When that many people screamed at once, Chris discovered, it battered at the mind as much as the ears. We're still animals somewhere inside, he thought, programmed to respond to the sound of another of our kind in distress. The worst thing was when one of the screams would suddenly alter in pitch and he'd know that someone else had been caught by the ravening horde behind them, and that they would soon be one of them. He no longer knew how many of the people around him were fugitives, and how many were pursuers.

The room stank, of sweat and fear and the raw meat smell of the human carnage behind him. He had to get *out*. The imperative overrode all other thought, and, for a while, he was just a mindless thing pushing itself out of danger.

And then he realised that the crowd in front of him had stopped. He advanced a few steps further, but he was soon pushing against an immovable mass of flesh.

'The doors are locked!' he heard someone ahead of him scream. 'We're trapped!'

The words were repeated back and back through the crowd, like a hollow echo. Chris felt bile rise in his throat, and for a moment he experienced the terrible urge to turn round and throw himself *towards* the bloody horde, just so it would be over. But then he saw a corridor snaking away towards his left.

'This way!' he shouted out, and began to shoulder his way towards it. He was damned if he was going to die here, killed by a hot-dog-eating champion. It would be too damn humiliating.

The Doctor looked at the scenes playing out on the bank of monitors in front of him. Chris had taken charge, as the Doctor had calculated he would, and was leading the crowd down a narrow corridor that led away from the atrium and towards the main bulk of the casino. The Doctor could see, as Chris probably couldn't, that barely a hundred people remained uninfected by whatever it was that was spread by that terrible bite. As he watched, one of the horde grabbed a small woman at the rear of the crowd and that was another one gone.

The Doctor looked at the door control, the security override designed to seal the casino in case of robbery. It was in the 'closed' position. He had closed it. There was a millisecond's hesitation, then he slammed down the switch, locking it in place.

He couldn't let this thing get out to the streets of Vegas. At least here, in the casino, there was some chance it could be controlled.

On the screens, another man fell under the howling, bloodied pack.

Bernice could taste the saltiness of her own sweat as it sluiced off her cheeks, down the runnels beside her nose and into her mouth. This was a good hand, a great hand – and she'd bet a whole stack of chips on it.

Slim was in it with her, Joan the blue-rinse shark, and icy blonde Betty, though Bernice was sure she was playing a bluff. She licked the droplets of sweat from her upper lip and squeezed up the corner of her cards again. An ace-king, suited. She was sure this was the winning hand.

Somewhere, vaguely, she could hear a faint thin sound that might have been distant screams. She tuned them out. She needed all her concentration for the game.

The casino was very much like a maze, though the Doctor had discovered that always taking the left-hand turn didn't produce a way through it. Eventually, though, he found what he was looking for: the entrance that led to the heart of the place, its nerve centre. And, no doubt, the cause of the screams that still rang in his ears.

Guarding the door were two pleasant-looking, blond-haired young men whose eyes studied him and saw nothing inside.

'There's no entry this way, sir,' one of them said, shifting subtly so that his body fully blocked the doorway.

'That's funny,' the Doctor said, 'that definitely looks like a door.'

'It is a door, sir,' the other said patiently, as if unused to sarcasm, or perhaps all too used to morons. 'I'm afraid it's off limits to guests.'

'Oh, well,' the Doctor said, and wandered vaguely away down the dimly lit corridor.

As soon as he was out of the sight of the men, he stopped. There was a camera scanning the area from one corner, a little red light blinking on and off as it watched. The Doctor tossed his hat casually to cover it. Then he began planning how to get past the guards.

Chris was at the front now, somehow elected leader by default. He would have liked to think it was because of his natural authority, but suspected it had more to do with the fact that he was taller than everyone else and had a louder voice.

The whole place was like a funfair maze – complete with tacky decor and piped screams. But finally, finally, he could see the corridor up ahead opening out into a broader, better-lit space. He forced legs that were wobbly with fear and fatigue to push him a few steps further, flicking backwards glances to make sure the other survivors were still with him.

They were, but there were fewer than fifty of them now. Of their pursuers, there was no sign. They'd been slamming doors shut behind them as they ran, wedging them with hostess trolleys and giant statues of insect-eyed aliens and whatever else came to hand. It didn't seem to stop their pursuers, but at least it slowed them down. Chris reckoned they had a few minutes' grace, during which he intended to come up with an actual plan rather than just run blindly in who knew what direction.

That all flew out the window when he realised that the room they'd just run into was the main floor of the casino. And that it wasn't empty. The poker and roulette tables seemed to have cleared. No doubt the croupiers had heard the screams and decided that minimum wage only bought you so much dedication. But sitting at the fruit machines were row after row of people.

For a moment, Chris didn't register the fact that they were human. There was something about the way they sat – buckets of coins beside them, feeding one in at a time, pulling the lever, watching the little numbers and figures spin round and round then scooping up the occasional win and dropping it straight back into the bucket – that was as mechanical and joyless as the machines themselves.

He ran up to the nearest, a middle-aged woman who looked like your best friend's mother when you were in school, and pulled on her arm.

'What do you want?' she said, never taking her eyes off the machine, never stopping feeding in coins.

'You've got to get out of here,' he told her.

'Just one more minute,' she said, her voice flat. 'I should be on to a big win soon.'

'There's no time!' Chris shouted. 'If you don't come now, you're going to die.'

'Just one more minute,' she repeated, and Chris gave up and ran on to the next man. This one he didn't bother speaking to, he just dragged him bodily away from the machine.

'What are you doing?' the man shouted.

'I'm saving your god-damn life!' Chris shouted back, but the man was a dead weight in his arms and he could already hear the sound of banging on the door they'd shut behind them, the danger closing in on them.

'Come on!' Chris shouted. The man looked at him, uncomprehending.

Giving up, Chris pelted towards the far corner of the vast chamber, all chances of an orderly retreat now gone. The other survivors pelted after him, though what they thought he could do for them he couldn't imagine. A few of the fruit machine players came too, but not very many.

It was a horrible place to run through, like an obstacle course composed of flashing lights and green baize. After a moment, he realised it would be quicker to run *over* the tables than round them and so he vaulted on to the nearest, the plastic markers crunching beneath his boots as he sprinted across it and on to the next surface. This was a roulette wheel, and he nearly lost his balance as it spun under his feet. At the last minute, he turned the topple into a leap and made it on to the next table, a long thin affair covered in dice. He had his pace now, leaping and landing almost fluidly. Behind him, his fellow survivors were following in his footsteps. One of them didn't have quite his stride though, and Chris saw him wobble precariously on one end of a table, then topple over backwards.

There was no time to go back and help him, not without endangering everyone else. When he was only halfway across, he heard the door give and the deep-throated roar of those who were following as they caught the scent of their prey. He thought they were finished then. The infected people moved horribly fast. But when he risked a look back, he saw that something had delayed them. They had found the people at the fruit machines.

Swallowing the bile in his throat and closing his ears to the gurgling cries for help, he focused on rescuing those who could be rescued.

In the end, the Doctor didn't have to do anything to get past the guards except wait. When the end of their shift came, their replacements failed to show up. It wasn't hard for the Doctor to guess why, but the guards seemed ignorant of the slaughter that was going on downstairs and decided that their comrades were merely shirking.

They waited an extra five minutes then shrugged and headed for the exit. As soon as they were off duty it was as if someone flipped a switch inside them, turning their humanity back on. One of them made a joke and the other laughed, throwing his head back in a carelessly happy gesture. The Doctor suddenly realised how young they were.

They walked straight past him but gave him only the most cursory of glances, even though it must be obvious he was loitering with intent. Clearly they weren't people to take their work home with them. He tutted to himself. You just couldn't get the same quality of mindless goon these days.

As soon as they were gone, he crept up to the door and started working on the lock. This was a less easy matter. The technology buried inside the simple keypad had never been invented on Earth and wasn't a type he recognised. It took him a whole minute to disable it.

He squared his shoulders as the door opened, tugging down the rumpled hem of his jacket, ready to face whatever was waiting for him.

The room was dark, but in the gloom he could make out more of the almond-eyed aliens he had seen earlier. They were clustered around something in the middle of the room, chattering and he thought laughing in their own unknown language. He allowed his hands to drop and drifted forward over the strange rubbery surface of the floor.

As he got nearer, he saw that they were eating, the table piled high with steaks and fries and cooked tomatoes, the staples of a standard American meal. The aliens were tucking into it with gusto.

'I'm sorry, is this a bad time?' he said loudly.

About twenty smooth grey heads snapped round to look at him. Unexpectedly, they all took a step back – as if *he* frightened *them*.

'I wouldn't normally interrupt,' he continued, 'but I couldn't help noticing that a lot of people are dying downstairs and I thought that perhaps you might be able to do something about it.'

'What are you doing here?' one of them finally asked. Bizarrely, the voice emerging from that unhuman head spoke in a deep Midwestern accent.

'I've come to tell you to take off,' the Doctor said.

'Take off,' another echoed.

'We're eating,' said a third, this one with a Southern twang. 'Please leave.'

'Of course, of course,' the Doctor said, nodding. Then he shook his head. 'I'll be very happy to go, just as soon as you remove your spaceship from this planet and take whatever disease you've unleashed downstairs with you before anyone else gets infected.'

'Spaceship?' another of them repeated. The Doctor began to wonder if their command of English was only an illusion. If their minds actually worked in such different ways that he only *thought* he was communicating with them, when really they were throwing ideas at each other that could find no purchase on the other person's world view.

'This spaceship,' he told them.

'But this is a casino,' the creature said, slowly, as if it thought he might be very stupid. 'It only looks like a spaceship.'

The Doctor smiled, but his smile slipped as he realised the creature wasn't joking.

Bernice had gone all-in, pushing all her chips into the pot in a reckless gesture that sent simultaneous shivers of fear and excitement down her back. She was quite sure by now that this game had nothing to do with money, which meant she had no idea what she might be about to lose. But she almost might be about to win whatever it was, and that tantalising prospect was the dominant thought in her mind.

Joan had gone all-in too. They both flipped up their cards at the same time. Bernice felt her heart lurch as the saw the other woman's: a pair of aces. With four cards on the table, one a king and one an ace, that meant that Bernice had two pair – but Joan had three of a kind. Unless Bernice could pick up a king on the final card, she'd lost. Then Chuck flicked over his cards and she saw that he had queen-jack. If he picked up a ten, he'd have a straight and beat them both. His expressionless eyes looked into hers, like mirrors that reflected nothing back at her except her own fears.

She felt the intense pressure of the other players' gazes on her, the ones who'd had the sense to get out of this hand early. There was something almost vulture-like about it, carrion eaters circling, waiting for the weakening animal to drop dead.

The pretty girl dealing the cards reached for the top one, moving slowly as if she enjoyed drawing out the drama of the moment. She smiled slightly at Chuck as she flicked it over. It landed on the table with the softest of whispers, but in Bernice's head it echoed louder than her heartbeat.

It was a king.

Bernice had won.

The surge of elation that swept through her was so strong she almost thought she might pass out. In her youth she'd taken drugs which didn't feel this good. She'd always despised bad winners, but she couldn't suppress the grin of triumph that seized her face.

Only after a second did she register the look on Joan's face. The fear. Because Joan had also gone all-in, and poker was a zero-sum game. Very slowly, Joan stood up from the table. Bernice saw her throat jump as she swallowed convulsively once, then again.

'Thank you for the game,' Bernice said, through a suddenly dry throat.

Joan didn't say anything. She just walked slowly towards the door. One of the goons took her arm as she passed, and Bernice saw from the strain on his face that Joan was resting most of her weight on him, as if she'd suddenly lost all strength in her body.

Leading her like an invalid, the goon took her out of the room, and the door swung shut behind him with a terminal thump. Every single person in the room stared at the door.

Bernice felt the smile slip from her face. She didn't want to think, didn't want to know, what she'd just done.

'We've heard of you, Doctor,' the alien said. 'We thought one day you might come for us. Before you do, hear our story.' The small mouth in its domed grey head twisted into an expression that might have been a smile.

'I'm all ears,' the Doctor told it.

The alien nodded, its too heavy head flopping on its thin neck. 'We lost our ship,' it said. 'We lost everything when we crashed in the desert near here in 1947.'

'Yes, yes, of course,' the Doctor said. 'The ship was destroyed?'

'Disabled. But it was all we had. It was all we had to sell to buy ourselves protection.'

The aliens sat in a ring around him. Their big, black eyes reflected him back at himself, distorted and strange, like an evil alter ego. They seemed... friendly, almost, but also wary.

'So you sold it to the government,' the Doctor said, but the aliens were shaking their heads even as he said it.

'How could we?' one asked. 'They wouldn't have been satisfied with the ship. They would have wanted us too. We needed someone who needed us. Someone who could act as an intermediary, sell the ship on to the government without revealing where it came from.'

The Doctor scratched a hand back through his hair. Dates, names, faces flitted through his consciousness, a jigsaw with a million pieces and all of them blank. But then, in a moment, they snapped into place. 'Bugsy Siegel,' he said. When the gangster who founded Las Vegas opened the Flamingo Casino there just after the War, it had been a disaster, bleeding his money into the parched desert sand. Then, suddenly, in 1947 it had all turned around.

There was a murmur of surprise or perhaps pleasure from the surrounding beings. 'And then, a few months later, he was shot and killed,' the Doctor murmured.

'Yes,' one of the aliens said, its voice ringing on a note of regret. 'Killed for our secrets, but he took them to his grave.'

'So here we were, in a desert so alien to our own home it took us five years to find a serum that allowed us to prosper in your atmosphere, to live a life at this temperature and at the humans'... excessive speed. And by then we were deeply in debt. We couldn't turn to the government, so we turned to the mob.' The others all nodded. Like many other peoples, both primitive and more advanced, the tale of their own history held a special power for them.

'Not so much alien invaders as alien illegal immigrants,' the Doctor said.

'Yes, yes,' the one with the Southern twang, who seemed to be their leader, said. 'But like many other illegal immigrants who came to this land, eventually we prospered.'

The Doctor glanced around at them, their shadowed, gleaming eyes and the grey skeletal forms of their bodies. 'But at what price?'

The alien shrugged, a totally human gesture. 'On our home world, we would have lived many hundreds of years. To survive here, by taking the serum – we can hope for no more than a human lifespan. It eats us up from the inside.'

The Doctor squinted at them, suspicious. 'But still you've stayed. Why?'

'Why?' their leader said, his voice high-pitched with disbelief. '*Why?* Because we could have lived our old slow lives, as bland as ice, but we wanted an existence with some flavour. We have seen this town grow from desert dust to the greatest resort on the planet. We've talked with kings and dealt with gangsters, and we've started at the bottom and risen to the top. Have you seen our new home, Doctor? Have you seen this place we've built with nothing but our own work?'

The Doctor blinked round at them, understanding. 'The American dream,' he said.

Finally, the alien leader's expression shifted into something that definitely was a smile. 'Live fast, die young, leave a beautiful corpse.'

It was the buffet that saved them. The infected were closing in on them too fast, but then Chris saw something out of the corner of his eye and, without even fully registering what it was, he swerved in that direction. There were only six other people with him now. He was faintly surprised to see that one of them was Tom, the man who had advised him to bet on the little guy. He let out a dry, painful chuckle as he remembered.

The swerve took him into another vast room and as soon as he entered it he knew what had drawn him here. The tables were heaving under a mound of food. Every food group, every country, every letter of the alphabet seemed to be covered, from avocados to zabaglione. It was the hotel's complimentary breakfast, but in any sane world it could have fed a small continent.

The infected humans fell on it with the same enthusiasm with which they'd earlier fed on flesh and bone. In the small amount of time that gave him, Chris saw a steel door and led his band of followers through it.

Even so, the food was finished before they were all through, and a second after he'd slammed and bolted the door shut after the last of his party he saw a drop of blood dripping down from a bite mark on her arm and a feral light growing in her eyes and he knew that things were about to go very bad very quickly.

Before he could even think about it, he went to the nearest table and, using a strength he didn't know he possessed, he tipped it up and on to the woman. She shrieked – a high, thin sound that pierced his ears and made all the hair on his arms stand to attention.

He didn't care. She was down, that was all that mattered. Except that she wasn't staying down. Astonishingly, the table began to lift. It was solid steel, it shouldn't have been happening, but somehow it was. Chris leapt on to the underside, right over the woman's chest, and still it carried on lifting.

'Help me!' he shouted out to the others.

They didn't move. He could see that they were on the point of turning tail and leaving him to it.

'She's faster than you. You'll never get away,' Chris said.

At that, finally, they moved, flinging themselves on to the table beside him. It heaved again then – mercifully – sank back down, allowing Chris to finally get an up-close-and-personal look at one of the infected humans.

Her eyes were bulging in her face, her mouth twisted into a mindless snarl of rage. The veins stood out all over her neck, so thick and ropy they looked like a vine growing beneath her skin. But the thing that struck him most of all was the heat. It radiated from her like a small furnace. She pushed up against the table again, but this time her arms seemed to fail, and her shrieking turned into a low keening, every bit as horrible but also somehow pitiable, too.

She was getting weaker. She was, Chris realised, getting smaller as well. The flesh seemed to be melting away from her bones, consumed by that unnatural internal fire. *She's eating herself up from the inside*, he realised, *consuming her own flesh to give her this terrible strength. No wonder they're so hungry. Their metabolism must be running at hundreds of times the normal human rate.* For the first time he began to consider what this infection could be.

'*Doping the other horses?*' Chris had asked, and Tom had told him it was the exact opposite.

He felt a terrible rage growing inside him.

By now, the woman trapped beneath the table had been reduced to a skeleton lightly hung with strips of skin.

Chris turned from her to Tom, whose unshaven face he now saw was twisted with guilt as well as fear.

There were only two of them left now. Bernice and the handsome man called Chuck. Chuck was winning; she could barely see him behind his stack of chips. Not that she'd been able to read him all night anyway. His face was like a mask.

She only had a jack-ten but she had no choice. She pushed all her chips into the middle, noticing that her hands shook as she did. All four goons had closed in round the table, engrossed in the action. Or perhaps they just wanted to make sure that she couldn't escape whatever fate was waiting for her when she lost this hand.

Chuck's mouth assumed its first real expression, a sharklike smile of triumph as he flipped over his own cards. A pair of aces.

Bernice was terrified. The terror sharpened all her senses. Her eyesight, so that she became very conscious of the slight line running down the hairline of Chuck's head, as if his whole face really was a mask that could be pulled off in one quick gesture. Her smell, so she realised that there was a faintly acrid odour in the room that seemed to be emanating from her fellow player. And hearing. She could hear the rasp of her own breathing – and of Chuck's.

'Well, this is all very fascinating and possibly salutary,' the Doctor said, 'but now it's time for you to give me the cure for the virus you're spreading.'

'What virus?' the alien leader said.

The Doctor had never met this species before, had no chance to learn the subtle physical and vocal cues that revealed the true thoughts and intentions of a speaker. But despite this, he knew it wasn't lying.

'What virus?' Tom said to Chris, but Chris could tell he was lying. His eyes kept flicking left-right, left-right, as if they were physically sliding off Chris's face.

Chris didn't have the patience. He grabbed Tom by the throat and shook him hard. 'What. Did. You. Give. To. Jimmy?' he asked, a shake on each word.

Tom looked more startled than afraid, as if he couldn't quite believe that anyone would dare to treat him this way. But he said, 'Hey, buddy, it wasn't me!'

'If it wasn't you, then who was it?' Chris demanded, stopping the shaking but keeping an iron grip on Tom's throat. 'And more importantly, what was it?'

'It was a... a friend of ours,' Tom said.

'What friend?' Chris shouted, shaking him again.

Though his teeth were rattling in his head, Tom managed to throw him a look of contempt, as if he couldn't quite believe he was this stupid. 'The mob,' he said with forced patience, when Chris stopped shaking him. 'The Mafia. The people who run this place owe them, they do them favours. Like, let them hold the competition here, or a poker game that isn't strictly kosher.'

'And what about this?' Chris demanded. 'What kind of favour was this?'

'It was just a scam, to fix the competition. We didn't know, I mean, how could we know, that this would happen?'

The remaining five survivors gathered round, staring at Tom with expressions that began as shocked and quickly transmuted into lethally furious. One, a big, bearded Midwesterner called Ben, looked on the point of homicide. Chris carefully interposed himself between the two men. Ben was welcome to kill Tom – *after* he'd told them all about the virus.

'So what is it?' Chris asked him.

But Tom shook his head. 'All I know is we got it from one of the owners of this place. He needed money as a stake in the big poker game, and he didn't want the other owners to know about it.'

'The virus isn't from Earth. It's extraterrestrial,' the Doctor said. 'If it looks like a dog, and barks like a dog...'

'But why would we do that?' the alien leader asked. 'Dead men don't gamble.'

The Doctor shook his head. 'Origin and intent are two different things.'

The alien leader shook his head too, even more forcefully. 'Impossible. We don't make viruses, we make money.'

The Doctor smiled, very slightly. 'So tell me again about the serum that speeds up your metabolism so you can survive on Earth...'

The aliens all went very still. Then one of them rushed to a small cupboard in the corner of the room. 'Gone,' he said, looking inside. 'Two vials.'

The alien leader's mouth twisted up in a suddenly very human expression of annoyance. 'How can this be? No one but us has access here!' In a sudden gesture of fury, he swept his arm over the table, scattering the fine china plates and crystal glasses to bounce dully on the rubber floor. That was a very human gesture too.

After a moment he calmed himself, and turned to the Doctor. 'I'm very sorry, we have no idea how this happened. But I don't think there's anything to be done now except wait for it to run its course. Contained here, the casualties should at least be limited.'

'You think it can be contained?' the Doctor asked. 'You think the doors will hold when the infected ones get hungry enough?'

The mottled skin of the alien paled from steel grey to white gold. 'No, no, that can't happen. That would destroy everything.'

The Doctor had opened his mouth to reply when his eyes were caught by something else, the flicker of a video monitor tucked into one corner of the room. 'What on earth is she doing?'

The aliens flicked their eyes to the screens, where two poker players were hunched over a table. The woman's face was beaded with sweat and taut with intense concentration. The man's was as blank as a mask. 'What on earth is he doing?' the leader asked.

The Doctor looked at him, then at the screen, another thousand-piece jigsaw snapping into place.

Bernice realised that she had to know. No matter how bad it was, it had to be better than all the things she was imagining. She'd clawed back Chuck's lead and, by her reckoning, their chips were now pretty much dead even. Now she had a hand she could go all-in on, decide the game on the two cards she was holding, a queen-jack of spades. End it, finally.

'Before I bet,' she said, 'you have to tell me what it is we're playing for.'

Chuck screwed his eyes tight as he inspected her, clearly suspecting this was some ploy. 'If you didn't know, you wouldn't be here,' he said.

Bernice grinned, but she knew that above the grin her eyes were wild. 'That would probably be true, except that I'm not the person who agreed to play here.'

She saw one of the goons looking at her pityingly, as if believing that she'd cracked under the pressure.

'No, really,' she said. 'I won the entry ticket.'

There was a subtle shift in the atmosphere of the room, a tension so palpable it seemed to physically thicken the air. Behind her, she felt one of the goons shift, and she knew his hand was drifting nearer to the gun that bulged out the jacket of his sharply pressed suit. The dealer, so impassive during the rest of the game, flicked sharp, startled eyes to her before dropping them back down to her card-sharp-fast hands.

'That's... unfortunate,' one of the goons said and Bernice realised for the first time that he was their leader, perhaps the man who had organised the whole game.

Bernice shook her head. 'Look, I could ask to be let out, and you'd tell me that it's too late and that by coming here I'd agreed to take part, and then I'd argue that that wasn't fair, and you'd tell me life wasn't fair and we could have a whole dull conversation about it, but I know you're not going to let me back out. All I want to know is what exactly it is I'm going to be forced to carry on playing for.'

The leader of the goons studied her closely, with a poker face more inscrutable, and a lot more frightening, than any she'd seen round the table that night. Eventually, he said, 'Sweetheart, you're playing for exactly what you think you're playing for.'

'Biggest stakes of all,' said another of the goons. He made a slashing gesture with a finger across his own throat, then grinned a feral smile at her.

Bernice nodded, light-headed with an emotion she couldn't distinguish between fear or relief or excitement. 'And what do I get if I win?'

Now Chuck looked up at her, his head twisting in a way no human should have been able to manage. 'You get to live.'

Bernice hesitated, just for a second, then pushed all her chips into the centre. 'Then I'm all-in,' she said.

Chris and the eight other remaining survivors huddled together in a corner of the echoing metal-lined room, arms wrapped around one another in an inappropriate gesture of intimacy. Even Tom was included, though Chris could see that the arms around him were white with tension, the fingers digging woundingly into his flesh.

Finally given a second's grace to come up with a plan, Chris had realised that the huge freezer at the back of the kitchen was the safest place for them to be. The metal doors were inches thick, enough to hold the infected hordes at least for a little while. And even if they broke down the doors, the cold might succeed in cooling down their lethal fever, perhaps even cure them, though Chris doubted that.

Of course, it wasn't an *escape* plan. It entirely depended on someone – and by someone, Chris meant the Doctor – coming to rescue them before the doors gave way.

He could hear the banging and the clawing on them now. And the muffled cries of rage or hunger from outside. Beside him, a young woman of twenty shivered, and snuggled tighter into his arm.

Come on, Doctor, he thought. Come on.

The game was finished. Bernice looked down at her cards, still not quite believing it. The one-eyed jack seemed to wink up at her. She looked at Chuck. 'I'm sorry,' she meant to say. But instead she just said, 'Why?'

It was the Doctor who answered, framed in the doorway like the answer to a prayer, though not necessarily hers. 'Because he needed the money for this game, and the only thing he had which the... organisers wanted was the serum. He couldn't ask his own people for the money because they wouldn't have let him play such a foolish game.' The Doctor's eyes looked into Bernice's, unaccusingly. Then they wandered back to Chuck.

'And he didn't really care what the serum would do if a human took it.'

Bernice looked at him, utterly baffled, then turned back to Chuck, just in time to see him reach behind his neck, flick some kind of catch – and peel away his human skin. The grey-skinned alien beneath blinked at her with huge black eyes more full of human expression than the blank blue eyes of Chuck had ever been. The goons didn't seem terribly surprised. They'd clearly known all along what one of their players was. 'The way you played, I thought you understood,' the alien said, still in the same soft voice. 'If you can afford to lose what you bet, you aren't playing properly.'

'But your *life*?'

'It was worth it.' There was a slight shake in his voice, but Bernice didn't think this was merely false bravura. He meant it. And she *did* understand.

'To you,' the Doctor said. 'The serum has spread through the humans like a plague.'

'I'm sorry,' the alien which had once been called Chuck said. 'If there was anything I could do...'

The Doctor just looked at him, his eyes filled with ice.

Bernice watched it all on one of the aliens' monitors, the aliens themselves crowded around her, very silent – witnessing something they hadn't seen since they'd come to this planet, she guessed. The death of one of their own.

Chuck – she still thought of him as that – took the same lift down that she'd taken up. He looked very frail, his too heavy head swaying on his spindly neck as the lift decelerated. There were no goons with him – when he'd understood what the Doctor wanted, he'd gone willingly.

It took him a while to find his way to the kitchen, where the infected humans were. Bernice saw that they were clustered round one wall, scratching at the metal surface of a large door. The Doctor had said that nearly ten thousand people had been infected, but far fewer of them were left now. She didn't like to think what had happened to the rest.

She couldn't believe how strong they were. Their fingers left deep gouges in the solid metal. The Doctor had told her that Chris was inside there, and she felt a horrible apprehension as she saw how far into the door the victims of the serum had dug, and she imagined what they might do to anyone they found inside.

But then Chuck arrived. Even in the grainy image of the surveillance camera, she saw him take a deep breath before striding purposefully into the room.

She looked away when the infected humans began to feed on him, to find the Doctor watching her.

'It's the only cure,' he said. 'The enzymes in his body will counteract the serum.'

'I know,' Bernice replied, but she still couldn't watch it.

Chris emerged to find that it was all over. The Doctor and Bernice were waiting for him, along with a bunch of grey-skinned aliens who looked like some ice-planet dwellers he'd met once from the outer fringes of the Empire. Surrounding them were the infected humans. He knew they must be, because their mouths and hands were smeared with blood, but the mad fire had gone from their eyes. Instead they were filled with bafflement and a dawning horrified realisation.

'You have memory-erasing technology?' the Doctor said to one of the grey aliens.

The alien blinked. 'How did you know?'

'Word gets around. For your sake, and theirs, I suggest you help these people forget what they've done or seen.'

The alien nodded and, without a backward glance, the Doctor led Chris and Bernice out, away from the remnants of the carnage.

'Is anyone going to explain anything?' Chris asked after they'd exited the casino and walked halfway back to the TARDIS without anyone saying a word. 'I mean, I have just spent the last few hours pursued by flesh-eating zombies and I'd quite like to know why.'

The Doctor looked at Bernice, who looked back at him with shadowed eyes.

'Because of a poker game,' the Doctor said.

Conclusion

The Doctor watched from a window as eight people walked away from the facility, little bowed by the terrible conditions outside. First, most eager, was the fat king. He hugged his skinny little wife to him as he hurried away, desperate to be off, shouting out words the Doctor couldn't hear. But the gleam in his eye was discernable even across the distance.

A serene-looking General Candy followed. She had an arm round the beautiful scarlet-clad woman, seemed to be comforting her, speaking words of peace and calm and hope. The vampire, for her part, walked as if in a daze, as if a great happiness had descended upon her and she could scarcely bear to think of it for fear it would vanish like a dream.

The moustached man had held back to let the others leave first, but now could be seen talking to the dumpy little financier, head bent deferentially to hear what she was saying. For her part, she was gesturing eagerly at the beauties that surrounded them: trees, birds, flowers, as if she'd never seen such delights before.

Only the good-looking chef seemed less than happy. His face seemed wan despite the tan, and he was hugging his arms to his chest. The moustached man had begun to offer round something from a paper bag: sweets or chocolates. The chef turned from him with a shudder.

The Doctor was happiest of all to see that the Time Lord was no longer stooping, was holding his head high. Had a spring in his step. Was smiling.

And when he had watched everyone leave, when he knew everyone was safe, he wandered off into the room he'd fashioned as a classroom, and sat down to wait.

It was some time before the Overseers arrived.

He'd convinced them he needed to be free to work in his own way. He had his own base in the facility, and he hadn't wanted them around, because however much he had to do this, he didn't have to like it, didn't want them looking over his shoulder.

And because he'd made a promise, and they'd made a threat, and because he was surrounded by their technology and their cloned Monitors, and because they thought the machine was indestructible, they'd let him work like that.

They were angry when they arrived, full of thwarted pride. The Doctor found that wryly amusing.

'The transmissions have stopped!' Penser growled, advancing on him.

'We've received no reports from our Monitors!' said another Overseer.

'Ah, no,' replied the Doctor, answering the second question first. 'Rather luckily, someone's just liberated them all. One of today's customers had strong – if now somewhat more humble – views on the subjugation of genetically engineered beings. He persuaded them they didn't have to serve you any more. They only stayed around long enough to help me finish my work.'

'Treachery!' cried Penser.

'Independence!' said the Doctor.

'We are referring to you,' said a third Overseer. 'This is treachery. You gave us your word. You would become master of the machine.'

The Doctor looked sheepish. 'I broke my word,' he said. 'I'm a bad man.'

'Then you will suffer the consequences,' he was told.

But the Doctor did not seem particularly concerned. 'You mean to tell me you will carry out your threat? That you will create misery wherever I tread unless I man your despicable machine for you?' He leaned back in his chair and crossed his legs.

He was surrounded by aliens who wanted to destroy his life and the lives of everyone he met – if they didn't destroy him there and then – and yet he did not even seem worried enough to stand and face them.

'I'm terribly sorry, though – I can't do that even if I wanted to.' Suddenly, he grinned. 'You'll never believe this, but I've only gone and destroyed your machine.'

There was a collective gasp, quickly stifled as the Overseers hastened to regain their dignity. Two hurried from the room. 'I'm not lying,' the Doctor called after them.

'You must be,' said Penser. 'The machine was indestructible!'

'Oh, indestructible, my foot!' said the Doctor. 'If a machine is created, it can be destroyed. And a computer more so than anything. How many supposedly indestructible machines have juddered themselves to death over a trivial bit of "the next thing I tell you will be the truth, but the last thing I told you was a lie"?' He frowned. 'I did try that on this one, but unfortunately it didn't work.'

He gestured at the semicircle of orange plastic chairs, inviting them each to take a seat. 'No? I'm going to explain everything; you might as well be comfortable.' He leaned over and prodded the hard seat of the chair next to him. 'Well, comfortable... ish.'

Failing to get a response, he continued. 'Anyway, I got to thinking. What would cause a machine full of misery to pull out its plugs and go to meet the great technician in the sky? A payload of happiness? Nope. An overdose of tragedy? Well, that seemed more plausible. But it was designed to suck in such vast amounts it seemed hopeless.

'And then I realised. Everything the misery machine captured grew from one or more of seven initial roots.' He jumped up, began to scribble on a blackboard. 'Sloth. Wrath. Envy. Lust. Pride. Avarice. Gluttony.' He underlined each word. 'These were the things that caused misery throughout the universe; these were things that made up the machine. And as Dante demonstrated, there was not one of them that could not be overcome, on the terraces of Purgatoria. No sinner cannot be redeemed.'

He drew a simple rectangle and wrote under it 'machine'. With swift downwards strokes, he divided it into seven sections.

'A simple overload wouldn't do it, but maybe if I could blow the circuits one by one... And perhaps I could redeem some sinners at the same time.

'I searched the lists of clients, put out feelers towards the sort of people I particularly wanted. They had to want the sort of service you – we – provided, but it had to go further than that. They must feel nothing – except one emotion. And that emotion had to rule them, had to be supreme in them, had to be all-consuming.'

'Then I selected events from my past that were particularly apt, where misery was created by each of those emotions. Each of those "sins". You had already done the groundwork. There were thousands of little bits of my life in your library, all there for the viewing pleasure of your sick clients. Easy to find appropriate ones.'

He drew a little circle above each of the seven sections; gave them hair or crowns or grumpy faces: the seven clients.

'I created a state whereby each client was taken to the limits of their vice – and then hooked up to the machine. They would feed from the misery therein. The machine would feed from the misery in them.' A line from the circle to the rectangle. From the rectangle to the circle. And another, and another, a fast scribble obscuring everything else on the board. 'Round and round and round and round, until it was more than man or machine could bear. And so... kaplooie. Seven lots of kaplooie, in fact. And a complete overload. Nothing left at all.'

On the chalkboard, he drew a big jagged star that took in the whole of the scribbled diagram. Under it he wrote: 'BOOM!'

Then he sat down again. The Overseers who had left earlier now returned. 'It is true,' said one. 'The Monitors are gone. The machine is destroyed.'

'Told you so,' said the Doctor.

Penser stepped forward. 'Then you have broken our agreement. And you must face the consequences.'

The Doctor yawned. 'Yes,' he said, 'you could pursue me for the rest of my lives, creating misery wherever you – wherever I – go. You could do that. Yes. Wouldn't serve much purpose, without the machine, but I understand that your wrath – your pride – demand revenge.'

He pulled out a sheaf of papers – contracts – from his pocket, and held them out to Penser.

'But it might be an idea to remind yourselves of just who your clients were for my Purgatoria project.

'King Loesin of Granneth. A man who was once so lazy he wouldn't move from his chair to save the lives of himself and everyone around him. He might be a bit busy for a while putting his kingdom to rights, but he does have a kingdom, he does have a lot of money, he does – now – have a lot of excess energy, and he does have a wife who is prepared to do just about anything to sort things out.

'General Candy, who, between you and me, is going to be a bit more sugary sweet from now on. Appalling temper, she had. Worried me a bit, that one, didn't want her blowing up the whole planet in a fit of rage... Wouldn't take much to wind her up, though, just a couple of minor, everyday niggles and she was ready to explode... Anyway, the anger might have pushed her on, but it wasn't responsible for her superb strategic brain and supreme courage. She is going to be even more formidable from now on, if you ask me, and that's saying something. She also has the military might of an entire solar system at her command.

'Tebediatroculozan. A Time Lord, like myself. Well, not so very like myself, if you want to be picky. He is a member of one of the richest and most powerful houses, and is one of the cleverest minds of our generation – far cleverer than me. But he allowed himself to be swallowed whole by envy. He wasn't content to be clever, he was desperate for so much more. He wanted to be the one stories revolved round, the centre of it all. He could have been great, but he was crippled by his discontent, gradually sinking into decay, feeling nothing. Now he's been freed from that. And I think he'll fulfil his potential at last. A future Lord President of Gallifrey, even, perhaps.

'Fiorla, the Vampire Queen. Once, she was entirely ruled by blood lust, and her whole planet was pacified to feed that lust. Now, I'll help her with a synthetic mix that will sustain her – well, let's call it her life, for want of a better word – and she'll no longer be a slave to her bodily desires, which means her people will no longer be slaves to her. Everyone's going to be a lot happier, but nevertheless, she will still have an entire planet at her command, and that's quite impressive, as I'm sure you'll agree.

'Pooh-bah. His very name means pride. Engineered to be proud through and through.' He looked angry for a moment. 'What price free will there? It's my hope that he should have a character now, rather than just *being* a character. He has command of all the poor creatures like himself. And now he'll be willing to deal with the humans, who knows? But I wouldn't be surprised if his power base grows.

'Miss Tabitha Dunhut has a flare for finance, but no longer a passion for profits. Whole economies are in her hands. She could ruin anyone – any organisation – as easy as winking.

'And Gilbert Fleshman, the King of Cuisine. Worshipped by housewives everywhere. Under that rugged exterior beat the heart of a callow youth. Several callow youths, in fact. That won't happen any more. He has considerable influence over the media, and via the media, although whether he'll care to use it any more is another matter.

'Every single one of them has shown they can endure whatever misery you care to throw at them. Oh, and they all also have riches beyond the dreams of avarice, and both you and I have seen for ourselves what avarice dreams of. Now they have no – shall we say, sinful? – whatnots eating up all their cash, they've got plenty to spend on other things. And, quite frankly, most of them are currently – and it's a bit embarrassing – thinking of me as their saviour and you as the big bad villain. So that's me with seven really, *really* powerful people, and by extension their companies, their vast networks, their planets, and all Rabbit's friends and relations, on my side, and no one at all on yours. Which means I walk out of here, safe, and you keep out of my way for ever.

'Just thought I'd mention it.'

He walked up to Penser, and jabbed an index finger in his face.

'You thought misery was so much fun. Now you'll have a chance to find out at first hand, without your machine, without the wealth and power and influence it brings. You threatened to surround me with misery if I didn't come back and control it, well whoops, who'd have guessed, it's all blown up in your face. Because I'm a spreader of misery, too. I spread misery to those who threaten, and bully, and revel in the pain of others. And now you'll stay here and write out a thousand times, "Misery is no fun", while I go to spread a little happiness instead, and finish clearing up your mess. This, you see, is where it ends. And people start to get their lives back.'

And, as the Overseers stared, the Doctor walked out of the room, walked down the corridor, walked out of the door of the facility, and walked into his TARDIS.

And as he went, he hummed a merry tune.

Afterword
David Bailey

'I promise you I will make it all better. Undo it. Put it right again. But... But I can't do it yet. One day, but not yet.'

It's now been so long, I don't know which are memories and which are simply figments of my imagination. Little bits of hope, given form and sense.

Someone gave me that promise, a long time ago. Someone who defied belief both times I met him. And he seems to have defied belief so vehemently, it has turned its back on him and left him stranded in imagination.

Which would explain a lot.

Maybe it's all a fiction, a lie that goes right back to me and Ellen hiding in the manager's office, her arm around my shoulder, lights off, breathing as quiet as we can. Monsters at the door. Scratching, snuffling, growling. Ridiculous, really.

Or maybe even before that. Maybe, when the chain broke and the lathe fell to the floor, mashing my legs as it went... Maybe it did more than that, and it mashed my life too. And this, this empty flat, this endless night, this incessant solitude, this is the afterlife. Hell.

The devil leaves me my mind, and a very imaginative sense of hope. And he sits on his throne of bone and blood, and laughs as he watches me weave a normal life out of this hope: a weft of this, a warp of the other, until it's some preposterous story of a traveller through time and space, who has promised to rescue me from the loneliness that took me when Ellen left. But she never got the chance to leave, did she? Because all I am is a shattered mess on the factory floor.

I mean, how desperate must I be?

So, if this is hell, I make my home here. I've still got the imagination and, since I've built everything on hope, why on earth should I stop now? I still have the stories, after all, however far-fetched. The devil leaves me those, too.

So, I start to build them again.

I hear a rattle at the door. Who will it be?

It's a sunny afternoon, and Ellen will take me to the park. Maybe we'll feed the ducks.

Or it's the dead of night, and the Doctor's here to fix everything. Or, better than that, he'll take me away. Take me into his time machine, and sweep me into the great beyond.

There's got to be a few stories out there, after all, and I am terribly bored of thinking about Ellen.

So that's what I do.

The door opens and there he is – and heaven knows what he looks like this time – smiling so much I can almost hear the joy. The front door is still open, and he holds a hand out, showing me the way. Outside, on the landing, the tall, blue shape that is my way out of here.

Together, we go. Maybe he's got another pretty girl with him, maybe he hasn't. It doesn't matter; I'm beyond such things now. I am a space adventurer! Brave and bold and ready for action! I welcome corners, because whatever's round the next one, I have the Doctor at my side and together we'll fight it.

And it isn't night any more. And I'll never have to see that flat again.